The Last Wingman

DAISY PRESCOTT

Copyright © Daisy Prescott 2019, All rights reserved.

No part of this book may be reproduced or transmitted in any form without written permission from the publisher, except by a reviewer who may quote brief passages for review purposes.

This book is a work of fiction. Names, characters, businesses, organizations, places, events, and incidents are the product of the author's imagination or are used fictitiously. Any resemblance to actual persons, living or dead, is entirely coincidental.

Cover Design by ©Heart to Cover

Interior Design: Jennifer Beach

Editing: Editing by C. Marie

Proofreading by JOs Book Addiction Proofing

First digital edition March 2019

ebook ISBN 978-1-7321330-4-4

Paperback ISBN978-1-7321330-3-7

For Whidbey,
I will always love you

We love the things we love for what they are.

Robert Frost

ONE

For years I've stood in a small hut, making coffee and chatting with people through their open car windows. I've probably had thousands of pointless conversations, words spewed back and forth to pass the time while milk frothed and espresso brewed.

Among the multitude of words, very few mattered. No one really listens to small talk with strangers. Weather, sports, politics, ferry lines. A heartbroken teenager ordering a frozen coffee through her sobs. The couple honeymooning, sex and happiness radiating off them while they sip twin cold brews. An exasperated mom, frustrated and exhausted, hoping a large mocha will give her enough sanity to make it until bedtime. The tourists and the day-trippers soaking up "island culture." (Whatever that is …) The guys who drink their lunch at the bar and stop by for a liquid dessert of the sobering variety. My regulars with their usual orders I know by heart and start making as soon as I spot their car in line. It's a constant stream of people, each believing in the individuality of their woes or joys, yet essentially all the same.

People ramble about things that don't matter because we're

too awkward, too afraid to share anything of importance for fear of being judged or mocked—or worse—ignored.

Always quiet, by middle school I became a stealthy observer, a ninja of human observation. It's amazing what a person can learn by not filling silence with unnecessary chatter.

Inside the hut, I play whatever music I want and no one messes up my crossword puzzle. Quiet and solitude have never bothered me.

Being alone doesn't mean being lonely.

Then she moved to the island and made me reconsider everything.

TWO

"We get one shot to make this work." I spread my arms wide to encompass the entire room. Construction debris, drop cloths, paint cans, and piles of random crap litter the open space. "Everything is a disaster."

"That's not true. No one expects success straight away. There's a learning curve, small failures. Bumps and dips are part of the journey."

I scowl at my sister. "Have you been reading inspirational quotes online again? If you put up one of those posters with an uplifting message and a pretty landscape background, I'm disowning you."

"Pfft, no. Those aren't a thing anymore. However, I do have my eye on some cross-stitches. One or two of them are even snarky enough for you to approve of—oh, and a couple of prints with fancy calligraphy."

"Ashley."

"Jonah."

We stare at each other. To a stranger, we don't look related. Her copper hair and hazel eyes contrast with my dark coloring. She's bright and colorful while I'm a somber monochrome.

Ashley blinks first and my big brother streak of winning

every staring contest with her remains intact. "Stop with the glowering and judgment. This place is supposed to encourage youth to reach for the stars."

"I think that's an old Casey Kasem line."

Her eyebrows draw together in confusion. "Who?"

"Exactly."

She squints at me and uses her hands to frame my face like she's a photographer setting up her shot.

"What are you doing?" I ask.

"Blocking out your hair and beard to see if you and Olaf are in fact the same curmudgeonly person."

"Haha. Last time I checked, I'm not a sixty-year-old misanthropic bartender."

She steps closer and touches my head above my ear. "Is that gray hair I see at your temples? Is that why you keep the sides shorter?"

Swatting her away, I sweep my hand over the buzzed hair and then run it through the longer strands on top of my head. "Stop it. If I were such a grump, why would I be opening a space for teenagers?"

"So you can yell 'Get off my lawn!' at them all at once instead of individually?" Her smile breaks free, followed by a laugh.

"I don't have time to stand around while you tease me. There are a million problems I needed to deal with yesterday."

"Okay, okay." She holds up her palms. "How can I help? Do you have a punch list?"

Pressing the heel of my hands into my eye sockets, I groan. "My lists have their own lists."

"What's the biggest issue?" Ashley walks around the counter and strokes the smooth, concrete surface. "These are nice. I should put these in the new house."

"Focus, please." My tone is more exasperated than I intend. "Sorry. We're opening next week and everything is already a disaster. Half of my games are on a truck stuck on the other side of the pass."

"That should be easy enough to fix. We'll organize a convoy of pickup trucks to go get them."

"Except the pass keeps closing due to snow."

"Then let's put that one in the 'out of your control' column for now." She pulls out her phone and taps on the screen. "What's next?"

"How much time do you have?" Grumbling, I stare up at the ceiling where light fixtures should be but aren't.

"It's going to be fine. This isn't your first business. Why so nervous, brother of mine?" Ashley leans against the counter and contemplates me. Her red curls are tamed in a braid today and it reminds me of when she was little.

"I want to get it right." I kick an empty cardboard box. The lack of weight makes the action unsatisfying.

"You'll figure it out as you go. That's why you have a soft opening—let everyone get their sea legs before the official launch."

"I'm crazy for thinking this can work." I pull out my phone and make a note to call the electrician later about installing the light fixtures.

"No, you're a dreamer and an entrepreneur. This is what you do."

"I should've spent my energy opening up a dispensary instead. There's a lot more money in cannabis than coffee."

Mouth hanging open, she gawks at me. "I don't even know where to begin with that statement. Are you crazy? First, this project isn't even a money-making venture for you. I thought the idea of this place was to be a fun way to give back to the community. Second, you think Langley would ever approve a pot shop on their picture-perfect main street? For one thing, the zoning regulations make it impossible."

"Not here, obviously. Give me some credit."

"Phew. For a hot second, I thought you'd smoked yourself stupid."

"You know most people don't smoke pot anymore. It's all about the edibles and oils." I neither deny nor confirm that I do either. "You're so old school."

"I am old, period, and a mom. My cool kid card expired a long time ago. Do you see the lines around my eyes? Those weren't there last year." She gestures at invisible crow's feet.

"Speaking of moms and kids, how's my favorite niece?"

"Rosie's good." Her tone softens. "She's hanging out with Ione this morning. Roslyn and the nanny are there too."

"If you need a babysitter, I'm happy to help out."

"You're busier than either of us, but thanks. Unless you need to borrow her for some sort of wingbaby activity again, the answer is no."

"One time and it was for a good cause."

She snorts. "Did it get you laid?"

"No, but it helped with some groundwork on a long-term project." Long-term might be code for pointless in this situation.

Her eyes narrow with suspicion. "Are you going to tell me the details?"

"No, and stop silently interrogating everything I say. I'm offering to help you out some evening. I'm around most of the time, and my offer is meant to give you and Carter a break for a date, something not involving coffee, goats, or babies."

She shifts her attention beyond my shoulder. "What is this life you speak of? Sounds vaguely familiar."

"If you can't remember, take me up on my offer."

"I'll check with Carter and get back to you. He's buying more goats soon, which means he'll be obsessing over them until they settle in with the rest of the herd."

"See? You'll need a break."

"Uh huh." Her focus drifts back to me.

"Stop with the suspicious side eyes. I'm being sincere. I want to spend more time with my niece. Quality bonding is important from a young age."

"You can't take her to clubs in Seattle. No concerts, and no Bumbershoot—not even with those cute noise canceling head-phones for babies." She aims her newly perfected mom stare at me.

I scoff. "Who brings a baby to a club or concert?"

"Hipsters." She gives me a pointed look.

"I'm not a hipster."

"Riiight." She stretches out the word before laughing. "Look around: vintage video games, pinball machines, turntable, and vinyl records. Paperbacks and comics and those other things you love."

"Graphic novels."

She nods, tight-lipped. "And is that Dungeons and Dragons set up on the table in the back corner?"

"Could be."

"Hipster," she whispers. "But I love you anyway. I have a little time before I have to pick up Rosie. Want to take me to lunch?"

"I have too much work to do." Staring at the empty box I kicked and the garbage needing to be removed, I resign myself to another long day of doing everyone else's jobs along with my own.

"Did you eat breakfast?" I shake my head. "Thought so. You're getting hangry. I'm going to let you take me to lunch."

"I'm covered in dust and paint." I gesture at my work jeans and dirty thermal.

"That's what sinks are for." She points behind me. "No more excuses."

"Yes, ma'am."

"Don't ma'am me. Quit dawdling."

There's no point in protesting when we both know I won't win. I wash my hands in the sink of the open kitchen area. "Where do you want to go? Pizza? Braeburn's? Useless Bay?"

She twists the end of her braid as she mulls over the options. "Let's decide on the way."

Outside, I pull out my keys. Brown paper still covers the windows to deter the curious and potential thieves looking to steal construction equipment. Layla, one of our baristas at Whidbey Joe's, decorated the paper with *Coming Soon* in artful lettering and drawings of the exterior.

After years of sitting empty, the building and my project are the focus of local gossip. Lucky me. Other than a couple of town meetings and permit applications, we're not disclosing the details until we're ready to pull down the paper and open the doors.

"Did you decide what you want?" I ask, fiddling with the key in the lock.

When I step out of the alcove for the door, she's right behind me and I bump into her.

"Stand closer, would you?" I say in annoyance, reaching for her shoulder to steady myself and make sure I don't knock us both over.

Only it isn't Ashley's shoulder I'm holding. The coat is green wool, not a black down parka. Dark hair spills out from beneath a pink, knitted hat topped by a pom-pom the size of a grapefruit. My heart misses a beat and I suck in a quick breath.

June blinks at me through her glasses. Today's frames are blue. "I'm sorry. I was trying to peek through the door when you were locking up. Busted. I should wear a bell or something so I can't sneak up on people."

Bell or no bell, with her brightly colored clothing and tendency toward oversharing, she'd make a terrible spy.

"Why are you sorry? I bumped into you. I should be the one apologizing." A bit of residual sibling annoyance lingers in my voice. "Are you okay?"

"Both fine and dandy. Thank you." She lowers herself slightly, one ankle behind the other.

Did she just ... curtsey?

Based on the awkward way she's smoothing her hands over the sides of her coat, I think she did. I find these little quirks adorable.

She's an odd, colorful bird of a woman. Since moving here a year ago, she's kept to herself, friendly-ish but distant at least with me. I'm sure she has friends, possibly even a boyfriend, although I've never seen her out with anyone.

She intrigues me.

Ashely stands off to the side, watching June and me like we're on the center court at the US Open. From the smile on her face, she's enjoying what she sees.

A warning flare fires. My sister is about a minute away from sniffing out my crush, the one I've carefully kept hidden for over a year, and once she does, she's going to meddle, which will only make an awkward situation worse—even worse than me almost knocking June into the gutter.

"Don't let us keep you." I pat June's shoulder before quickly stuffing both hands inside my jacket pockets.

She focuses on where I touched her green coat for a second and then says, "Sure."

"We're going to lunch. Want to join us?" Ashley prods, simultaneously friendly and cunning.

June adjusts her bag on the opposite shoulder, the one unsullied by my touch. "Thank you, but I have to get back to the shop. I'm just returning from a quick bank run, although there was no running involved." She laughs. "More of a bank walk."

To confirm her story, she points around the corner in the direction of the one bank in town.

"Another time?" A happy grin brightens Ashley's face. "You and Jonah should go to lunch together soon, given you're neighbors now. You'll probably run into each other all the time—daily even."

Wondering if it would be too obvious if I clamped my hand over my sister's mouth, I nod and smile. "Yeah, cool. I'll see you around."

What is wrong with me? I sound like I'm going to run into her in the halls of high school, or worse, middle school. At least my voice didn't crack when I spoke to her.

We watch June cross the street and walk a few doors down to the yarn shop, In the Loop. I should say, my focus is on June while Ashley studies my profile with a smug grin plastered on her face. Ignoring her, I tuck my arm in the crook of her elbow and turn us in the opposite direction. Not until we're around the corner do I speak.

"Weren't you just saying you were starving? Let's go to the Braeburn."

"Nice try." She squeezes my wrist. "Tell me everything."

"Nothing to tell."

"Ha. I'm not that easily deterred. I saw the look you gave her."

"There wasn't a look."

"You may have a stoic poker face, but even the best players have a tell. I know yours."

"What is it?" Over the years, I've practiced my ability to hide my emotions and reactions.

"No way. If you know what it is, you'll train yourself to avoid doing it, ruining all my fun."

I dip my chin and stare at her.

"Not going to work. You don't scare me. You're all growl and no bite, like an adorable baby bat."

"Bats aren't adorable. People fear them. They're creatures of the night," I grumble.

Her giggle forces a smile from me. "I'm not being funny."

"Doesn't mean I don't find you hysterical."

"Whatever. If I'm here for your amusement, you can pay for lunch."

"Fine with me, and for the record, you do like her. You're crankier than usual, a sure sign you're smitten with her—or someone. Given you've been working non-stop on the new project, it's doubtful you've been going to Seattle much."

"I'm not cranky, just hungry and tired."

She squeezes my arm again. "The place is going to be amazing. All your effort and stress will pay off."

"I hope you're right. The whole idea might be a disaster."

"Or the best thing ever."

"If I can reach one kid, make a difference in one life, it will be worth it."

"Imagine if you had a place like this when we were growing up," she says, voice tender with memories of our not-so-idyllic childhood.

"I have. I've been thinking about this for twenty years."

She rests her head briefly on my shoulder as we walk. "I know. Mom focused on saving my virginity and my soul while ignoring every bad thing Dad did."

"At least I was away at UW when things exploded." I pull away so I can see her eyes. "I'm sorry."

"It's okay … now. We both turned out fine. Our lives are good."

"Says the married woman with a husband and a baby," I tease. "The same one who also swore she'd never get married."

"I know. Every once in a while it hits me that Carter and I ended up together even after everything with Dad."

"Can we stop talking about Ron Curtis? I'm losing my appetite." We've arrived at the cafe and I hold the door open for her.

"Deal. I'll even let you off the hook about June." She pats my shoulder. "For now."

"There's nothing going on there. Trust me, I'm confident she hates me."

"Stop. You always assume people don't like you, and hate is a strong word. She's probably just awkward, like you."

THREE

Second Saturday of the month means catching the seven a.m. boat to Mukilteo. There have been many nights where I slept in town after a show to buy myself another hour of sleep, at times, staying with old friends on their old couches in random apartment rentals, or with the occasional short-term relationship with a warm bed. Some of those relationships didn't last a weekend and weren't worth the extra hour of sleep. Mostly, I prefer to find a spot on a quiet street to park my camper and crash alone.

Bert gives me a salute when he directs me to the middle lane on the deck, a prime spot for unloading first. I appreciate the gesture and grab a bag of coffee from the box to give him as a thank you. It's become our tradition.

Once the engines engage and we're on our way, I join him on the deck.

He accepts the bag from me with a thanks. "Thought you might miss the boat. You oversleep this morning?"

More like couldn't sleep. "Had to take care of some things at the worksite in Langley."

"Ah, the mysterious new business you're keeping under

wraps. You know there's a rumor going around you're opening up one of those pot shops."

"I've heard that rumor, and I'm pretty sure Connie started it when she tried to snoop on my paperwork at the bank."

He chuckles and nods. "That's who told me. I set her straight about zoning laws and city council approvals. You'd think a gossip like her would attend every meeting on the island. A person can learn a lot by sitting in the back of public hearings."

I don't miss his pointed look. "Then you know what I'm up to without me saying anything."

"I have an idea." He tugs on his white beard. I remember when it was brown. When did he get old?

"Sometimes I use my powers for good."

"You should let more people see that side of you. All this metal and ink and whatever it is you did to your earlobes is just a disguise."

"You think so?" I rub my jaw. "I've spent years developing my personal style and I'm pretty fond of it."

"Hmph."

"That sounded a lot like judgment. Et tu, Bert?"

"All I'm sayin' is you walk around looking like a punk-ass kid. How old are you now? Pushing forty by my calculations."

"Thirty-five is not quite forty." Annoyance prickles the back of my neck.

"Eh, close enough. Time to grow up," he grumbles. "When I was your age—"

"Yeah, yeah. I know." I cut him off before he can give me his speech about marriage and kids and pensions. "Things have changed. We don't all march to the same beat. Some of us aren't cut out for the same old definitions of being a man."

He eyes my arms even though my tatts are hidden under the sleeves of my leather jacket. "Don't waste your life trying to hold on to your youth."

He reminds me of Olaf. "You and Olaf ever think about

writing a book of cantankerous wisdom? Probably be a New York Times bestseller. You could call it *Kids These Days* or *This Generation is the Worst*. Maybe go with the classic, *Shut Up and Get Off of My Lawn*."

Narrowing his eyes at me, he sniffs the bag of beans. "Smartass. It's a good thing you make great coffee."

"You're welcome. Thanks for the chat." Chuckling, I pat his shoulder. "Always good to see you, Bert."

On the upper deck, I find an empty spot at the railing near the stern, always preferring to face the island whether I'm coming or going.

Bert's been saying the same thing to me since I was a teenager. In high school, he badgered me about my grades. When I got into UW, he warned me not to squander my chance by getting drunk and chasing skirts for four years. After I moved back to the island, he chastised me about throwing away my opportunity to do more with my life.

Reviewing the hundreds of conversations we've had, I realize Bert's taken on a fatherly or concerned uncle role in my life, giving me solid advice, which I've often ignored. Some of his input did stick, though. Work hard. Be a good person. Earn respect. Keep my tallywacker wrapped.

That last one he shouted at me across the car deck of a full ferry when I was eighteen.

Sometimes, I wonder why I stay on the island with its small-town mindset.

As the ferry crosses the narrow channel, I feel the shift in energy inside me as I anticipate arriving in Seattle.

Traffic. Delays. Stress.

I love what the city has to offer in terms of culture and distractions, but there's no way I could ever live there full time. Tried it once, lasted a year after college finished.

Living on the island gives me the best of both worlds: easier to disappear when I need to, close enough to civilization to keep life interesting.

Bert gives me a wave as I drive off the boat in Mukilteo.

Seattle traffic is only mildly horrible this morning as I weave my way downtown. With a glance at my phone after I park at the hospital, I confirm I have half an hour to spare—plenty of time to drop off more coffee to the nurses station and chat with Vicky at reception if she's working.

———

I'm tired but happy when I pull out of the parking lot a few hours later.

The best way to get out of a funk is to do something that helps others. I've been following this advice for a few years, and a few dozen conversations with Dan on the subject inspired the new shop idea. Through a secret real estate trust, he bought the old building, saving it from an investor who wanted to convert it to a burger chain.

Dan being behind the trust is one of the worst-kept secrets on the island, but we all pretend we don't know it's him. Stuff like this is why he's the local Bruce Wayne and why the rumors about a pizza mafia never quite go away.

Instead of driving back to the ferry, I decide to go to one of my favorite places in Ballard for a late lunch. I might even stay in town and see a show tonight if anyone good is playing. Ashley is right about needing a break before I explode from stress. Good food, good beer, and good music will help.

Inside the minimalist restaurant, I find a seat at the corner of the bar near the wide picture window. All the tables are full while the sound of cutlery and conversation creates a loud din. Doesn't bother me. I'm not here for conversation.

I know the bartender and greet her by name. "Hey, Ceci."

She responds with a broad smile on her full lips. "Hey, yourself. Finished at the hospital already?"

"Yep. Good day when the ward isn't full."

Ceci's gaze softens. "What can I get you, Mr. Potter? We have your favorite saison on tap."

"Sounds good."

"Food?"

"Dozen oysters, please. Your choice." A glint of metal in her eyebrow catches my eye. "New piercing?"

She touches the spot gently. "Yeah. Based on your recommendation, I went to Hillary inCapitol Hill last week. It's still tender."

While she pours my beer, we chat about piercings and tattoos. Ceci's been working on a back piece for over a year, and colorful ink covers the tawny skin of her arms and hands. She probably has more than I do. I realize it's more than a year since I got a new piece and the thought makes me crave the feel of the needle and the look of fresh ink.

"How are Ansel and Naya?"

Her eyes light up. "Good, really good. I never thought being a family of three would make me so happy. Look what I got to celebrate Ansel's birthday."

After she places my pint in front of me, she stretches the collar of her shirt down, exposing more of her chest but not flashing me her bra. In the center is a small, red A above her heart.

"Love it," I tell her. "Works on several levels."

"That's the best part. I want to call my parents and tell them I'm putting my English degree from U-Dub to good use." The joy in her eyes fades with her sigh.

"Want to talk about it?"

"No. I pay enough to my therapist for her to listen to me. Aren't bartenders and baristas supposed to be the listeners?"

"That's been my experience. Sometimes I think people confuse a coffee hut with a confessional." I lift my glass in a toast. "To being good listeners."

She rests her palms on the bar and studies me. "How is Neverland these days?"

Her nickname for the island draws out a chuckle. "Good. Busy."

"Someday we'll have to make the trip and check it out."

"It's really not that far away," I grumble.

"You have to take a ship to get there. Do I follow the second or third star from the right?" The corners of her eyes crinkle when she smiles at me.

I chuckle. "You and Naya would love it. Most of my friends have little kids. You'd fit right in."

She pops her mouth open as if surprised. "It isn't an island of lost boys who fled the city to live out their days in the woods, stomping around fires and fighting battles with pirates? Way to destroy my illusions."

"I'm not lost." I sip the cold beer.

"I know. I'll stop teasing and put in your order." She taps the counter and pauses for a second. "It's good to see you. Been a while."

Our flirty banter—if that's what it is—comes naturally but there's no fire behind it. No direction or goal in mind. I've known Ceci and Naya for a long time. Doing the math in my head, I realize we first met over a decade ago. Fifteen years should be cause for celebration. Waiting for her to return, I mull over the ebb and flow of our friendships from college campus to now.

A head of dark hair catches my attention near the door. When the woman turns, familiar pink glasses confirm what I already knew: June's here. I'm always happy to see her but surprised she'd be hanging out in Ballard.

Out of the usual context of seeing her in Langley, I consider her like she's a stranger.

Today's outfit is a vintage-style dress that flares out from her waist. Studying the pattern, I notice what I first thought were white polka dots on the gray background are actually bunnies. A purple cardigan covers her top half, and a pink coat rests over her arm. The color combination is stolen straight from a cloudy winter sunset.

Lifting my attention back to her face, I realize I've been busted staring. Her wide eyes and frozen pose recall an actual rabbit caught in the garden. She's not smiling, and I'm not even sure she's breathing.

To break her trance, I raise my hand in a friendly wave.

"Do you know him?" a middle-aged woman behind her peers at me over June's shoulder. Glares might be the better description. "Why is that strange man waving at you?"

Her voice isn't loud; she's not shouting, but the acoustics near the window deliver her words crystal clear like she's standing next to me instead of a dozen feet away.

"June? Is he a friend of yours?"

I realize the woman is an older version of June with similar glasses and warm hazel eyes, her dark hair streaked with gray. Must be her mother.

My hand loiters in the air like I'm hoping for the teacher to call on me. I drop it and pick up my beer instead.

"Uh, he's from the island. Hi, Jonah." She mirrors my awkward wave. "Funny seeing you here."

I avoid saying I come here all the time and she's the one who's out of place. Instead, I meet her eyes and give her a friendly smile. "They let me off the island sometimes. Whidbey's not Alcatraz."

"Was that a prison joke?" Older June chokes out a laugh that is more nerves than amused.

"It was." I lift my glass in a one-sided toast. Seeing myself through her eyes comes easily to me. The black leather jacket slung on the back of my stool. Black jeans, black thermal. Boots, tatts, piercings. Lopsided, weird hair. Her disdain for my appearance is funny to me. We may not know each other, but I've done this dance enough times to know the routine by heart. "For the record, I've never done hard time. Never been arrested or even charged with jaywalking."

June's mouth tightens like she's pulled the ends of a bow. Narrowing my eyes, I try to decide if she's fighting laughter or biting her tongue.

"Oh, I'd never assume you were a career criminal based on a leather jacket and some tattoos. Or in a gang," her mom explains.

Uh huh. Sure.

"Lots of people wear leather jackets now. I own a leather jacket," June says.

"That doesn't seem like your style. Next, you'll be telling me you've joined a biker gang and taken up smoking." Older June laughs at the absurdity of such an idea.

From her description, I believe her only point of reference for this situation is imagining her sweet daughter is the Sandy to my Danny Zuko. It's fascinatingly out of date. I want to ask her if she gets out much, but I'm not going to be rude to June's mother.

"Mom, this isn't a musical production of *Grease*," June groans.

Given I was just thinking that, I grin at the possibility of being on the same page as her. *See? We're not so different.*

"Don't be silly. We should probably go. The meter will expire soon. I'd hate to get a ticket." Mom places her hand on June's shoulder and addresses me, "Lovely to meet you."

"Same." Funny that we weren't actually introduced. Does it still count as a meeting? My attention lingers on June for another moment. "Good to see you."

Her eyes blink a few times and then she bites the corner of her bottom lip. "See you around."

After they leave, I'm still wondering if she meant to mimic my words from the other day back to me.

"Here you go." Ceci sets a large plate of oysters on ice in front of me.

Distracted by June's random appearance, I forgot I ordered food. My pint sits on the bar, almost full.

"Uh, thanks."

"Jonah?" Ceci says my name, her amused expression telling me it's probably not the first time she's spoken it.

"Yeah?" I give her my attention.

She pretends to rub her forehead. "You have something on your forehead. When you first walked in I thought I'd forgotten Ash Wednesday again, but it's Saturday."

Using my thumb, I rub my skin to wipe away the mark. "Gone?"

"Not quite, but better, less obvious. Now it looks like you had lipstick on your face instead of half of a swastika."

"What? No." My tone is sharper than I mean. Grabbing my knife, I study my forehead in the reflection of the polished metal. Sure enough, what was once a lightning bolt is now a faded smear of dark red. "Did it look like I was cosplaying Manson?"

Well, shit. No wonder June's mother was worried about her daughter talking to me.

"Not really. I knew it was a lightning bolt." Ceci pats my arm where my Dumbledore's Army tattoo decorates my wrist.

"And if you didn't know? Psychotic cult leader and mass murderer would be the first thing to pop into your mind, right?" Bringing Manson to mind is not the best way to make a good first impression. The fact that I'm even worried about her mom liking me is a sure sign I'm screwed.

Instead of reassuring me, she scrunches up her face and then winces. "What are you worried about, scaring off the tourists? Keeping Seattle weird is a good thing."

My mouth opens as I debate explaining the epic fail of the encounter between me, June, and her mother, but I think better of it and drink my beer.

Ceci gives me a concerned look but leaves me alone.

FOUR

I feel like I'm living inside a fishbowl. Given that I worked in a small hut for years, this shouldn't bother me, but it does. There's a lot more foot traffic in downtown. Every time someone walks by, the movement catches my attention and I glance up, not because I think it might be June. That would be ridiculous.

We pulled the brown paper off the windows this morning. In addition to our official signage, Layla painted new decorations on the glass. Her original artwork was such a big hit, we've decided to have her do a regular rotation of window designs. We might even have a contest for the kids to create art, logos, and screen-printed shirts or bags. The possibilities are endless.

The polished concrete floors and reclaimed wood on the counter are almost identical to the design of Whidbey Joe's. We wanted something akin to our existing space, but that's where the similarities end.

Old school video games and pinball machines will line one wall. A collection of five hundred vinyl albums fills a large stack of cubes near the turntable, and we also have wireless speakers set up to encourage the sharing of playlists. Two bookcases are currently filled with copies of some of my personal favorite books. None are for sale; it's more like our version of a free library based on the honor system.

There's also an espresso machine, a soda fountain, and fridges filled with beverages. The small kitchen is stocked and ready for snack orders.

My vision is coming to life.

Layla's hand-lettered illustration of the house rules fills a narrow wall between two windows:

No staring at your smartphone or tablet screen.
If you ever decide to use your phone for calls, do so outside.
No fighting.
Don't be a jerk.
Bullies will be banned.
Don't cheat, lie, or steal.
Bring back the books you borrow.
Don't scratch the needle on the turntable.
We're not your parents.
Be respectful of yourself and others.
Ask for help.
Don't assume.
Remember you're amazing.

I'm sure we'll add to the list as we figure out what we're doing. Part clubhouse, part after-school hangout, this space is as much for the kids as it is for me and my teenage self. Ashely's one hundred percent right: I would've loved a place like this as a teen, somewhere that wasn't school or home, somewhere safe where I could be myself and have a community. God knows I didn't have many safe spaces when I was in high school.

I just hope now that I built it, they will come. If a baseball diamond in the cornfields of Iowa can forgive the ghosts of a man's past, I hope this space can right the wrongs of my own life.

We'll open the doors and fire up the espresso machine for a few hours a day this week to test the waters. Then the community open house and party will be on Saturday afternoon.

My task for the day is stopping by the neighboring businesses to personally invite them to the celebration.

Roslyn Porter's PR firm is handling the press for the event. She's been instrumental in shaping the mission statement and branding for The Place. We wanted to give a nod to the old name but remove any association with the former restaurant.

Not going to lie, I had a crush on her a few years ago before she and Dan got back together. Way out of my league, but I do love a smart, strong woman.

Walking counter-clockwise around the block, I hand out flyers to every store, restaurant, and shop that's open. If they're not, I slip the piece of paper under the door.

My route means the strip of buildings closest to the bluff will be my last stops, with the Dog House being the final one. Of course, Olaf already knows about the open house and grand opening. He's complained about it on multiple occasions.

Planned or not, I save In the Loop for last.

An old-fashioned brass bell jingles when I open the door to June's store. The narrow space is made even tighter by the floor-to-ceiling cubbies that line the two long walls. In the back of the store, a picture window frames a view of Saratoga Passage like a painting.

Tucked in the corner near the window is a comfy-looking wingback chair, and next to it, an oversized basket filled with balls of yarn. The shop is cozy and feminine, comfortable like a sweet grandmother's house.

A grandmother who listens to "Sex and Candy" on low volume.

Not what I was expecting.

"Hello?" I call from my spot near the door. There's no sign of June or anyone else inside. Double-checking the door for a *Be back soon* note and not seeing one, I step farther into the space. "Hello?"

A soft thump followed by more thumps comes from the desk area. Metallic pings and something heavy hitting the floor precedes a feminine voice yelping "Ouch" and "Fuck!"

June doesn't seem like the type to drop f-bombs. Maybe she's hired a '90s-music-loving teenager with a foul mouth.

"Everything okay?" I follow the noise to the partially open door near the register.

"Fine. Fine! Nothing to see here! I'll be with you in a second. Thanks for your patience." What sounds like rapid-fire bean-bags hitting a cornhole board contradicts her words.

As I see it, I have two options. I can ignore whatever is going on inside the closet and wait, or I can ignore her lie and step in to help.

I go with the second choice.

Swinging the door open, I'm greeted with a scene of colorful chaos. A box balances on its side on the edge of a high shelf, most of its contents now on the floor around June's feet. She's keeping the box aloft with both hands, but doesn't have the height to shove it back into position.

"Here, let me help you." I step into the small space behind her and reach above her head to stabilize the cardboard container before she ends up concussed.

"I don't need your help." Reluctantly, she releases her grip.

"Okay." Disappointed and a little hurt by her obvious annoyance at my presence, I give the corner a final shove to guarantee we're out of danger. "You're welcome."

"I said I was fine." Continuing to face the shelves, she doesn't turn her head to speak to me. In fact, she sounds down-right angry.

"Got it. Well, I'll get out of your way." Resigned, I decide to abandon my mission and retreat to the safety of my own business, both literally and figuratively.

What happens next is more her fault than mine. Had she

used a step stool and not tipped the box over, there wouldn't be balls of yarn strewn across the floor, creating a minefield. Easily-tripped-over round objects that cause me to lose my balance and reach for the closest available thing to stop myself from landing on my ass.

Unfortunately, I grab June by the waist, surprising her. She's not prepared to act as my anchor. Unstable, we both stumble backward.

Lucky for June, I break her fall. Unlucky for me, she lands on top of me.

We've never even hugged before this moment. I think we might have shaken hands once when Dan introduced us, but the memory isn't clear. There wasn't an electric shock when we first touched or met eyes, no love-at-first-sight zings upon initial contact—unlike now when my body is on high alert that we're not only touching but lying flush against each other.

"I'm so sorry!" June wiggles, her movement drawing my attention to her clothes. How did I not notice she's wearing a full skirt made of thin material? My imagination easily erases its existence altogether.

"Don't apologize. This was completely my fault." My words come out a grunt as I try to catch my breath.

My hands still grip her waist, making this position more awkward by the second. Unbidden, my fingers flex against her softness. Bad idea. Feeling my dick thicken, I tell myself not to move, not to even breathe. Oxygen is overrated.

Shifting on top of me, she bends her knees and gets her feet under her enough to stand up in a single, ninja-quick move-ment. Instead of waiting for me to stand or extending a hand to help me, she exits through the door and closes it behind her.

I'm left sprawled out on the floor, balls of yarn and possibly a needle poking me in the back. "No good deed goes unpun-ished," I mutter to myself as I scramble to my feet. "Don't worry, I'm fine."

My hand is on the knob when the door opens again.

June's hair is disheveled and there's some purple fluff on her shoulder.

"Can we swear an oath to never speak of this again?" She points to the box and then to the floor and finally at me.

"I have no idea what you're talking about. In fact, I have no memory of how I even got in this closet." My lips curl into an amused smile.

She steps aside and gives me room to pass. "Thanks for your help with the box."

"What box?" I give her a wink. Winking isn't something I do on a regular basis. Neither is showing up to assist a woman in a precarious situation like some sort of white knight.

June's eyes narrow.

I'm guessing the wink was too much. Best leave the winks to grandfathers and lecherous men in bars.

"What can I help you with?" Putting the checkout desk between us, she's all business.

"Uh, right. I'm here for a reason." No idea what that could be right now, but I know I didn't randomly wander in here searching for crafting materials.

She waits, quiet.

"Right. Right, I already said that. So …" Fuck. I'm not asking her to the dance in the school gym. I'm here for professional reasons. "I'm stopping by all the businesses downtown to let everyone know we're having a soft opening this week at the new space. The official grand opening party will be on Saturday and you should come by in the afternoon. In the meantime, I wanted to invite you to check us out whenever you want."

I cease speaking because I can sense myself starting to ramble nervously. I'm perfectly capable of chatting with women without going off the rails—except around June, that is.

"Check you out?" Her eyebrow arches.

"The new space, not me specifically." I give her a half smile to convey how friendly and harmless I am.

Not since the awkward years of school have I been unable to

find my footing around a woman, stumbling around without a clue—both literally and figuratively given the closet incident.

"Thanks for the invite." Focusing on the mess of her desk, she picks up a pile of catalogues and organizes them into a neat stack.

"You're welcome." My friendly grin remains in place as I try to salvage this moment. "Stop by any time. I'll give you a tour."

She meets my eyes, her tone flat when she says, "Sounds great."

The way she says it makes me think she'd rather do anything else.

"Okay, then …" I pause, trying to think of something to charm her. Nothing comes to mind and I end up saying, "See you around."

"Probably will." She nods, not smiling.

Whatever that encounter was, it wasn't a success. Resigned, I decide I should give up on trying to win her over.

I swear half the people here just want the free food and drinks. The others are curious to see what we've done to Mike's old place. If I drew a Venn diagram of who is here because of our mission, it would be a tiny sliver between those two groups and a third: the teenagers looking bored with their parents. Nothing kills the cool vibe when you're a teenager than your parents hanging out with you.

Mixing and mingling aren't really my thing. I've probably spoken more words in the last hour than I do most days—and some entire weeks. In hindsight, I should've printed up FAQ cards and handed them out. Would have saved me from having the same conversation and answering the same questions over and over and over again. Despite my pledge to give up on June, my eyes continually scan the room for her.

Ashley sidles up to me and slings her arm around my shoulder. "You should give your speech now."

"No one wants to listen to me talk." I rest my arm on her shoulder, pulling her into a half hug.

"Didn't you prepare something?" She ducks out of my hold. "It's a grand opening. Where's the ribbon for cutting?"

"In case you didn't notice, everyone is already inside. Too late for a symbolic moment."

She twists her mouth. Tonight's lip color is a deep red, and with her curls down, she's a fire goddess not to be messed with. "We can still christen the building with a bottle of champagne or something."

"Given this is a teen hangout spot, booze probably isn't a good idea." I scan the crowd and smile at a few people.

"Oh, that explains the lack of adult beverages at this party. How about smashing a bottle of kombucha next to the door instead?" She's serious, even though her tone is joking.

"The after-party will be at the Dog House, although I suspect a few people here stopped by there first."

"If you're not going to cut a ribbon or christen the building —and it's probably too late to get a lamb to sacrifice—the least you should do is give a speech."

My eyes bug out. "What? How many coffee hut openings have we done? We've never cut a ribbon or spilled the blood of an animal."

"Seeing if you were paying attention. For the record, we did a ribbon cutting at the Mukilteo location."

"I think I was in Mexico for that. If you need to cut something, I'm sure we have packing tape and a box cutter somewhere around here."

"Speech it is." She lifts her hand to her mouth, cupping it like a megaphone. "Hello! Can I get everyone's attention, please?"

A few people turn to face us, but her voice barely carries over the volume of the pinball machines and old-school arcade games.

Ashley tries clinking her glass with her wedding ring, forgetting she's holding a plastic cup. "No one can hear me." She sighs, resigned.

"That's too bad," I drawl, sarcastically.

"Use your loud man voice." She nudges me in the ribs with her elbow. "Or you could whistle."

"Do I have to?" I ask through clenched teeth, offering a smile to the random people staring at me. I hate being the center of attention.

"Yes. A few words and it'll be done."

Placing my thumb and index finger up to my mouth, I blow. The sound is sharp, loud, and impossible to ignore.

Conversations cease as all eyes shift to me.

"Hello and welcome to The Place. I'm Jonah Kingston and I guess we're all here tonight because I had a crazy idea."

Clapping and loud whoops force me to pause.

"Jonah's the man," Erik shouts while pumping his arm above his head.

Layla, Amber and the rest of the Whidbey Joe crew begin chanting, "*Jo-nah! Jo-nah! Jo-nah!*"

They're making it worse. Heat spreads across my face.

"Okay, okay." I sweep my arm from high to low to get them to quiet down. "Sorry about that. Uh, I'm going to keep this short. Thank you for being here. This building has sat empty for way too long. I'm humbled and grateful that I've been entrusted with bringing a part of Langley's history back to life. The bene-factor who made my dream a possibility when he purchased the property wishes to remain anonymous, so I won't call him out with a public thank you."

Resisting glancing at Dan, I scan the room, making eye contact with Erik and Carter.

Near the back of the room, which is really the front by the door, June stands with her arms crossed. My heart rate quickens at the sight of her and the rest of the room disappears as my focus narrows to only her. Still wearing her thick, pink coat, she doesn't look happy to be here. Maybe it was something I said?

"This place is for our community, especially the teenagers who need somewhere to hang out with their friends." I brush my hand over my beard and tug on my ear lobe. "That's really it."

"No parents allowed?" a kid in a black hoodie asks, causing a wave of laughter.

"We're not going to ban parents, per se … but our vision is that this is a place you can come on your own and your parents will know you're safe."

A few of the parental figures in the room clap while others exchange doubtful looks.

"We'll figure it out as we go. For now, enjoy the games and snacks. I'm here if you have questions. Thanks for all your support." I clap my hands together once and make a small bow.

Ashely gives me a thumbs-up along with a cheesy grin. "Well done."

I thank her and the others who step up to congratulate me.

After shaking a few hands, I manage to escape the well-wishers, wiggling free from the circle that's formed around me like we're all about to do the Hokey Pokey.

June still lingers by the door, wearing her coat. I haven't seen her chat with anyone since I noticed her and realize she may not know anyone here. The fact that she showed up renews my hope that I can get her to warm up to me.

When she sees me making a beeline for her, her eyes widen and she slips her yellow knit hat over her hair.

"Hi," I say, stepping in front of her. "Thanks for coming tonight."

"I was just leaving." She points to the door behind her.

"You should stay. We're going to kick everyone out soon then some of us are going over to the Dog House. Join us."

"I wouldn't want to crash your celebration with your friends."

Her reluctance feels like rejection.

"You know most of them. Diane and John are here. So are Tom and Hailey, and Erik and Cari. My sister, Ashley, and her husband should be around somewhere."

"Are all of your friends paired off in couples like they're boarding the ark?"

She's right. "I hadn't really thought about it that way, but yeah, I guess so."

"Do you only hang out with couples?" She tilts her head to the side and peers up at me.

"No." I sweep my finger over my eyebrow. "Maybe."

"Isn't that awkward?"

"Not really. I've known most of these guys my entire life. Relationships happen." Lifting my left shoulder, I shrug off her insinuation of being a third wheel. "They're good people."

"I know. Diane gave me my first job when I moved here and she introduced me to Cathy at the yarn store. Probably wouldn't own the shop now if it weren't for Diane."

"Good timing with Cathy retiring."

"I never imagined being a shop owner, but she made me a deal I couldn't refuse."

"Better than waking up to a horse head in your bed?"

She doesn't laugh.

"*The Godfather*? The guy finds a horse head..." Seeing the horrified expression on her face, I don't finish my sentence. "Movie reference."

"Decapitation seems to be a theme around here."

"How so?" I rock back on my feet, confused about the dark turn this conversation has taken.

"Ask Erik."

I chuckle. "Erik has a thing for horror movies, in case you hadn't picked up on that."

"I've noticed. Well, good luck with the space. It's nice to see someone doing something with the building instead of letting it slowly rot from neglect."

"Uh, thanks. We're hoping to make a difference."

She pulls on a pair of gloves and straightens her hat.

I want to remind her the invitation to join the group still stands, but I don't want to get shot down again.

Instead, I say good night and return her wave through the window. We've yet to have a normal conversation that doesn't end in awkwardness, and I'm not sure who's to blame at this point. Even with her rejection, my crush lives on, defeated but not demolished. The fact that she showed up at all gives me enough hope to delude myself into thinking the keys to winning June over are proximity and time.

SIX

Along with opening the new space, I try to keep up with my share of the coffee roasting business with Erik.

Late on Monday afternoon, we're standing around the packing tables in the warehouse. Erik's girlfriend, Cari, is here, labeling bags of freshly roasted beans for our wholesale business. Being a freelance photographer, she has the flexibility to help us when we get slammed, or pick up my slack when I've been focused on the new project.

"Any plans tonight?" Cari sticks the label on the last bag for tomorrow's deliveries.

"Eat. Sleep." I stack boxes on the dolly to take out to my VW bus when we finish. Last year we bought a cargo van for bigger orders in town, but I like to drive the bus for the island deliveries. "I'm living an exciting life these days."

They exchange a conspiratorial look.

"Why? What's going on?" I ask, wary.

"It's pub quiz night at China Ruby in Freeland and we need another person on our team. Want to join us?" Erik asks while Cari makes a begging gesture with her hands.

"Thanks, but I'm going to pass." An evening of hanging out

at the better of the two Chinese restaurants on this end of the island isn't something I've done since my early twenties.

"Please? With sugar and cream and strawberries and chocolate sauce and chocolate sprinkles—or rainbow if that's your jam because no one should judge anyone's sprinkle preference—on top?" Cari exhales after presenting that list.

"Why do I feel like in this scenario, sprinkles aren't simply dessert toppings?" I eye them both with suspicion.

"I'm not implying anything. I'm just a universal sprinkle lover." Cari grins. "Sprinkles for everyone."

Erik clears his throat. "Getting back to this evening's event—you should come. Do something fun instead of work nonstop. When was the last time you went out?"

I tug on the gauge in my earlobe as I think. "What's the date? January thirteenth?"

"Fourteenth," Cari corrects.

"Right. It's only been two weeks. I went to a show in Seattle on New Year's Eve." I was on the ten o'clock boat back to the island and asleep by eleven-thirty, but I don't tell them that part. Instead, I go on the offensive. "Since when do you two play bar trivia?"

"Started in the fall. We're trying to support new and exciting things happening on the island," Erik says. "Live local and all that."

He quotes the new motto of the chamber of commerce like a cheeseball.

"If team trivia is your idea of excitement, you need to go to Seattle more often."

"Blah blah blah … city blah. So, are you in? We can share a pu pu platter and get the spare ribs." He speaks in a sing-song voice as if tempting me with pork will change my mind.

They're ridiculously relentless when they latch onto a new idea. It will be easier to escape by giving them a vague answer. "Maybe. What time do the festivities begin?"

"Seven," Cari interjects. "But if you're going to bail, let us know ahead of time so we can replace you. Things get competitive and we don't want to lose to the knitting ladies again. We'll need to call in another ringer."

My eyebrows lift and I ask, "You want me to be your ringer?"

Cari twists a lock of hair around her finger. "Maybe. It isn't fair that they have June on their team. We tried to lure her over to our side, but she's fiercely loyal to her lady gang."

The chance to see June changes my perspective. Evidently, I'm a glutton for awkward situations.

I brush my fingers over my beard near the corners of my mouth. "Okay, I'll be there, even though I should go home and crash. I've been living off an average of five hours of sleep for weeks—months, probably—but what's one more night?"

"Who needs sleep?" Erik shrugs.

Cari grins like she's won a bet. Knowing the two of them, they probably did have a wager on whether or not I'd agree.

Erik laughs. "All we had to do to get you to go was mention June?"

"Nah," I lie. "I like the idea of being a secret weapon."

———

The bar area of China Ruby is more crowded than I anticipated. Guess all the cars in the lot should've clued me in. If we're going to win tonight, I better be on top of my game.

Red upholstered booths line the two walls of windows forming an L around the bar area. They're filled, along with a bunch of the four-top tables occupying the center of the room.

Cari waves from one of the booths. She's wearing her dark brown hair in a pair of braids and I spy the back of Erik's short blond hair across from her.

I weave through the other tables to get to them. After shrugging off my leather jacket, I take a seat next to Erik. I recognize a few faces in the room, but most are unfamiliar to me. "Who are all these people? Are all the teams importing their own ringers from off the island?"

"No idea. I heard people were driving down from Coupeville and even Oak Harbor to play." Erik waves at some random guy in a Gonzaga sweatshirt.

"Seriously? Can't they just stay home and yell *Jeopardy* answers at the television from the comfort of their own couch?" I flip over the laminated menu on our table and scan the drink options.

"We already ordered a double scorpion bowl. We can get another straw if you want to share it." Cari points her long straw at the enormous yellow tiki bowl decorated with dancing hula girls that dominates the center of the table.

Using an extra straw on a cocktail meant for two is the ultimate third-wheel move. No thanks. Maybe June has a point about hanging out with couples all the time.

"I'm good with a beer." Scanning the room, I notice most of the tables are filled with groups of four people.

"Who else is on our team tonight? I'm seeing most teams have at least four people."

"She'll be here soon," Cari answers.

"She?" Cold dread settles in my veins. "Hold on—this isn't a set up, is it?"

Cari chuckles. "No, mostly because bigamy is illegal."

"And John would kill you," Erik adds, straight-faced.

"Diane's our fourth?" I ask, surprised, although I'm not sure why.

"She is." The brunette in question sits down opposite me. "Ready to kick some random-knowledge-of-obscure-facts ass tonight?"

"Always." Cari holds up her hand for a high five.

After reciprocating, Diane turns to me. Like Cari, she's dressed casually in jeans and a sweater. Her dark hair is twisted into a knot on top of her head, and her warm brown eyes are serious.

"Jonah, what are your areas of expertise?"

"He's our geek expert," Cari announces.

"I guess." I shrug.

"Give me your top five strengths," Diane prompts.

"No pressure or anything." I think for a few seconds. "History, comic books, graphic novels, literature, music. Bonus: random facts about Volkswagen Campers and their parts, plus Ikea furniture assembly. Also, coffee, but I'm assuming Erik can handle that area, and way too many other random, useless facts taking up space in my brain."

Diane nods approvingly. "All good additions to our knowledge base."

Around us, other teams chat, and their excited banter reminds me of my years competing in the academic decathlon in high school. I think we each won a hardcover Merriam Webster's dictionary and thesaurus, an odd prize based on the assumption that we'd already owned a dictionary and thesaurus given we were brainiacs.

In the corner closest to us, a larger booth for six remains empty with a *Reserved* card defending it from interlopers.

"Who gets the big booth?" I point behind Diane's head.

"Yarned and Dangerous. They're undefeated and therefore get to reserve the best table."

From the name, I'm guessing this is June's team. My pulse quickens in anticipation of seeing her.

"Do we have a name?" Add this to the list of things I should've asked before agreeing.

"Ebey's Head."

My mouth literally drops open. "You're not serious. You named yourselves after Issac Ebey's head, which was chopped off and stolen in 1857? Gruesome. You guys are hardcore."

June's comment about decapitation makes more sense now. I chuckle at the memory of our mutual confusion. No wonder she thinks we're a bunch of weirdos.

Cari elbows Erik. "See? This is exactly why we needed him on our team. He knows random stuff like this."

High-stakes pub trivia and a team named after the missing noggin of one of the island's founders is not a typical night out for me. "I feel like I've stumbled into an alternate reality. Are we still in Freeland? It's Tuesday, right?"

"Still Tuesday." Erik gives me a thumbs-up before proudly saying, "I came up with the name. Head, brain … get it?"

"Got it," I reply. "I should've known given your obsession with zombies and horror movies."

"We vetoed a lot of his other suggestions before settling on that one." Diane flags down the waitress to order drinks and food.

After ordering, Cari leans forward over the table, whispering, "Here they come. Get your game face ready."

I twist in my seat to see if she's talking about June, but the waitress blocks my view of the door.

Disappointed, I face Cari again. She's flattened her expression and narrowed her eyes like she's going to psych out the competition through the power of her stare.

"Your girlfriend is intense," I tell Erik.

"A little," he confirms with a laugh.

"Hello, June," Cari says as June passes our table with her team.

"Cari. Erik. Diane." Each one of them gets a nod of acknowledgment and a friendly, albeit smug, grin. Then June sees me and her voice goes flat. "Jonah."

No nod. No smile. It's almost like she's deliberately icing me out. Perhaps the lady doth protest too much? I grin at the thought. "It's great to see you."

A tiny flash of surprise widens June's eyes before she narrows them in suspicion. "I didn't know you liked trivia."

Nervous, I laugh at the over-the-top seriousness of this evening. "I'm the king of useless knowledge."

Something she would know if she ever had an actual conversation with me.

"He has a photographic memory," Cari brags.

"That's not true," I correct her.

"Near photographic. He's a history whiz, knows the dates of everything, and he can do complex math problems in his head, lightning fast. Prepare to be awed," Cari continues.

I appreciate her attempt to intimidate the opposition. "The math part isn't true either. However, I will stand by the warning to prepare yourself to be amazed." I give June a cheeky grin, hoping she knows I'm not really serious.

"Good for you. Have fun tonight. May the best group win," June says as she follows the group of older women to their table.

I can't tell if she's being overly polite because of her teammates or if my presence here has thrown off her game.

"Did you notice they're all wearing matching cardigans? Are those hand-knit sweaters? We don't even have T-shirts. We should remedy this. Can Whidbey Joe's sponsor us?" Cari asks Erik and then turns her attention to me. "No, wait—The Fellowship of the Bean. Actually, that might make people think of flicking the bean. Can't have that. This is a family show. Oh, I know! The Place should be our sponsor. Good advertising for you, better branding for your business, than say, sponsoring a baseball team or some other sporting event."

Erik removes the straw from Cari's hand. "No more scorpion bowl for you. You can't get sauced before we start playing. We need to stay sober enough to pay attention."

She releases her grip and slides the entire bowl closer to him. "You're right." Cracking her knuckles and rolling her neck, Cari focuses.

Across from me, Diane whispers, "Don't worry, I'm not nearly as serious about all this as these two. I'm just happy to be out of the house and not being called Mom every three seconds. Welcome to Ebey's Head."

I tap my glass of water against hers in a toast. "I'm not sure how I feel about being associated with a dead man's missing head. Can I see how tonight goes before taking the required blood oath or pledging my allegiance to the cause?"

Erik and Diane nod.

Cari sips her water. "Absolutely. You may suck. We're not making any permanent commitments. Think of this as your audition."

This is my life now: a probationary team member for trivia night. I think my days of hanging out in the clubs and going to the coolest concerts in Seattle might be behind me. Not sure when that happened, but I'm surprisingly okay with the change.

A slim, blond man with a patchy ginger beard, glasses, and a piano tie taps a microphone. After going over the rules of engagement and pub quiz etiquette, he declares the fun officially begun.

The woman, who took our drink orders—whose name is Cassie I think—drops off pads of paper and pens to each table.

"What are we supposed to do with those?" I ask, confused.

"For our answers. We each write what we think is the correct answer on our pad then show them to the group to come to a consensus," Diane explains.

"Why don't we just, oh, I don't know, say the answer out loud?" I scrunch up my brow in confusion. Trivia night is going to give me wrinkles.

"Spies," Cari whispers, tipping her head back and to the side to gesture at our neighboring tables. "A few months ago, there was a sting operation that caught several teams eavesdropping for answers."

"Months ago? How long have you all been coming to this?"

"How old is Mac?" Diane counts back the months on her fingers. "I needed a break from two kids and something to help with the mommy fog. Delicious spring rolls and trivia seemed like a good combination. First, I recruited Hailey Donnely, but she dropped out because of pregnancy brain. She roped these two in."

"So you're the ringleader?" Should've known. "Why not drag your husband here?"

"Someone needs to stay home with the kids. We swap nights. Tuesdays, I play trivia. Thursdays John plays pool with Tom Donnely at the Dog House. Everyone wins, and by winning, I mean keeps their sanity."

A flash of color at June's table catches my attention. The waitress delivers a tall glass of pink liquid decorated with a paper umbrella stuck into the straw and a long kabob of pineapple and maraschino cherries.

Not surprising given her love of bright colors and vintage dresses, it seems June likes girly cocktails. Along with being on a pub quiz team, I add this new fact to the small, but growing list of things I find charming about her.

In high school, I was a state champion wrestler in my weight class. Competing at a whopping hundred and twenty pounds, I was a lightweight, more agile and nimble than a larger wrestler using his bulk. I've experienced literal throwdowns as well as underhanded techniques employed to win a match.

I suspect that tonight will feature plenty of both.

My previous pub quiz experience is limited to boisterous bars in Seattle where people randomly shout out the answers to fairly easy questions like "Name a British punk band who wants to save the queen" or "List three grunge bands out of Seattle with at least one dead member" and so on.

This is nothing like that.

We've entered the Thunderdome of trivia.

SEVEN

"Who are these people? Is there some sort of secret, island brain trust? A local Mensa group I don't know about?" I ask my team.

Cari snorts. "I told you it was intense."

We're only on the fourth question and there's already been a loud vocal altercation between two other teams about parliamentary procedure. Another team was disqualified for using Wikipedia on a phone under the table.

"Is there serious money involved?" I could understand the vibe in the room if the winning team walks away with cash.

"The only prize is bragging rights," Diane clarifies. "Doesn't cost anything to play other than the price of drinks and food."

"Wait, we don't even get a ribbon or a trophy? What's the point?" As a millennial, the generation of the participation award, I want accolades for showing up.

"You get our sincere thanks?" Erik suggests earnestly. "You really came through on the question about the date of the DB Cooper disappearance."

"You're welcome, and for the record, I one hundred percent believe he survived the plane crash and was smart enough to disappear with the ransom money." I'm not a conspiracy nut,

47

but some things make sense. Extraterrestrial life, yes. Dragons, yes. Big Foot, possibly.

While we play, my attention keeps drifting over to the round booth in the corner every time I hear June's laughter. Her team consists of three older women. If I had to guess, I'd say they range in age from late forties to early sixties, but it's hard to tell their exact ages. The oldest one is Alexis, the owner of the local independent bookstore. She's an institution in Langley. Between the public librarians and her, they saved teenage me through their book recommendations and quiet places to hang out when I needed to escape home.

The other two aren't as familiar, but I've seen them around downtown. Best guess is they're all part of the same knitting group … or coven. Or both?

Alexis catches me staring at their group and smiles, wiggling her fingers in a friendly wave.

I return the gesture, feeling a fondness for her after all these years.

June glances between Alexis and me, a frown on her face as she says something to her teammate. Still smiling at me, the older woman ducks her head to hear better over the din of the bar.

Whatever June says makes Alexis laugh and pat her arm. Shaking her head, she responds and points at me.

I wish I read lips so I could find out what's obviously being said about me. My cheeks warm.

"Okay, we're moving on to the next question," Simon, our host, announces. "Name all the members of the '80s Brat Pack. First and last names required or your answer will be disqualified. Bonus points if you can also name anyone in the earlier Rat Pack that proceeded them."

I know this.

Frank Sinatra, Sammy Davis, Jr, Dean Martin, Peter Lawford; and … shit, whatshisface.

I'll come back to him.

Ally Sheedy, Molly Ringwald, Emilio Estevez, Anthony Michael Hall, Judd Nelson, Andrew McCarthy, Demi Moore, Rob Lowe.

After I scribble all the names I can remember, I place my paper in the middle of the table.

"Wow. That was fast." Diane high-fives me.

"Unless 'whatshisface' is someone's actual name, I didn't get all of the Rat Pack. Hoping one of you can fill in the blank."

June's also done writing on her paper. When our eyes meet, she lifts her glass in a toast—or a challenge.

"Jerry Lewis!" I shout before I remember the rules. "Shit."

Simon chuckles into his cordless microphone. "Someone's a big fan."

Embarrassed, I check June's reaction to my outburst.

Amusement pursing her lips, she shakes her head.

Was that an *I can't believe he just yelled out the answer* no? Or a *No, Jerry wasn't cool enough to be in the Rat Pack"* headshake? Would she warn me about being wrong? Why would she help us? Giving information to the enemy would seem to be against the spirit of trivia Thunderdome.

Diane scoops up everyone's papers and silently reads them.

"Okay, we have consensus on all the members of the Brat Pack but only agree on four out of the five OGs."

"Anyone else have Mr. Lewis?" I whisper. "Or can we pretend I was deliberately misleading our competition?"

Diane shows me the rest of the slips of paper.

"Right. That guy." I point at Joey Bishop.

We hand over our final answer to Cassie. Simon announces, "The only two teams who had the answer right are Yarned and Dangerous and"—he holds up the card like he's already forgotten the second team—"Ebey's Head, which means we have two teams tied for first place."

Smug my outburst didn't derail us, I grin at June. Her acknowledgment is a slight dip of her chin.

I grin to myself. Maybe she doesn't think of me as an enemy after all.

We alternate winning rounds until the final question. Simon announces the category is arts and crafts.

All three of my teammates groan.

"I swear they somehow rig this whole thing, probably bribing Simon with mittens and extra thick socks," Cari mutters.

"We're doomed." Erik rests both of his hands on top of his head.

"Hey, I've got the art part down," Diane reassures them.

"Ready?" Simon asks. "This type of embroidery was widely popular in Britain during the seventeenth century and can feature threads of precious materials like gold and silver as well as wool."

Erik puts his pen down. "I'm out."

Cari and Diane stare at each other, brows scrunched in thought.

Instead of paying attention to my own team, I watch as June writes something on her paper and folds it in half with a sharp crease.

Costumes and fashion aren't my wheelhouse, but I've read enough fantasy fiction in my lifetime to be familiar with some terms. It's a long shot, but I scrawl a single word on my page.

All three pairs of eyes stare at me.

"What?" I place my paper in the center.

"You confident about that answer?" Cari points at the only page on the table. "Because you're our only hope."

"I've still got nothing," Diane agrees. "I'm not crafty at all."

"Do we still get bragging rights for coming in second?" I ask.

"Not really, but allegedly tying brings on a sudden death round."

"Allegedly?" I clarify. "No one has ever tied before?"

"Not even once," Diane says.

"Nothing to lose but losing. Let's go with this one." I tap the middle of the table.

Cassie shows up to collect our answer.

Unable to stop focusing on June, I notice she raises her eyebrows at me after Cassie takes their paper. I swear she mouths, "Bring it."

"The answer we're looking for is crewelwork. Let's see if anyone got it correct." Simon takes forever to read the responses, and his dramatic pause draws grumbling from the various teams. "Well, this is exciting. For the first time in our history, we're moving on to a tie-breaking sudden death round between Ebey's Head and our reigning champions, Yarned and Dangerous."

June's jaw drops so far I'm worried she's going to bang it on the table.

My own team sits stunned, all eyes on me while I grin in triumph.

"How did you know that?" Erik asks.

"Reading books." Pleased and enjoying June's shock, I shrug off their surprise.

Cari holds out her fist for a bump. "Inviting you tonight was the best decision I've ever made."

"Hey now, what about me?" Erik crosses his arms.

Leaning across the table, Cari kisses his cheek. "Okay, okay. After coming to Whidbey on a whim and then moving here permanently, this is right up there."

"We haven't won yet," I point out.

"I have a good feeling about this," Diane says. "If Jonah can stop staring at June long enough to really focus, we might win."

Busted, I bite the corner of my mouth and drop my focus to my hands on the table.

"Thought so," she mumbles, amused.

Simon's voice brings our attention back to him. "Okay, each of the tied teams will appoint one person to be their player for sudden death. I'll ask a question and the first person to respond with the correct answer wins. If you say the wrong answer, the other team will automatically win."

"No pressure or anything," I joke. "Which one of you is going to do it?"

They make eye contact and nod.

"You," Erik declares.

"Me? I'm the new guy. This might be our one shot at glory. Are you sure?"

Cari speaks for all of them. "A hundred percent. You're our good luck charm."

"Who are our players?" Simon asks.

"Jonah for us." Diane lifts her arm and points down at my head.

"And for you?" Simon turns to June's table.

"Me," June says, eyes on me.

"Come on up." Simon swings his arm, inviting us to join him near the DJ booth.

As our teams cheer for us, I enjoy the view of June walking ahead of me. Her full skirt makes her waist appear narrow, exaggerating her hourglass shape. Some men like athletic and thin women, but I prefer a woman with curves and softness to her body.

We face each other in front of Simon like this is an impromptu wedding ceremony, which is now the weirdest though I've had during this very strange evening.

"Introduce yourselves." He holds the mic in front of June and then me.

"Okay, June and Jonah, are you ready to fight to the death to become champion of China Ruby trivia?"

Dramatic, much?

"Yes," we both agree as if murder is something we're completely comfortable with in order to win a competition that doesn't even give out a trophy.

"Either of you have questions before I read the clue?"

"I do." Keeping my focus on June, I ask, "Do we have to wait until you've read the entire clue before answering?"

Simon chuckles. "Eager, are we? No, feel free to share your

guess as soon as you think you know it." His tone tells me he fully expects a premature exclamation from me. "Any more questions?"

"No. I'm good."

June stares at me, her cheeks flushed. Standing with her hands on her hips, her shoulders back, and her chin lifted, she's in a classic power pose, showing me I don't intimate her.

She's adorable. I've always been a sucker for vintage Wonder Woman.

Simon lowers his voice, sounding like a TV gameshow host. "Sudden death begins now. I'll say the clue only once, so listen carefully."

June's teeth worry the corner of her bottom lip. Distracted by the deep rose color of her lips and thoughts of kissing her, tasting her, I momentarily zone out and miss the first words of Simon's clue.

"… beloved by the French, this American was also a vocal advocate for—"

"Jerry Lewis!" For the second time tonight, I yell out that name.

June's lips part but she doesn't speak. No one says anything. *Oh fuck.*

"That's correct!" Simon slaps me on the shoulder. "Looks like we have a new champion. Congrats to Ebey's Head!"

"Holy shit!" Diane shouts and jumps out of our booth. Cari and Erik quickly follow, high-fiving each other and other teams as they walk toward me.

June extends her hand. "Congratulations. Great game."

Like her smile, her words are genuine. A happy feeling settles in my chest at getting complimented by her.

"Thank you. You were tough competition." My longer fingers engulf her warm hand. "Sorry, my hand is cold."

"Crewelwork, huh?" She tilts her head to the side, studying me.

"Told you I'm the king of random information."

"Rematch next week?"

It's a challenge, but one I'm happy to accept. I feel like I'm beginning to crack her tough outer shell.

Cari slips between us and hugs me while Erik grips my shoulder, rocking me back and forth. "He'll be here. He doesn't have a choice."

"You're one of us now." Diane joins our group hug.

"What about Hailey?" I ask once we break apart.

"Other than her savant knowledge of the Backstreet Boys and other '90s pop bands, she doesn't compare." Erik eyes me. "How are you with boy band trivia?"

"Not my kind of music. Sorry."

"No worries, I'm pretty good." Cari's tucked her arm through mine and leads me back to our table. "We'll see you next Tuesday, right?"

Diane snorts. "She makes that joke every week."

Trying to find June in the room, I half-heartedly chuckle at whatever they're saying. "I'll be here."

Alexis walks by our table and smiles at me. "Congratulations on your win. Enjoy the big booth, but don't get too comfortable in it."

After she leaves, I ask the table for confirmation. "Did she just put us in the one-and-done category? Like this was a one-off win?"

"Completely." Erik pulls out his wallet to pay.

I do the same.

"It's on us tonight. No trophy, but you did get free beer and an egg roll."

"Okay, next time we win, I'm paying."

June might not be my biggest fan, but this could be a way to break down her defenses and find out why.

EIGHT

There's another car in the lot at the trailhead when I arrive. After a week of non-stop rain, I thought the promise of sun and blue sky would draw more people outside this morning, hence the reason I'm here just after dawn. I prefer my walks in the woods to be solitary. This is where I think and plan and sort through daily life. I can do the full five-mile loop on the trails in Saratoga Woods and still be the first one at work.

A few minutes into my trek, I notice a tiny door filling a gap in the roots of a cedar near the trail. Complete with hinges and a small window, the arched wooden door is perfectly scaled down to fit the natural curve of the tree.

"Hello there," I say to it then immediately feel ridiculous, but not enough to stop talking. "What are you hiding?"

Squatting down, I manage to disengage the latch and open it. Tucked into the small space is a real bird's nest containing three tiny eggs. At first glance, I think they're real eggs, too, but when I pick one up, I discover it's a painted rock.

Someone put a lot of time into crafting the details of the door and its hidden treasure.

Carefully, I replace the egg back and close the door's latch, leaving everything as I found it for the next observant hiker.

I reach the crest of the trail and find a woman sitting in what I've come to consider my spot. There's a large cedar log that's become a makeshift bench at the turnaround point near the enormous glacial boulder, and it's occupied by June. I recognize her dark hair and the curve of her body even though she's not in her typical feminine clothing.

Once I recover from the surprise of seeing her and calm my racing heart, I find my voice. "Good morning."

She startles. "What are you doing here?"

As I step into the clearing, I notice she's not wearing a dress. I don't think I've ever seen her in anything other than a dress or a skirt, but this morning she's sporting dark purple leggings and a pair of hiking boots splattered with mud. Now I understand the Victorian fascination with calves. This feels intimate, seeing the full outline of her legs from ankle to hip.

I don't realize I'm staring until the soft sound of a throat clearing breaks the trance of June's lower half. Realizing I didn't answer her question, I reply, "This is my favorite spot for an early morning hike. Never seen you here before."

"I'm usually more of an afternoon hiker. I love the slant of afternoon light through the trees, but the rain is supposed to return later today, so I thought I'd enjoy the sun while I can. I didn't know you'd claimed the rock as your own. Should I go?"

"No, of course not." I walk up the path and settle on a round outcropping of the boulder. "I had the same thought, about the rain. Seize the moment and all that."

"Do you come here often?" She wrinkles her nose. "That sounded like a pick-up line. It wasn't."

Disappointed she's not using a cheesy line on me, I chuckle. "Thanks for clarifying."

"I didn't want you to get the wrong idea." Her laughter sounds more nervous than amused.

"Trust me, I knew you weren't trying to hit on me." Exhaling, I decide to be honest. "I get the feeling you're not a fan of mine."

"Why would you think that?"

"Are you?"

"A fan? Do you have a lot of fans?"

"Why are you answering my questions with more questions?"

"Am I?" Her lips twitch with amusement.

I laugh. "Well played."

"Do you want me to be one of your fans?"

"No." Images of a Naked Whidbey calendar hanging in her house flash through my mind and I cringe. Moments like this are why I should've given more thought to posing naked for charity. "It's a figure of speech."

Adjusting her green glasses with the tip of her finger, she clarifies. "So what you're really asking is why don't I like you."

Her straightforward words and steady gaze do a much better job than I do of getting to the point. Feeling like I've been physically punched in the gut, I focus on my breathing.

A droplet of water falls on my head from the large cedar tree above me. I'm pretty sure it's rainwater and not bird shit, but given the direction this encounter had been heading in, the latter might be more appropriate. I swipe my hand over my hair and am relieved to see clear liquid.

"Guess I am."

"Does it matter if I don't?" She tucks her hands into the pockets of her parka.

"Like me?"

She nods.

"Was it something I did? Or said?"

"We're just very different." Her gaze shifts to a spot over my shoulder.

"How do you know?"

She points at her eyebrow, earlobes, and forearms.

"Ah, judging a book by its cover?" She's not the first to make up her mind about me based on physical appearance. Most of the time, I don't care what people think. If they want to be superficial assholes, let them. June doing it annoys me, though, and apparently, I can't let it go. Whether or not she likes me, I'm smitten with her.

"We might have loads of stuff in common. We both enjoy a cutthroat pub quiz night and hikes in the woods. We could share an unquenchable love for ramen, or a mutual hatred of golf."

"Those seem oddly specific."

"I don't like golf, but I wouldn't say it's reached hatred level. Please don't tell me you were varsity golf state champion."

"Never played more than mini golf as a kid."

"Phew. So that's one thing."

"And I do love ramen," she replies, tone thoughtful.

"Have you tried Oodles on Second Street?"

"They're next door to the Pilates studio, so I eat there all the time. Pretty sure I've had everything on their menu."

"What's your favorite?" I want to keep her talking and sharing about herself.

"The spicy miso ramen." She sounds pleasantly surprised to learn I like the same place she does. "I swear it has magical properties. Liquid sunshine in a bowl."

"Also my favorite." Feeling a positive shift in the dynamic between us, I continue, "Okay, that's four things in common. See? Not so different after all."

Are we turning a corner? Whatever negative preconceptions she's had about me can be dispelled by getting to know each other better.

"I hate video games." She lifts her chin in challenge.

Whoa. Here I am thinking we're starting over on common ground and she's firing arrows straight at my heart. "Why? What did they ever do to you?"

"Seems like a pointless waste of time." Her dismissive shrug is another shot.

"Ouch." I rub the imaginary wound in the middle of my chest. "Video games saved my life."

I might be exaggerating slightly, but they did provide an escape when I needed one.

"See? We're very different. I'd rather make tangible things than hide away in an alternative reality, fighting fake bad guys or driving imaginary cars for points that don't matter."

My jaw has literally dropped open in shock. "Do you feel the same about pinball?"

"Probably."

"You're not sure?"

Even June has flaws. I realize in this moment that I've put her on a pedestal of perfection. Too concerned about impressing her, I hadn't stopped to consider if she's the right woman for me. Pinball is life, so this might be an issue.

"Until your grand opening, I'd never seen an actual machine. Outside of old movies and TV shows I didn't know they still existed," she confesses. "They seem loud, obnoxious and pointless. Randomly moving a ball around using flippers doesn't appeal to me."

"Don't knock it till you try it. Some people find them satisfying and stimulating. There's skill involved, hand-eye coordination. Pinball is about mastering physics." I'm determined to change her mind about something I love.

"Physics?" Her voice mirrors the doubt on her face.

"Gravity, velocity, momentum, friction, kinetic energy." I pause. "Want me to continue? I can also discuss game theory, if you'd like."

"No thank you. I know myself well enough to know they're not my thing."

I stop myself from explaining real-world applications. Whatever I'm trying to sell, she's not interested. A Girl Scout trying to sell cookies to robots might have more success. I go for another tactic. "Have you ever surprised yourself?"

"No." Her answer is quick, perfunctory, a door slamming shut.

I feel a little sorry for June.

"I can see why you love knitting instead of games."

Her eyes narrow. "Why's that?"

"You like following instructions and rules, using the same pattern because you know what to expect." I might be poking the bear a little, but if she's made up her mind about me, there's nothing to lose. "You're afraid of being out of control or outsmarted."

She purses her lips and twists them to one side.

"Hit too close to home?" I ask.

"I don't see any of that as a negative. Life's easier with a plan."

I arch an eyebrow. "Did you plan to move to Whidbey and run a yarn store?"

"No, that wasn't in my imaginary life plan." She sighs. "Doesn't mean I'm going to suddenly develop a passion for pinball."

"Never said you would." Rolling my lips together, I avoid a gloating smile.

Quiet, she worries her bottom lip with her teeth. "What about you?"

I lift both eyebrows. "Me? No, I've never had a timetable for my life. Business plans? Yes. Personal life plan? Always find them to be a waste of time because there are too many unknown factors that easily derail things."

"Interesting." She says it the same way my grandmother did when she didn't approve of something.

"I never want to get to the point in life where nothing surprises me anymore. Means I'm not pushing myself or caring enough to pay attention."

Shoving off of the rock, I brush my hands over my ass.

She remains silent as she observes me like she's not sure what I'm going to do next.

"It's okay if you don't like me or want to be friends with me. I get that I'm not everyone's taste, but you're missing out on a vast ocean of possibilities if you don't open yourself up to people and things that are different than you. Since we're standing in the woods, I'll bring up Robert Frost's lines about taking the path less traveled."

"I wasn't expecting you to be familiar with his poems." She sounds surprised, and maybe even a little impressed.

"Not expecting a guy with tattoos and piercings to quote classic American poetry?" I grin. "Might you even say I … surprised you?"

Her signature move of narrowing her eyes and pursing her lips makes me laugh.

"I can see I might have to reevaluate," she murmurs, more to herself than for my ears.

"Then my work here is done." Hoping we've at least moved past the enemy zone into neutral territory, I ask, "Want to hike back to the parking lot together?"

"Thanks, but I think I'm going to sit here for a while longer."

"It's starting to rain." I point up at the sky in case she's forgotten where the wet stuff comes from.

"I'll be fine. I like my own company." She zips her jacket and pulls up her hood.

"Suit yourself. If you ever get curious about the joy of a simple game of pinball, you know where to find me." I adjust my hoodie to cover my head.

"See you around, Jonah."

Even though I've been dismissed, there's a pep in my step on the way down the trail. Cracks are forming in the glass box around June. We're not exactly friends, but I don't think we're adversaries either. This thought makes me happy.

———

My good mood lasts all the way to the trailhead and through the drive home.

The old Sears Kit cottage was moved to Columbia Beach by

barge from Seattle over a hundred years ago. When someone bought the property and wanted to tear down the small structure, a local group rallied to save it from destruction. Basically, the house was free to a good home as long as the new owner had land to put it on.

The purchase of a few acres in the woods and a crazy plan to move it by flatbed truck later, I owned my own place. The house isn't much to look at and doesn't have a lot of space, but it's perfect for me. A living room, a bedroom, an office, bathroom, and small kitchen are all I need, plus there's plenty of space to park my camper in the open carport I built close to the house. My friend John brought over his logging equipment to clear the timber from the land and returned the former trees as cords of wood, ready to be chopped for my wood stove. Along with a propane tank for the gas stove and water heater, I'm pretty self-sufficient.

Ashley calls it *The Homestead* and is always asking me about canning. One summer, I got so carried away making pickles I can never live it down, or eat bread and butter pickles again … or pickled beets, pickled asparagus, dilly beans, or—the worst mistake—pickled eggs. I worried people might stop speaking to me after everyone got pickles for Christmas that year. Lesson learned.

Cell service is spotty in the woods, so I have an old school landline for emergencies. I think four people have the number. Besides my sister and mom, Erik and Layla know to only call for work emergencies.

I like being able to turn off my cell and disconnect. Unfortunately, this isn't something I've been able to do for a while. When I can't get away physically, I hide out here and avoid the rest of the world.

After months of working seven days a week, I finally have a day off. No plans, no meetings. No one to manage, no customers to serve.

Sounds like heaven. Dropping my keys in their bowl on the

kitchen counter, I make a beeline for the fridge to grab a beer. Open bottle in hand, I settle on the couch in the living room.

"Ah." I exhale after taking a long sip, slouching down to rest my head against the back of the couch.

Normally, the silence is comforting.

Closing my eyelids, I wait for a sense of calm and peace to spread over me. Instead of gratitude for the stillness, I'm feeling antsy. It's too quiet.

I shuffle through the events of the day and the last couple of weeks. Other than my short hike, I haven't spent enough time outside, and even then I couldn't escape June or my thoughts about her.

Every time I think I'm making progress with her, one of us ends up saying something awkward.

I've never had issues getting along with women. My sister, my friends' wives and girlfriends, and Ceci and Naya from college can all vouch for me. Should I have them write letters of reference for me and send them to June?

I take a long draft of beer, wondering for the hundredth time why her opinion matters when so many others don't.

There isn't a logical explanation.

All I know is that it does, and I'm forever frustrated by it.

NINE

Upholding my promise to Cari and the team, I return to trivia night and bring my A game to the corner booth. Ten texts to confirm I'd show up tonight from Cari and one from Erik's number that I suspect was also from Cari and here I am. Even arrived early.

"I have a question." I lower my voice. "Diane, if June worked part-time at your studio, why didn't you recruit her to your team?"

Evidently, I can't get June off of my mind.

"I know, I know." Diane sounds exasperated. "I didn't think to ask her. The first time we played, she showed up with her knitting group. Trust me, I've tried to bring her over to our side, but she's loyal. Great in an employee and friend, but not so good when I want her to switch teams."

"Epic fail. You should've locked her down right away. Otherwise, you only have yourself to blame if someone else comes along and puts a ring on it," Cari scolds, wagging her finger in Diane's direction over a half-empty scorpion bowl. "First rule of dating and trivia teams."

"Erik? You want to comment on that?" I slyly ask, knowing he's been thinking of proposing.

His eyes flash to mine. "No, nothing to add."

I don't know why he's waiting. They've been together for over two years and seem solid, not that they need to get married to be happy together. God knows a wedding doesn't equal a happy life.

"Hey, it's Jerry Lewis." Simon joins our table. Hot dogs have replaced the crazy piano tie from last week, and I'm a little sad to discover he's a quirky tie guy instead of trapped in an '80s music video.

"Actually, it isn't. Jonah is fine. Sadly, it's one of those names that doesn't have an automatic nickname."

"I'm sure we can come up with something." He strokes the fluffy puffs of beard along his jaw.

"Eh, that's okay. Not really the nickname or pet name kind of guy." I shrug.

His expression morphs from overly cheerful wide eyes and too many teeth to annoyed. "Okay. All right, no need to get testy about it. Just being a friendly host."

Opening my mouth to argue that I'm not testy, I realize the irony of doing that and shut it. No point. I have nothing to prove to Simon Says. Instead, I show my teeth in a fake smile.

After he moves on to be friendly to other teams, Cari groans, "Ugh, why is it always the guy who swears he's just being friendly who turns out to be the biggest creeper?"

"The worst," Diane agrees. "Most likely to send you a dick pic while telling everyone what a nice guy he is."

Cari gags. "Please tell me you're speaking figuratively."

"Yes. Oh dear lord, yes, at least when it comes to Simon."

Erik and I exchange uncomfortable looks.

"For the record, I've never sent anyone such a picture," I reassure them. "My dick is like Big Foot—zero photographic evidence."

The women laugh, but Erik remains quiet.

Cari faces him. "Erik?"

"The whole world saw my naked ass," Erik brags. "Not sure if that counts."

"Probably not all seven and a half billion people." Cari laughs at her lame attempt to reassure him. "And it doesn't count, because I'm the one who took that picture."

It's nice they can laugh now about the viral sensation started by a picture on Cari's phone three years ago. At the time, I was certain Erik's head was going to explode. Instead, they fell in love. With the help of Dan's wife and PR genius, Roslyn, Erik and Cari spun the attention into a multi-million-dollar charity fundraiser. Not a bad ending for a story that began with public nudity.

"Moving on from talk of unsolicited, virtual flashings—what's Simon's beef with me? Was it my imagination or was he being a jerk? He was friendly to all of you."

Diane and Cari meet each other's eye. "Probably because you unseated his girlfriend from her throne as trivia queen."

"Who's his girlfriend?" Alexis is married, but I don't know the other women's relationship status. "Hold on, you don't mean June, do you? June's dating Simon Says?"

What the hell? I glance over at the Yarned and Dangerous table where he lingers, chuckling and smiling down at June.

That's her type? Guys who wear piano ties and host trivia nights at random bars? Does he even get paid for these gigs? How does he make a living?

You know what? What do I care? June barely speaks to me. I have no claim on her. Hell, we don't even know each other.

That said, a blind man in space could see she's way too good for him—out of his league, above his pay grade. She deserves more. If they are dating, someone needs to take her aside and tell her she can do better.

"Is that why you think the game is rigged? Because Simon makes sure his girlfriend's team always wins?" Disbelief frays my voice. "Why doesn't someone complain?"

"Whoa." Diane holds up her hands. "We weren't serious. June isn't with Simon."

Cari giggles. "The guy obviously has a crush on June, but she couldn't be less interested."

She could. I've experienced it.

"*Is* she dating anyone?" My curiosity gets the better of me. There is no logical reason why I can't shake this crush. If I've developed a thing for knitters, I'm sure I could find hundreds of single women in Seattle who knit and don't hate me. Okay, at least dozens. If I bothered with dating apps or was interested in diving back into the dating scene, there are millions of single brunettes looking for love. Unfortunately, no other woman has the same effect on me. Unable to rationalize away my feelings about June, I've accepted that the heart defies logic.

Diane's lips flatten into a thin line and she seems annoyed. "Not that I've heard. We don't really gossip about our personal lives, but she's never mentioned anyone. Then again, she's not really putting herself out there by spending all her time with grandmothers."

"Ever?" Cari asks. "She's lived here for how long? I know the pickins are slim ..." Her attention flicks to me. "No offense, Jonah. There are a few good men on the island, though."

Diane's frown switches to a smile. "Are you single these days?"

Wary of where she's going with this, I pause. "Haven't had time for a social life lately."

"Interesting." With a nod and a wicked gleam in her eye, it's plain she's about to start scheming.

Cari perks up. "What's interesting?"

"*Nothing,*" I stress, keeping my gaze steady on Diane's face. We don't know each other well, so I'm surprised she's thinking about playing matchmaker. However, she probably knows June the best out of all of us and could be a good ally.

She doesn't glance away. "We can discuss this another time. Look! Simon's getting ready to start."

"I'm not sure I can handle the pressure of defending the big booth," Cari announces. "If I choke tonight, don't hate me."

My attention drifts over to June's table. Tonight's cardigan is cardinal red, a power color and the same shade as her lipstick. She's here to reclaim her place as trivia queen.

Good.

I like a challenge. Obviously, I still haven't been deterred by June's chilly behavior toward me.

That's the fun of not being a knight in shining armor or Prince Charming—no one expects me to play nice.

If she wants to do battle, I'm ready. Our mutual passion for winning only proves we have more in common than she wants to admit.

I lift my beer. She does the same with her fruity cocktail. We silently toast. Instead of glowering at me like last time, she allows herself a wry smile. I mirror the expression back at her.

Across from me, Diane turns her head to see whom I'm looking at. When she catches my attention, she nods conspiratorially.

————

"I can't believe we won!" Cari holds up both of her hands for a group high five. "Not even a tie-breaker."

"What are you doing?" Erik asks her, watching as she wiggles on the banquette.

"Claiming this spot by creating a butt groove like Sheldon on *Big Bang Theory*." She grinds on the upholstery.

"Don't jinx us." Diane laughs at her. "We've only won twice. Yarned and Dangerous has a lot more wins than us—by a lot."

"Yes, but now we have Jonah and they can suck it." Shaking her head, Cari stops her seat marking. "I might be too invested in trivia night."

Erik slings his arm around her shoulder. "Just a little bit."

June and Alexis stop by the table to congratulate us.

"I can see we're going to need to up our game," Alexis jokes. "All those hours you spent loitering around the bookstore have paid off, Jonah. Nicely done on the Robert Frost quote."

Her praise makes me uncomfortable. "It's also from one of my favorite books growing up."

"I remember."

"*The Outsiders* by SE Hinton," June says softly. "That was one of my favorites, too."

I twist my lips to the side and fiddle with the ring in my ear. "You don't say."

Yes, I'm flirting. Yes, I'm pleased she realizes we have another thing in common.

Diane breaks the silent tension between June and me. "There's always next week. I'm sure we're all looking forward to seeing each other again … for another fun night of trivia."

She's more perceptive than I'm comfortable with. Maybe Ashley's right—maybe I do have an obvious tell.

TEN

Two weeks after opening, we hold an anti-Valentine's party at The Place, complete with a playlist competition for the best songs for the bitter, lonely, heartbroken, disinterested, and resigned. Layla came up with the idea, but I'm all in.

Halsey's "Bad at Love" has been played at least five times on as many different playlists. One more and I'm going to have to step in and put a moratorium on the song. TLC's "No Scrubs" has already been banned.

CeeLo Green's "Fuck You" has inspired an impromptu dance party. Probably not parentally approved, but I'm not about censoring what music the teens listen to because of some cursing. A few f-bombs aren't going to damn anyone to hell or a life of crime.

On the other hand, me losing my shit over "No Scrubs" might accomplish both of those. Apparently, all things '90s are back to being cool.

The kids hung up a dartboard with a picture of Cupid over the bullseye. Amber and Layla baked heart-shaped cookies and then cut them all in half. Some resemble broken hearts and they decorated others with Be Fri and St Ends, which they explained to me are BFF heart charms. The things I don't know.

No flowers or hearts allowed. Chocolate, however, is still acceptable. We're not heathens. I glance out the window, down the street at June's store. Unlike our black crepe streamers and hearts, the windows of In the Loop are decorated in the more traditional style appropriate for a holiday celebrating all things love. We're the Nightmare Before Valentine's Day versus the delicate, handmade, paper heart garlands sweetly adorning June's windows.

That's the two of us perfectly summed up. We're opposite ends of the spectrum, parallel lines that will never meet.

Which is probably for the best.

Any more pink and In the Loop would rival Dolores Umbridge's office at Hogwarts. With all the dark decorations in here, we could be hosting a Victorian funeral or a gathering of Death Eaters.

"You've turned all the little Whos of Whoville into emo goths," Amber says in awe. She fits right in with her black jeans, black Whidbey Joe's hoodie, and a striped black and white top.

"This wasn't even my idea," I remind her. "Layla suggested it and the group voted. I had nothing to do with it."

Amber grins. "It's brilliant and you should take credit. We should make it an annual event."

"I admit Valentine's isn't my favorite holiday, if it even qualifies as one, but I'm enjoying today." My goal was to create a safe, welcoming space for the weirdos and misfits, the oddballs and nonconformists. "I'd say our first party is a success."

"Gold Digger" blasts through the speakers, inspiring another dance party.

"Okay, who played this?" I use the remote to turn down the volume and stop the windows from rattling.

One of the teens, Theo, sheepishly lifts a finger.

"How old were you when this came out? Two?"

This earns me a laugh from the group.

"What do you know about gold diggers?" I'm only a few

steps away from talking about that one time in Nam like Olaf or one of the older guys at the VFW clubhouse in Freeland.

Crossing his arms, Theo widens his stance in challenge. "FTR, some girl used to hang out with me during lunch in middle school because she knew I'd give her my fries and cookies. What do you call that?"

"Total gold digger. Was that Tasha? She borrowed a pen from me and never returned it." Lara jumps in to take his side. "Didn't she move away?"

Not interested in getting involved in their gossip or weird attempts at flirting, I stroll to the other side of the service counter to give them some space.

In the back near the commercial triple sink, Layla's pulling a rack of clean glasses from the dishwasher, and I offer to help. With her overalls and her blonde hair in braids, she doesn't look much older than the kids. She's cute and nice, but I don't date employees.

We stack glasses and mugs on their shelves, the sound blocking out the teens' conversations and Kanye's voice.

"You think there's something going on between them?" she whispers to me, tilting her head in the direction of Lara and Theo.

"I'm no expert in the mating dance of teenagers, but I think Lara would like there to be. If Theo's anything like I was in high school, he's clueless and oblivious."

She sighs. "It's sweet."

"You've worked for me for this long and I never knew you were a romantic?" I ask, returning an empty rack to the machine.

"I can't help myself—it's Valentine's Day." With an embarrassed lift of her shoulders, she says, "Have any plans? Or are you firmly in the anti-Valentine's camp?"

"I am and these are my plans. You?"

"I'm meeting Daryl for pizza when we finish here."

"Daryl? Do I know him?" I feel protective of my employees and am fine sounding like a dad.

"He works at Donnely Boats." A faint blush tinges her cheeks. "It isn't serious."

———

We settle into a rhythm at The Place. Layla and Amber take turns training Lara, Dax, and Theo on the espresso machine. Our plan is for them to be up to speed and working a few hours a week during the spring so they're ready to work the busy summer season. Best way for them to feel a sense of pride and ownership in this place is to give them some responsibility for its success.

On a dark and rainy afternoon with zero foot traffic, we play a random game of ad-libs. Layla writes answers on a pad of paper while a group of four teens yell random words.

"Keep it PG," I shout after one of the guys suggests eggplant. "I'm onto you and your emoji codes."

Jesus, I'm a hot minute away from hoisting my pants to my ribs and handing out Werther's Originals.

What fool thought working with teens would keep me young and hip? All I want to do is go home, eat a cold can of soup and go to sleep by nine. This exhaustion reminds me of being camping tired, rising with the sun and crashing a few hours past sunset. Since we're still technically in winter for another week, that means going to bed by six. I should get an award for making it until late evening.

Running both the Fellowship of the Bean and Whidbey Joe's with Erik has never been as exhausting as this project. I should apologize to Erik for all the times I called him immature.

Then again, his naked ass went viral, so I'm not sure if he's ready for the adulting award.

"After this round, we're closing. Given the weather, I doubt we'll get any more customers. Let's start cleaning up," I tell the crew. "It's five o'clock. You don't have to go home, but you're not staying here."

"Man," Dax moans. "What happened to having evening hours? You know five o'clock is still technically the afternoon."

He makes a good argument. "Add it to the list, along with open mic night, the co-ed sleepover Theo suggested, movie night, and the DJ competition. We'll discuss everything at the monthly meeting—except the sleepover, because *that's* not happening."

"You're so old fashioned. Even church camp is co-ed and we sleep over," Theo mutters.

"Theo, you're going to make a fantastic lawyer someday. Today, though, is not that day."

"Fine." He grabs a broom and starts sweeping in the corner near the front windows.

While we don't turn away anyone who wants a coffee, the general vibe here is definitely geared toward teens. This is *their* place. The few tourists and local adults who wander in grab their drinks and leave. In fact, I've been thinking about adding a walkup to-go window on the side of the building.

"You don't have to stay and babysit us, Jonah. We're perfectly capable of closing up on our own," Dax suggests. "Isn't that the whole point of this place? Teaching us responsibility? Layla's an adult, but like a cool adult."

"I agree with all of that, but today, I've decided to close early. End of discussion." It's no secret that I might need to work on my control issues. "Is there a reason you don't want to go home, Dax?"

He blusters and postures. "No, not at all."

I'm not sure if I believe him, but I won't press him on it in front of the others.

The front door swings open and a chorus of "We're closed" greets June.

She hasn't been here since the grand opening party and I'm surprised but happy to see her in the doorway.

"Ignore them. Come inside." I smile and motion her in. "We're cleaning up for the day, but I can make you something."

Aware of four pairs of eyes watching my every move, I act like she's any other customer.

"No coffee for me, but I have a favor to ask." June toys with the end of her pink scarf.

"Shoot." I keep my tone casual when I already know the answer will be yes to whatever she needs.

"Can you give me a ride home? My car was acting weird yesterday so I took it to the shop this morning, and they need to keep it another day for a part to come in. I would've asked Alexis, but she's already gone."

This is huge. June's asking *me* for a favor. I want to pump my fist over my head in triumph. She's obviously moved on from thinking I'm an evil troll who lives under a bridge if she's willingly asking to be trapped in a small space with me. *Hello, hope, my old friend. We meet again.*

Instead, I play it cool and ignore the soft "Oooh" from one of the kids—Theo probably.

"Uh, sure. Mind waiting while we finish? Or I can swing by the shop when I'm done in about twenty minutes." I'm giving her an escape.

"That sounds good. Just honk and I'll come out. Thanks so much." She pauses for a second, seeming on the verge of saying more, before she changes her mind and leaves.

"Look at old man Jonah getting a date. You've still got it, you dog." Theo gives me an exaggerated thumbs-up.

"Theo." I glower at him. The kid is a walking hormone.

Dax joins in on the teasing. "That was totally a date setup. You shouldn't honk though. That's rude. Show some respect and walk up to her door."

The two of them are practically twins in their retro grunge flannel shirts, droopy jeans and boots—hip, teenage versions of Tweedledee and Tweedledum.

"Trust me, it isn't a date. In case any of you would like to know, for it to be a date, one person has to ask the other person to go out and do something, like see a movie or have dinner, maybe go to a concert. This is a friendly favor. Big difference."

I could explain how June and I aren't really friends. We've barely waived the white flag to call a truce in the war I never understood.

"You should ask her out on the drive home. Then you can go to dinner and it'll be a date." Lara suggests. Her eyes cut to Theo as she speaks. "A date doesn't have to be a big deal."

Ignoring the tension between them, I declare, "New rule: my social life is not up for discussion."

Theo smirks. "From the sound of it, you don't really have one."

The others snicker at his comment, including Layla, who tries to cover her amusement with a hand over her mouth.

My temper flares for a second before dissolving. He's right. All work and no play.

I should check the calendar for concerts this weekend in Seattle, go to a few shows, see some friends. I need to have conversations about music and art and life that don't involve work, family, or teenaged nuisances.

ELEVEN

"So?"

June buckles her seat belt and twists to face me. "Yes?"

"I need to know where you live if I'm going to drive you home."

"Oh, right. Of course." She sounds embarrassed. "You can just drive me to Ken's Corner. It isn't a far walk from there."

"That's silly. It's pouring and you don't have a hood or an umbrella. You'll be soaked, catch a cold, die from pneumonia, and I'll live out my days in guilt and shame. Besides, if you're close to Ken's, you're on my way."

"Really, I don't want to put you out." Her fingers worry the edge of her sleeve.

"You're not, unless you insist on walking in the rain." I tease.

We ride in awkward silence while the defroster blasts warm air, the wipers squeaking when they begin their return arc across the windows.

On the shoulder of the road near the fairgrounds, June spots a group of rabbits hanging out in the grass. "Poor, sweet bunnies."

"Clearly, you've never read *Watership Down*." I tease.

"Apples and oranges. That's like saying all pigs are evil

because of Snowball in *Animal Farm*." She crosses her arms, releases them a second later to straighten out her skirt before crossing them again.

I like that we're bickering over literary references. I've hit a nerve, but why? "They're fine. If they weren't, they'd find a place out of the rain."

"Do you think they're happy?" she asks, sincerely.

The idea never occurred to me. "You know they aren't pets, right? Completely feral by this point."

"I know." She frowns. "But they're from genetically domesticated rabbits. You can't just release domestic animals into the wild and think they'll know how to survive."

"I'm not sure how to count rabbit generations, but those are the descendants of the rabbits that figured out how to live in the wild and if they're sitting in a field in the rain, so be it." Briefly, I glance at her, and she's glaring out the front window with her arms crossed. "Yes?"

"I didn't figure you to be so cold-hearted, Jonah."

"Was it the tattoos and piercings that gave it away? The all black wardrobe?" My tone is sarcastic. "Or because I'm not going to let my heart break for wild animals doing their thing?"

"Hmm ..." She dramatically taps her chin. "Your cold, black heart?"

"Excuse me?" I choke out a laugh. "Why do you say that?"

If anything, my heart is more tender than ever.

"From Valentine's Day? Your place only had black decorations. What was up with that?"

I'm curious as to why she's shifted the conversation from bunnies to my beliefs on Hallmark holidays. "We had an anti-Valentine's party."

"Why? Are you anti-love?" She twists to face me, resting her shoulder on the seat back.

"No, of course not. The party was the kids' idea. I have a heart and I believe in love, but I don't need a holiday to tell me how I should express my emotions or make me feel un-loveable if I'm single. I don't need corporations making me feel less because I don't have a date on a random Monday."

Behind her glasses, her eyes widen before she blinks rapidly. "I, uh …"

"Yes?" I wait for her to say more.

"Never mind." She pats the dashboard. "What year is this thing anyway?"

"The bus?" I stroke the smooth texture of the oversized steering wheel. "1978, but the engine's been rebuilt and the interior reupholstered within the last three years."

"I like it." She glances over her shoulder at the mini kitchen and bench seat in the back. "Although, you do need better curtains."

"These work fine." I had them made from canvas drop cloth material. "They block the light when I camp. That's all I need."

"They're functional, but they're boring." She catches my eye and slyly says, "You're not boring."

"Was that a compliment?" I fight the upward curve of my lips.

"Don't let it go to your head." She straightens and faces forward, smoothing out her skirt.

A quiet settles over us. I'm not sure if it's a natural pause in the conversation or another awkward moment.

"For the record," I say, breaking the silence, "those adorable bunnies eat people's kitchen gardens and dig warrens that cause people to trip. Someone could sprain or snap an ankle. I guess I'm more of a pragmatist."

"What does that make me?"

Glancing away from the road for a second, I meet her eyes. "You, June Moxee, are a romantic."

"Because I want to protect the rabbits?"

"No, because you have a tender heart."

"And that's a bad thing in your eyes?"

"Never said that. Protect it. It's more precious than all the wild bunnies in Langley."

"Ugh, please stop." She giggles and rolls her eyes. "You sound like my mother talking about my virginity."

Full-out staring at her, I forget I'm driving for a few seconds. We've drifted over the center line on a curve. Thankfully there's no oncoming traffic.

"Please pretend I didn't say that." She shakes her head, her cheeks pink.

"Sorry. I wasn't expecting that turn in the conversation." Feeling too warm, I adjust the defroster and crack my window for some fresh air.

"I can't believe I blurted that out. For the record, I've had sex." She moans and tilts her head back, focusing on the ceiling as she mumbles, "Way to make this more awkward."

Inwardly, I fight the urge to ask her to expand on her declaration. How many men? Has she had boyfriends? Where are they now and can I challenge them to duels out of pure jealousy?

Instead, I make light of her random confession by teasing her. "Was it awkward to begin with? Until you brought up sex, we were simply a couple of local business acquaintances sharing a ride and discussing the local fauna. What's awkward about that?"

"Nothing." Her voice shifts to exasperation.

"There's something in your tone that disagrees."

"It's just ... different here." She sighs.

"How?"

"I don't know how to explain it. Islanders are both helpful and friendly but also kind of standoffish and keep to themselves. Not sure that even makes sense."

She nailed the description. "Pretty accurate if you ask me."

"Why do you think it's like that?"

"Summer people. It's a love-hate relationship. We need them, but sometimes we resent them."

"So ... friendly, but standoffish."

"Exactly," I say. "Warm, but keep to ourselves."

"Good to know it's not just me. I was beginning to wonder." She picks at a thread on her coat.

"Don't take it personally. How long have you been here?"

"A little over a year." Her fingers tap in the air. "No, closer to eighteen months."

I didn't realize she'd been on the island for six months before I noticed her.

"You're still new. Most of us take a while to warm up to people. One of the favorite local pastimes is figuring out who's been on the island longer. Anyone who moved here in the eighties is still considered new. Sorry to break it to you. No prizes, only gloating rights."

"Let me guess who wins—the Donnelys?"

"Bingo, and they can be insufferable about it." I roll my eyes. "Not really, but don't ask Tom about his family history on the island. He'll talk for hours."

"Tom?" She presses her hand to her chest. "No! I can't imagine."

We both laugh.

"Obviously, you two have met."

She nods. "What about your family?"

Her question is a natural continuation of the conversation, but my jaw ticks as I try to think of a neutral answer. Given she's new, she doesn't know the whole lurid tale.

"I grew up here … and my parents grew up here, too."

She hesitates, maybe waiting for more details from me, before she speaks again. "When I first moved here, I went to the Smugglers Inn near the ferry one night to check it out. I wanted to try new things, get out of my comfort zone."

"How'd that work out for you?" Smuggler's isn't a place I can imagine June.

"Other than the bartender and a drunk guy with hairy ears, no one spoke to me." She groans in disgust.

"Did the drunk guy hit on you?" My protective instincts kick in even though I have no reason to feel protective of June other than the fact she's a woman who shouldn't be hanging out in bars near ferry docks.

"Sadly, no. He asked me if I wanted to give him a twenty for pull-tabs. With his slurring and my ignorance of pull-tabs, I did think he was trying to pick me up until the bartender explained pull-tabs are a game of chance."

Her answer surprises me. "Did you want to be picked up by a man with hairy ears? If that's your thing, I'm not judging, just curious."

"It's always nice to be asked to dance." She flashes a half-hearted smile.

"I'll keep that in mind." Relieved to hear she's not trolling for the lowest hanging fruit available in a dive bar, I focus on driving her home. I stop at the red light. "Which way to your house?"

"Keep going on Cultus Bay. I'm off of French Road."

I gape at her. "That is not close to here."

"I don't mind the walk."

"It's over a mile to French Road, in the rain, with no sidewalk. You *should* mind it." An idea settles into my head. "If you don't want me to see your house, I can drop you at the end of your drive. Don't feel obligated to invite me in."

"You assume I live in a house." Her grin is cheeky and a little teasing.

I like flirty June and flash her a grin. "Well, now you have my interest piqued."

<h1 style="text-align:center">TWELVE</h1>

"This place is …" I pause, trying to think of the appropriate adjective without going over the top and giving myself away.

"A dump?" she asks, her voice gruff like she's beaten me to the punchline of a joke about herself.

"Perfect." I meet her eyes. "Nothing dumpy about it at all."

We're stopped in front of a mint condition Airstream Flying Cloud. Shaped and colored the same as a blimp, this is the gold standard for vintage campers. Judging by the collection of needles on the roof and the moss growing on the tops of the tires, it's been here a long time—a lot longer than eighteen months.

"How did you find this place? I had no idea this was back here."

"When I decided to move to the island, the price was right. I've updated the interior but haven't done anything to the outside—as you can tell."

"Can I see inside?" The words fly out before I realize I'm inviting myself into June's home.

She sits still, a bemused expression on her face.

"You can say no. It's just I love vintage trailers." Because I'm a weirdo who says weird things like this. "That's not a pick-up line. I really do love vintage campers. It's the reason I'm driving this bus."

"I, uh, I guess so." She hesitates for a moment longer. "It's kind of a mess."

"I'll wait outside if you need to straighten up, or I can come back another time. No pressure."

"No, it's fine. Just give me a minute." She gathers her things and hops down from the VW. With her bag over her head, she jogs to the front door and unlocks it.

A few minutes later, she reopens the door and motions for me to join her.

Inside is everything I'd hoped. A few updates have been made to the upholstery and cabinets, but otherwise, the interior is all original and in pristine condition. My opinion of June has grown exponentially in the ten seconds since I entered.

"This is amazing."

She picks up a copy of the local newspaper and folds it neatly before fluffing a bright green pillow on the small built-in couch upholstered in sunny yellow fabric. "I'm not used to having company."

"What about when your friends come over?" I hover near the front door while she flits around the narrow space, tidying up an already spotless room

She karate chops a turquoise velvet pillow. "I usually meet them in Langley or go to their house."

"Family?"

"None local and if they come visit, there's no room in here, so I book them a room at one of the local B&Bs." She's refolding a neatly folded, rainbow-striped knit blanket for the second time.

I'm delighted that her home is as brightly colored as her outfits.

My attention lands on a sleek wood stove tucked in the corner between the living area and the kitchen cabinets. I'm glad to see she has a reliable heat source. "Sounds like your personal fortress of solitude."

"Not sure if that's supposed to be a compliment."

Confused, I shift my attention to her. "The fortress part or the solitude part?"

"Both?" Her forehead creased, she pats the blanket and sets it in the corner of the small sofa.

Sensing something but unable to pinpoint if it's awkwardness or insult, I explain. "I call the coffee hut my fortress of solitude, which is a total misnomer if I think about it. Yes, there are moments of quiet, but it's a stream of people asking me for things. Like if Superman became a celebrity superhero and now his Smallville refuge is a tourist attraction complete with a gift shop selling mugs and T-shirts."

"Do you sell a lot of those?"

"You'd be surprised." I meet her eyes. "I meant it as a compliment—in case I didn't make that clear. I love your place."

"Um, thanks?" She frowns again. "Sorry. Not sure why everything that comes out of my mouth right now sounds like a question. Thank you."

"You're welcome."

The tiny space shrinks under the weight of our silence.

"I'd give you the grand tour, but unless you want to see my bed and a tiny bathroom, you've already seen the highlights."

The toilet I could skip. Asking to see the bedroom feels like crossing a line but that doesn't stop me from being curious about it.

"I've always wanted an old Airstream." I tap the original cabinet next to me. "How could anyone not want something called both a flying cloud and a land yacht?"

"Really?" She leans a hip against the sofa. "Why?"

"How long do you have?" I joke. "I have a '78 VW bus and some people think I live in it."

"Why would they think that?"

"Because sometimes I do. When life becomes too stressful

and the walls begin to close in, the best solution is to remove the walls. I'll camp for a few days, and that seems to right the world again."

"Oh!" She straightens. "I'm being a terrible hostess. I should offer you coffee. No, you're probably tired of coffee and I'd worry about messing it up. Tea? Is that an insult? I do have some cookies. They're gluten-free gingerbread. I should warn you that they're made with almond flour, in case you have a nut allergy."

As she speaks, she opens cupboard doors and closes them without removing anything.

"Tea would be fine, but you don't need to serve me anything. You needed a ride and I was there. Island code."

"Take some cookies. Think of them as a thank you—unless you're allergic to nuts. If they might kill you then please, don't feel obligated. I'd feel terrible if you died from politeness." She's flustered and turning pink.

The space is so small, I take two steps and am able to wrap my hand around her wrist, stilling her nervous movements. "Tea is good. Cookies are even better."

She pulls out an old-fashioned, round, metal tin and places it on the counter. "Take this one."

Curious, I lift the tin and the weight surprises me. "All of them? I can't take all your cookies."

"I have more." She opens the cupboard and sweeps her hand in front of it. Five similar tins fill a shelf.

"Are all of them full?" She's a cookie hoarder.

"To some degree." With a shy smile, she explains, "I can't bake here because the oven's too small to really accomplish anything. I'd have more success with an Easy Bake Oven. So, I'm forced to use the kitchen at the church. As long as I leave a dozen or two for the staff, they don't mind me baking there."

Huh. June spends a lot of time at the church. Nothing against church people, they've just never been my people—not that I'm anti-religion or God. Like George Michael said, you gotta have faith. I'm just not a fan of organized conformity.

I eye the other tins. "How many dozens do you bake at a time?"

"Five or six. What's the point of making twelve cookies? Pfft. Amateurs." She gives me her soft smile again. My stomach clenches at the idea that she knows the effect she has on me.

Curious about her baking skills, I remove the lid and inhale the scent of warm spices. "Reminds me of my grandmother's gingerbread houses."

"Try one. If you hate it, just tell me. You can spit it out in the sink. I won't judge."

"Stop. They smell incredible and if they taste half as good, it'll be one of the best I've ever had." I select a cookie and break it in half before biting into the soft texture. Spices, butter, and molasses explode on my tongue. In spite of having a full mouth, I manage to say, "Wow."

"Good?" She picks at a few crumbs.

After swallowing, I gape at her. "I was right—definitely one of the best cookies ever. What else do you have? Are they all gingerbread?"

She points at the open cupboard. "No, I have chocolate chip and snickerdoodle."

"I should probably try them all." I take a seat on the banquette.

"Are you sure? Don't force yourself." She laughs, but it sounds nervous.

"Please don't make me beg, because I would. I'm not above begging, but I'm trying to play it cool."

"Should I put on the kettle?" She hesitates again, but I spot a flash of pride in her eyes.

A glance at the clock on her microwave confirms what I don't want to be true. I'm out of time. Not overstaying my welcome is probably a good thing, though.

"Actually, I can't stay. I'm babysitting my niece tonight."

"Oh, that's totally fine. Take the cookies to-go as a thank you for the ride." She tries to cover the disappointment in her eyes with a smile.

I hate that I can't say yes. The thought occurs to me that maybe June's a little bit lonely like me.

"I will." I take a chance to see if she'll spend more time with me. "How are you getting to work tomorrow?"

Blowing out a breath, she gives me a sheepish smile. "I hadn't thought that far ahead. Bus? Walk?"

"What time should I be here?" I dismiss her nonsense with a teasing glower.

She shakes her head in protest. "I can't ask you to come pick me up."

"You didn't ask. I'm offering."

Embarrassed but also maybe a tiny bit pleased, she says, "Does nine work for you? Or I can call Diane."

"I'll be here at nine. How do you take your coffee?" I tuck my tin of cookies under my arm.

"You really don't have to bring me coffee."

I dip my chin and stare at her. "I know."

"But … if you were going to bring me something, a dirty chai latte would be nice."

Accepting the small victory of providing for her, I decide to leave on a high note.

"Got it." Opening the door, I pause. "See you at nine. Thanks again for the cookies."

At the end of June's driveway, I notice another fairy door inset into a tree trunk that also serves as her mailbox. It can't be a coincidence that it's similar to the one I found in Saratoga Woods. I love the idea that June is making these doors for the island fairies. Classic Hufflepuff behavior.

———

At 8:58 the next morning, I make the turn onto June's long driveway.

I'm halfway out my door when she exits the Airstream. With a friendly wave, she quickly walks over to where I'm parked.

Today's outfit is a burst of sunshine with yellow tights under a multicolored plaid dress and topped with a yellow striped scarf. I'm wearing black. Our streak of appearing as polar opposites is unbroken.

"Morning," I tell her as we both climb into the van. "One dirty chai latte."

She takes the drink from me and examines the name on the side. "Did you go by the Fellowship of the Bean this morning to get this?"

"I did. If you wanted coffee, I could've made it at home, but I don't drink chai."

She takes a sip and sighs, content. "Wasn't that out of the way?"

"Not by much." Concentrating on reversing, I hope she doesn't make a big deal about something as simple as me getting her tea. "Had to stop by and pick up the bank deposit anyway."

"Okay, thank you." She holds the cup with both hands. "How was babysitting?"

"Fine. She slept the entire time. Kind of boring, but better than screaming for three hours."

"That sounds horrible." She visibly cringes. "Babies are scary."

I cast a sidelong glance at her.

"What? They are. Ask anyone."

"Aren't babies a big part of your business model?"

"Baby stuff is, but not actual living, breathing, tiny humans. I try to avoid those."

Nodding, I add this to the list of things about June that surprises me. I guess the times I borrowed Shaw Donnely and Rosie and took them to the shop didn't help my cause.

"I sound like a terrible person saying I don't like kids." Pausing, she blows on the top of her cup. "Women are supposed to have a gene that makes us love all infants and huff their baby essence like it's the elixir of life."

"I'm not judging." Downshifting, I slow to take a tight curve. "And I won't tell anyone your secret."

"You seem to like the tiny humans—even voluntarily hanging out with them."

"It's different when they're family. A lot of my friends have had kids over the past couple of years. Hard to avoid them."

"Is that why you stopped by the shop with other people's babies?" she asks, a slight curl to her lips.

Busted. "You have a good memory. I stand by my story. I needed to buy a baby gift and wasn't sure about sizing."

She laughs. "That's why we give people blankets—no sizing needed. Did the gift work out?"

I think about Ansel and the tiny Sorting Hat I got for him.

"It was perfect."

"Did you have anything to do with the new Naked Whidbey calendar baby theme?" She eyes me, not hostile, but not exactly happy.

"It was Ashley's idea. Most of the time, women act like their ovaries are exploding when they see a hot guy holding a baby."

"Apparently."

"Not you, though," I say softly.

"I'm immune or I'm missing that gene." She shrugs and sips her drink.

"Yet you make blankets for newborns." None of her pieces fit neatly together. She's an enigma of contrasts.

"Easy to do and quick to finish. The knitting circle at the church has made them for years. The blankets are part of being a member."

"Can't you find another knitting group? There's more than one church on the island."

She slurps the last of her drink. "I've tried all of them. The ladies in Langley are the nicest and most normal."

"You interviewed church ladies?" June continues to surprise me.

"Of course, I'm glad I did. The Episcopalian women in Freeland were more about making body pillows than knitting. A few dressed their pillows in flannel shirts and a couple even added fake fur beards. I never went back." A small shudder ripples through her.

"Did they resemble anyone in particular?" I ask, fearing the answer and wondering if the local gossip brigade are Episcopalians as I imagine Sandy, Connie and Sally sewing man pillows then cuddling them while they sleep. Delete, delete, delete.

"Now that you ask, a couple had brown beards. No tattoos though, so I think you're safe."

I pull to a stop in front of her shop. "We're here."

She presses her glasses higher with her index finger. "Thanks."

"My pleasure." I shift into neutral and let the engine idle.

"Well, thanks again."

"You're welcome." I tap my fingers on the steering wheel. "Let me know if you need a ride home. I'll be up at the warehouse this afternoon."

"Will do." She meets my eyes and I see an unexpected shyness in them. "Guess I should go now. See you at trivia night this week?"

If I didn't know better, I'd think she was lingering.

The idea makes me smile as I drive away.

Tuesday night at China Ruby, June stops by our table to chat. When she leaves, Diane grins at me.

"She seems especially friendly tonight. In fact, she was in a great mood during class yesterday, laughing and smiling.

Haven't seen her like that in months. I wonder what's changed." Her gaze settles on me for a beat.

Erik chuckles. "My guess is she's getting laid."

Cari groans. "That's not the answer for every good mood."

For a guy who's supposed to always have my back as my partner and my wingman, he's terrible at his job. "Pretty sure she's single."

Diane tightens her lips into a thin line, suppressing a smile. "As far as I know, she's not seeing anyone."

"Fresh batteries," Cari whispers. Both women giggle.

My eyes cut over to June's table. All four women are knitting while talking. For whatever reason, June prefers the company of old women. She's beautiful, funny, interesting, and kind—and hangs out in church basements, knitting. There's a story there and I want to know if she's hiding from love like I am.

THIRTEEN

The elevator doors open and I exit into the lobby of the hospital. I plan to say goodbye to Vicky before heading back to the island. Today's the first Saturday since opening The Place that I haven't been there, and I'm anxious to get back and check on things.

Only partially paying attention, I stop short when I spot June standing in the middle of the open space, four enormous brown paper shopping bags in her hands.

"What are you doing here?" she asks. Eyes wide with shock, she bobbles and almost drops her tote.

After last time, I made sure my face was clear of any signs of makeup before I left the bathroom after changing into my regular clothes. Conscious of June staring at me, I rub a circle on my forehead in case there's any lingering imprint.

Unable to place it in the right emotional column, I stare back. Is she mad I'm here? Surprised to see a familiar face? Annoyed we're running into each other yet again off the island, like it's bad enough she has to see me in Langley and now she can't escape me in Seattle either?

Rather than giving her an explanation, I answer her question with a question. "Why are you here?"

"I ..." She studies the bags as if trying to figure out what's inside. "Just dropping off some blankets."

"Did you make them?" Curious, I lean forward to peer more closely at the patterns of multi-colored yarns.

"No, of course not, at least not all of them. There haven't been that many births on the island recently. We have too many blankets and we keep making more."

It's a lovely story but doesn't quite explain her presence here. "You could stop. Is anyone forcing you to continue knitting? A modern day Penelope?"

Her bright pink lips purse. "Penelope never finished. That was the whole point."

"Touché. So, you're donating your surplus?"

Her eyes scan the lobby, nervous. "I've never done the drop-off before but Hilda had cataract surgery last week. She's normally the point person and makes the donation on her way to visit her kids in West Seattle."

The wording she uses reminds me of a drug deal. I arch an eyebrow and wait for her to refer to herself as a mule.

Yarn Mule would make a good band name.

Sadly, she doesn't continue. Blowing out a deep exhalation, June scans the lobby with a sad, worried expression heavy in her eyes.

"Let me guess: you drew the short straw and hospitals freak you out."

"Uh, is it obvious?" She shifts her attention to me.

"A little." Holding up my thumb and index finger an inch apart, I then widen the gap between them. "Nothing to be afraid of down here. Want me to show you where you drop off donations? Or do you have an appointment?"

"Are you like a hospital ambassador or something?" She points at my badge on the lanyard. "You didn't say why you're at the hospital so early on a Saturday. Oh, no, is it Rosie? Is she sick? Is it serious?"

Her worry about my niece is genuine but misplaced.

"Huh?" I touch the small hoop in my eyebrow. "Rosie's fine. Completely healthy."

"Oh good. Good. I'd hate for her to be sick. Nothing's sadder than sick kids." Her bright smile falls after a second and she grimaces. "Oops. Probably shouldn't say that in a place full of ill children."

"To answer your question, I'm a volunteer, been coming here for years, and know my way around. Here, let me take some of your bags, or all of them." Stretching out my arm, I reach for the handles in her left hand. My fingers brush hers as I encourage her to release her grip. A small frisson of electricity sparks at the point of contact.

June must feel it too because she glances at our hands for a few seconds before speaking.

"I have four more and a box in my car. I left it in the valet parking area." When she spins toward the door, she knocks my legs with the other bag. "Oops, sorry."

"That's a lot of blankets." I peer inside the two bags I'm now holding. "Leave these with me and go get the rest. Might as well drop them all off at once."

"Are you sure? I don't want to bother you or take away from your volunteer hours."

"Not a bother. I'm done for the day."

With a quick thanks, she dashes outside then returns with the box and more bags dangling off of her arms.

"I think this is everything." The box tucked under her chin muddles her voice.

"Allow me." I shift my bags to one hand before removing the box from her grip.

"You really don't have to help."

"And yet I am. It isn't a big deal." I tip my head toward Vicky at reception. "We're going right over there." When I don't hear June's footsteps on the polished stone floors, I turn to see what's holding her up. "Is there a problem?"

"You mean all I had to do is drop these at the desk?" Her hair slips in front of her face as she shakes her head.

"It's Saturday, so Vicky's your best bet to get these where they need to go. If you came during the week, you'd be sent upstairs to Volunteer Services."

"Oh." Her brows draw together. "Well, that was a waste of an anxiety attack."

I study her for a moment. "Did you think you'd be hand-delivering these to the kids on the wards?"

She nods and chews on the corner of her bottom lip.

"And that gave you anxiety?"

She confirms my suspicion with another dip of her chin.

"Because you're afraid of all children?"

"No, worse." Her cheeks redden.

"Oh." I pause until she meets my eyes. "Just sick kids."

"I'm a horrible person." She presses her hands together in front of her mouth, her eyes apologetic. "This shouldn't be about me and my feelings. There are really sick kids in this hospital, tiny babies hooked up to machines. Someone might even die today." The waterlines of her eyes turn pink as tears form.

All of what she said is true, but crying about it in the hospital lobby isn't going to help anyone, and telling her everything will be fine will only make me a liar.

"You're doing something nice and bringing joy to people. Focus on that." I want to hug her but my arms are full, and I'm also not sure if we've crossed into the intentional touching zone. "Ready?"

I lead her over to the oversized reception desk with its dark contemporary steel and glass design then introduce her to Vicky.

"June has some hand-knit blankets she'd like to donate." I act as the go between even though June never asked me to. "Can you make sure they get to the right place?"

One glance at June and Vicky's eyes soften. "Oh, isn't this

lovely. A lot of effort must've gone into making so many blankets. Isn't that kind of you to think of us."

"I didn't make all of them. We have a knitting group." She rambles to Vicky about the baby boom and drop in births on the island.

Vicky pats June's hands. "Then your surplus is our blessing. Can I hug you?"

Never once has Vicky asked to hug me. Not so much as a shoulder squeeze in two years. A little put out, I step out of her way when she rounds the corner to wrap her arms around June.

"No crying, honey. All we can do is say our prayers and have faith in the strength of the kids. Our doctors here are the best in the world, and I'll fight anyone who says different."

I didn't realize June had started crying until Vicky spoke.

This should be my cue to escape, but I find myself frozen by the spectacle of June's emotions.

"On behalf of all the children and their families, we're so grateful for your donation. Please pass along our thanks to the rest of your knitting group." Vicky finishes her speech with another hug. "Feel free to bring more blankets anytime."

June sniffles and swipes her fingers beneath her glasses. "Thank you. I mean, you're welcome."

Her soft laugh of embarrassment earns her another hug from Vicky. "Come back whenever you like. Jonah, bring her with you next time. She can be your assistant for the magic show."

My explanation is automatic. "I'm a wizard, not a magician."

The words sound even nerdier leaving my mouth than they do in my head.

June's head snaps in my direction, shocked. "You're a what?"

"Another time."

Her look tells me she's going to ask for details as soon as possible. Time to go.

"If that's all, I have a ferry to catch." I reposition my backpack on my shoulder. "Vicky, see you next month."

"You betcha." She sends me off with a wave.

————

There is one major reason above all the other smaller and more petty ones why taking a cruise doesn't appeal to me: being trapped on a boat with people for long periods of time with no escape—people who I don't like and don't like me, people who are nosey and ask a lot of questions.

Normally, the short ferry ride between the mainland and the island is brief enough to avoid the aforementioned major reason, and if I spot someone I wish to avoid, I stay in my vehicle and don't go up on deck. Islanders respect this boundary. If you're in your car, that means you don't want to socialize. A quick wave and be on your way.

Islanders know the unspoken rules about socialization on the ferry.

June is not an islander.

When I spot her bright red Prius in line in Mukilteo a few lanes over from where I'm waiting, I figure we'll end up in different sections of the car deck and I'll be able to avoid her for the short trip home. Today's steady wind blowing rain sideways should also keep most people inside their vehicles.

Normally, I'm grateful for the center lane spot that means I'll be one of the first cars unloaded.

Not today.

Not when I notice June's car to the left of mine.

Most days, I'm happy for a glimpse of June from afar. You'd think I'd be giddy to run into her not once, but twice in one morning.

The opposite is true.

Vicky may have spilled the beans back at the hospital. There's only one way to find out if my secret's been blown. Before June tells her knitting circle and they in turn share it with the local gossip bunch, I better do damage control.

Briefly closing my eyes to rally myself, I'm surprised by a knock on the window near my head. With one eye still closed, I cast a glance at the glass.

June waves. "Hi, again."

Even though my plan was to leave the safety of my van and approach her, I only crank down the window so we can speak easier. "Hi, yourself."

The cold, damp wind off of the water blows June's hair into her face. Tiny droplets of water linger on the surface of her glasses. She hops from foot to foot, teeth chattering.

I change my mind. "You must be freezing. Get out of the rain." Leaning away from the window, I pop open the passenger door.

Not needing to be asked twice, she jogs around the front of the bus and hops inside.

"Hey." I shift in my seat to face her. A gap between the front chairs provides a nice buffer.

"Thanks for your help with the blankets." Her knees bounce and she blows on her hands. She seems nervous.

"Sure." I keep my tone neutral. "Guess you're wondering why I never answered your questions about what I was doing at Children's."

"It's none of my business. I think it's great you chose to volunteer at the hospital. How many hours do you have left to do?"

"Sorry?" I'm confused by her overly friendly, chipper tone and presumption I spend time volunteering because I *have* to.

"For your community service. Not judging you—at all—and don't worry, I'm not going to pry or ask why you have to do service in the first place. I understand. My cousin got into some trouble with the police a few years ago and avoided jail by agreeing to volunteer."

"Excuse me?" *Is she trying to bond with me about being a criminal making amends?*

Her smile dims. "Sorry. I shouldn't have said anything. I just wanted to tell you I think it's great you're volunteering with kids. As you saw back there, I could never do something like that."

"Hold on. Back up."

She snaps her mouth closed, presses her lips together.

"I think you're under a misapprehension or two about me."

"Vicky said—"

"Want to hear my version? Since this is about me?" I'm not angry, per se, but the interior of the van feels smaller by the minute. Why did I invite her inside? Not wearing proper rain gear is on her, not me … I decide to go with that.

"First, why aren't you wearing a raincoat?"

"What?" Her eyes widen until she resembles a barn owl.

"It's raining. You should have something waterproof. Maybe a hat, too."

She blinks at me through her water-speckled glasses. "You're really good at deflecting. Has anyone ever told you that?"

I stare back at her. "No."

That isn't true. The counselor I saw in high school told me the exact same thing.

"Second," I continue, proving her right, "I'm not volunteering because some judge ordered me to do community service."

Her face falls and she removes her glasses to wipe the lenses on her pink skirt, which is decorated with tiny roses. "Wow. I really blew it."

Without the colorful frames, it's easier to see the swirl of gold and green in her irises.

"I'm sorry. I … I made an assumption. Why the children's hospital?

"Escaping my own head is part of why I volunteer with the kids. Easiest way to put my own bullshit into perspective is to be around them. Whatever issues I think are insurmountable pale in comparison to a kid with cancer."

"And you do magic tricks for them? Like a show?"

"Promise this doesn't leave the ferry? Or even better, my bus?"

She nods. "I definitely owe you for the court order assumption."

Her preconception about me is still frustrating, but I'll deal with that later. "Have you ever been to the Emerald City Comic Con?"

"No."

"But you've heard of comic conventions, right?"

"Sure. Of course."

"Well, in my twenties, I got really into cosplay, short for costume play."

"Like role-playing?"

"In the non-sexual sense, yes. Custom costumes and masks, the works."

"This is … a secret?" she asks slowly, clearly confused.

"I don't really talk about it with the guys on the island. If you hadn't noticed, some people prejudge me based on my appearance."

Her mouth opens and closes twice before she nods. "Point taken."

"I wanted something that was mine and not related to the island or my family." I stop myself from saying more about my family. "When I discovered cons, I knew I'd found the thing that was just for me—and the thousands of other people who show up.

"A couple of years ago, I decided to quit going to them. Being a nerd or a geek became mainstream, and the magic got lost. Too expensive, too much drama around getting tickets. Even after spending all that cash to go, the lines for the panels were out of control. Maybe I got too old."

"What does this have to do with sick kids?" She smiles, encouraging me to explain more.

I'm loving that she's interested in all of this. "Patience," I tease. "I'm getting there."

She pretends to lock her mouth and then throws the key over her shoulder.

Amused by her pantomime, I continue. "One of my online friends started volunteering at her local library in her Wonder Woman costume as part of a youth literacy program."

"That sounds cool. Why not do that?"

"Who's to say I haven't?"

"At the library in Langley?" Her eyes widen in surprise. "Recently?"

"No. Separation of real life and nerd life, remember?"

She nods in understanding.

"To answer your question, friends had a sick kid who spent time at Children's. Visiting him, I felt helpless. Instead of wallowing, I saw an opportunity to give back and brighten someone's day."

I leave out the part about the sick kid being my godson Ansel, Ceci and Naya's son.

"Who are you?" she asks, her voice barely above a whisper.

"Some Saturdays, I'm a superhero. On others, an older Harry Potter."

"Harry with a beard and tattoos?" she clarifies, disdain in her voice as she pushes her glasses up her nose. "They buy that?"

"Luckily, my wizard robes hide my tattoos. Kids see the glasses and the lightning bolt and know who I am. They're so happy for the attention and distraction that they're willing to suspend disbelief about the beard and my age."

She's quiet, contemplative. Processing. I feel uncomfortable about how worried I am she doesn't approve.

"So …" I blow out a breath. "That's my big secret. No criminal activity, just an aging nerd who still likes dressing up in costumes."

"I feel like I'm having my own superhero reveal moment, like when Clark Kent opens his shirt and exposes the mighty S, or when Mary Jane figures out Peter is Spiderman. Or … insert another example here." She laughs. "Wow. I completely misjudged you."

My heart stutters with her confession that she's finally seeing me as more than a guy with piercings and tattoos. Sure she can see the truth of my emotions all over my face, I only manage to ask, "How so?"

"In my head, you've been the villain, not the good guy." Her nose wrinkles.

I'm not sure if I feel relieved to be right or not. "If we're being honest, I could tell—especially the time we ran into each other at the Orca when you stared at me like I was the devil."

"Sorry." She gives me a sheepish smile. "In my defense, you had a weird red mark on your forehead." Using her index finger, she makes a line on her forehead.

"Like Manson?"

She nods, scrunching up her nose again. "It crossed my mind, but it didn't make sense. You're not a monster."

"Your mom acting like I was a greaser trying to steal your virtue probably didn't help." I let my lips curl into a smile at the memory.

Groaning, June covers her face with her hands. "I don't know what was wrong with her. She isn't usually not like that— at all. Also, it isn't the first time she's seen you, so I don't know what her problem was. Trust me, that was on her, not you."

"Not the first time I've scared a parent and probably won't be the last. If it helps, I test high for Slytherin on Hogwarts quizzes."

"Interesting but not surprising." June's eyes crinkle and her cheeks round with her teasing smile.

"Haha. Just so you know, I identify as a Ravenclaw."

"I can see that too." She nods. "Want to guess my house?"

"Hufflepuff," I state without hesitation.

Her mouth forms an O of surprise.

"What? Am I wrong?" I know I'm not wrong, unless she self-selects as Gryffindor because of Hermione. I can see that happening.

"No, you're right. I'm a proud Hufflepuff."

"I know. You have a yellow and black scarf."

Her eyebrow lifts slightly. "I could be a fan of bumblebees."

I worry I'm exposing myself and all the trivia I've collected about June. "That's a very Hufflepuff thing to say."

"Do you sort everyone you know into their Hogwarts House?" she asks, amused.

"Not everyone. You've met my sister—Ashley is definitely a Slytherin. Carter is a Gryffindor. So is Dan, and Roslyn is Ravenclaw like me. Erik and Cari are probably both Hufflepuffs. You can form a club."

She nods in agreement. "What about Olaf at the Dog House?"

"Hmm," I brush the tip of my finger over my mouth, "He's the rare combination known as a Slytherpuff. Hufflerin? Loyal but prideful and probably a bonafide misanthrope. He doesn't tolerate fools or Kelsos."

We continue listing houses for other islanders we know. During our talk, we've steamed up the windows. To clear them, I blast the defroster, but without air conditioning, it will take forever to work. I open the window to bring in cooler air.

"People are going to think we've been getting hot and heavy in here." June clamps her hand over her mouth.

Images of us kissing fill my head: her ruby lips pressed against mine as we stretch across the gap between our seats. It would be easy to lean into the space that separates us and kiss her. If only she didn't appear appalled by the thought.

"Does that horrify you?" I ask, my voice low. "Are you afraid I'm going to ruin your reputation?"

The loudspeaker squawks to life, announcing our arrival in Clinton and instructing passengers to return to their vehicles.

"I should get back to my car." Her hand is already on the door handle. "Thanks for trusting me with your secret. I promise to keep it."

Before I can tell her we have at least five more minutes until the walk-on passengers are unloaded, she hops down and closes the door. Waiting until she crosses in front of the bus, I lean my elbow on the window sill and tell her, "For the record, I don't care what people think, and you shouldn't either."

Her pace falters but she quickly recovers with a friendly wave and a fake smile.

Makes me wonder if June's the hero or the villain in her own story.

FOURTEEN

After the conversation with June on the ferry, I take the dating advice of snarky teens and decide to ask her to dinner. On Monday morning, I walked over to her shop with a plan. Except In the Loop is closed on Mondays.

Fail.

Tonight is the pub quiz at China Ruby, and there's no way I'm going to ask with witnesses. There's a strong possibility she'll turn me down. Walking back to The Place, I debate whether it would be better to ask her before or after we play trivia. Yarned and Dangerous has only won once since I started playing. Another loss could push June and I backward into hostile acquaintance territory. Our friendship is a baby giraffe on wobbly legs.

On Tuesday, I make a dirty chai latte. I let Layla know I'm running an errand as I walk out the door with two paper cups. The shop is dark when I arrive, so I sit on the small bench in front to wait.

Early mornings during the week are quiet. Other than the cafés and the market, most of the shops don't open until after ten. I count six cars that drive down the street in the fifteen minutes I wait.

When she arrives, the first thing I notice is her colorful outfit. The next is that I've already finished my coffee—and that hers has cooled.

No one should drink tepid coffee, so I set the cup on the ground by my feet and then stand. Slightly nervous, I push my hair out of my face and sweep it back.

"Morning." I greet her with a smile, which she returns without hesitation.

"Is that coffee for me?" Her eyes brighten when she points to the cup in my hand.

"Uh … yours got cold." I drop the arm holding my cup to my side. "I'll bring you a new one."

Her delight fades a little as she tilts her head. "How long have you been out here?"

"Fifteen, twenty minutes?" Pressing my lips together, I shrug off the time. "I wanted to catch you before you opened and got busy."

She laughs and flips her keys for the right one. "Busy is relative. I doubt there's going to be a mad rush on yarn this morning, or that there has ever been one. There was a brief phase when every other woman and her sister were making pink hats in 2017—peak yarn market days. Too bad they happened before I took over the business. Typical Moxee family luck."

She sounds so wistful. I cannot repress the urge to cheer her up. "You never know when the next knitting or sarcastic cross-stitching craze will happen."

"True. Good thing I'm not in this business for the money." She pauses on the threshold. "Sorry to ramble. What did you need to talk to me about?"

Given she wasn't rambling, I wonder if June's insecure about her business and what she perceives as a lack of success. Although cold coffee and struggling business blues aren't the setup I imagined for this moment, I plow forward anyway. She may shoot me down, but I won't know unless I ask.

"I was wondering if you want to get dinner with me sometime." I lean a shoulder on the door frame. "Obviously not now."

"Like on a date?" she asks, surprised but curious.

I nod. "I'm asking you to go out with me. Just dinner."

She nods and then smiles. "Okay, but we'll split the bill."

If she needs to pay her own way to prove it isn't a date, so be it. Labels don't matter. "Fine by me."

"Where should we go?"

Good question. "Somewhere on the island. Mind if I keep it a mystery for now?"

At least until I actually figure out where I'll take you.

Shifting her bag from her shoulder to her hand, she regards me. "A place that serves food, right? If so, I'm good."

"Definitely serves food. Are you free on Saturday? I can pick you up at six-thirty at your house."

"Whoa. You're serious about this being a date." Her eyes widen. If I had to describe her face right now, I'd say she's surprised, but delighted. Okay, that might be a stretch. Pleased with the idea. Amused? Let's go with that one.

"Is that a yes?" I swear my heart is beating faster, loud enough she can probably hear it.

"Sure. Yeah. Of course." Her smile widens into a grin I can't help mirroring.

"Great. I'll be back with your coffee." I scoop up the cup of cold dirty chai from where I stashed it under the bench.

"You don't have to bring me another one." She reaches for the disgusting drink in my hand.

"I do. Life's too short to drink bad coffee. Plus, it gives me an excuse to come back." Still facing her, I take one step, then another away until I'm in the middle of the sidewalk.

She's warmed up to me, and now I want to figure out how to get her to thaw completely.

"Do you have any of the ginger scones this morning?" she asks as I continue.

"And if we do?"

"I'll take one of those too." She pauses, a tentative yet sly grin curving her lips. "If you're already going to be coming back."

"One ginger scone for the lady. Anything else? T-shirt? Travel mug?" *My heart?* Because I'm pretty sure she's already stolen a big piece of it.

"Let's not get carried away." For the first time, I'm certain she's deliberately flirting with me.

As promised, I arrive at her house around six-thirty on Saturday evening. After I cut the engine, I lean forward over the steering wheel to stare out the window at the Airstream.

The days are growing longer and the warm, rose-tinted evening light allows me to see more of her property. Ferns and moss-covered fallen trees give the forest around the narrow meadow a wild feel. The sleek, Machine Age design of the aluminum siding glows against the dark green of the trees, like the camper was dropped here from another time period.

A red and white striped awning running along the front provides shelter from the rain. I don't remember it from my previous visits and wonder if it was folded up. On a hot summer day, I can imagine June sitting in the shade, knitting, with me reading beside her.

Lost in my fantasies, I miss June descending the steps. She's halfway across the driveway when I finally notice her. Beneath her green coat, tonight's dress is black with small red roses. Her glasses are the red frames and they match her lipstick. My breath hitches at the sight of her. I wonder if she knows red is a power color and how lovely she looks wearing it.

I hurry to jump down from the bus and run around the front to get her door for her.

She grins. "All the stops, huh?"

"Too much? I can close it and let you open it yourself." I pretend to release my hold on the handle.

Shaking her head, she accepts my palm to help her climb inside. "It's nice."

I hide my grin as I close the door before jogging back to my side. *I can work with nice.*

"Honestly, I'm out of practice with dating. The line between chivalry and being an overbearing alpha keeps shifting, and I'm not sure how good I was at it to begin with," I confess once I navigate us onto the main road.

"Huh. That surprises me."

I check her expression in the fading light and find it to be genuine. "Really?"

"Based on first impressions, I thought you were more of a bad boy." Her eyes flick to mine and then out her side window. "Not like you were in a biker gang, but tough, with an attitude, and maybe a little dangerous."

The final word of her sentence is softer than the rest, like maybe she didn't mean to say it out loud.

"Does that opinion still hold? I've already confessed to being a Potterhead and do-gooder. I think that means I basically have a halo." To emphasize this ridiculous statement, I draw a circle above my head.

"Somehow I don't buy that. Or, if it's true now, it hasn't always been the case." Shifting in her seat, she twists to face me.

"You should believe me. I'm practically a saint." Monk is the word I'm looking for, but I don't correct myself. Even if I confessed my recent complete and utter lack of a social life and my chosen celibacy, I'm not sure she'd believe me. "But … you've got a point. I haven't always been the good guy. That said, people are capable of change. Whether or not they follow through on taking the steps to better themselves and their lives isn't a given."

Nodding, she says, "Who I was in my early twenties isn't at

all who I was in my late twenties, or who I am now. Thirty-year-old me doesn't have everything together, but I'd like to think I'm less of a disaster."

Her statement confirms the insecurities I picked up on outside her shop earlier in the week.

"I don't think you're a mess at all." I touch her hand where it rests in her lap.

"Thanks for the compliment, but you don't really know me well enough to make that statement." Her tone flips back to defensive.

I thought we were making process, but her walls have snapped back into place. One step forward, two back.

"No one has their shit together the way we think they do. Some people are just better at pretending than others." I take the turn at 525 and head north up the island.

"You might be right." Doubt creeps into her voice. "Where are we going? Or is it still a secret?"

"Have you been to Bush Point?" I ask.

"When I first moved here, I drove all the main roads on the island to learn my way around, but I've never eaten at the restaurant there."

"That's going to change tonight. It was one of my favorite places growing up, mostly because they gave me extra sour cream and bacon bits for the baked potato. They have some of the best seafood on the island or anywhere in the Pacific Northwest."

"Gotta respect establishments that don't scrimp on the extras." She winks at me.

I'm happy she agrees about the importance of substantial toppings.

"The interior is nothing fancy, so keep your design expectations between medium and low—unless wooden seagulls and desiccated starfish are your favorite."

"I'm sure it's going to be great." She touches my arm. "Thanks for inviting me out."

I'm not sure what I said before that raised her hackles, but I'm glad she's swung back to being excited to spend the evening with me.

"Thanks for saying yes." I place my hand over hers for a second before focusing on the road again.

FIFTEEN

The Hawk's Nest spans the second floor of a 1970s era building at the very tip of Bush Point. Surrounded on three sides by water, the views of the shipping lanes and the Olympic Peninsula to the west are some of the best on the island.

"Who cares what the food is like! This view is *incredible*." June's face glows in the light of the candle on our table, making her even more beautiful. "Are you trying to impress me?"

"Might be." I scratch my temple. "Is it working?"

"Most definitely."

Feeling emboldened by her happy mood, I say, "Do you remember our hike in Saratoga Woods?"

"You mean our accidental rendezvous by the boulder?" she asks, sounding a little sassy.

"That's the one. I asked you why you don't like me, and after deflecting by answering my questions with questions, you finally said it was because we're too different."

"I remember the conversation," she answers, cautious.

"Do you still feel the same way?"

She doesn't respond right away. "No. Well, except the

Hufflepuff vs. Ravenclaw issue, but I think we can overcome our house differences."

A waitress appears at our table. "Can I get you something to drink? Beer? Wine? Cocktail?"

"I'll have the Full Sail amber. June?"

"Water's fine. Thanks," she tells the waitress, who leaves with a promise to return with our drinks and take our orders.

"If you're worried about needing to be our designated driver, I'm only going to have the one beer. Feel free to have a cocktail, or wine." I hope she's just a stickler for sober drivers and not worried that I'll take advantage of her if she drinks. I wouldn't. I've never done that. Because I'm not an asshole.

"That's not it at all. I don't drink." She's utterly unapologetic.

"Anything?" I know I've seen her consume liquids before. "You had one of those frou-frou drinks at China Ruby at trivia night."

"I mean alcohol. That was a Shirley Temple. Most people assume it's a vodka cranberry and I don't have to explain why I'm not drinking."

Curious myself, I want to ask why, but whatever the reason, it's none of my business.

"No problem. Soda? Water? Iced tea? Shrub? Kombucha? Mocktail?" I list off every non-alcoholic beverage on the menu. "There are a lot of options. If I remember correctly, they make a mean Shirley Temple here, too."

After a loaded pause, she answers my unspoken question. "Alcoholism runs in my family, so I've seen the destruction of addiction up close. A few years ago, I realized my social drinking was less about having fun and more about needing a drink. A glass of wine turned into two or three, or the bottle. I didn't like drunk June and woke up too many mornings with regret about something I did or said. So, I stopped."

I wasn't expecting this confession from her, but I admire her self-awareness and her bravery for not giving into social pressure.

"You know you didn't have to explain why. It's none of anyone's business, but I appreciate your honesty."

"I guess," she says slowly. "But it makes socializing harder and less fun, especially when everyone else is toasted. Being the solo sober person in a group isn't as amusing as you might imagine. It's kind of like having to be the chaperone at a school dance."

"I've attended plenty of concerts as the designated driver, or the only driver if I'm flying solo."

"You do that a lot?" She scrunches up her face.

"What? Go to concerts by myself? Sure. I prefer my own company for the most part, with a few exceptions."

"How come men are allowed to say that and women can't?" she muses.

"Huh? Why can't you?" I'm confused.

"One word: spinster."

I groan with disgust. "What century is this?"

"Single men of a certain age aren't eyed with pity the same way."

"Says who? I can introduce you to at least half a dozen women on the island who worry I'll die alone. Granted, most of them are my sister's friends or have known me my whole life." I switch to a falsetto to mimic their teasing. "Jonah, the loner bachelor who doesn't even have a dog to keep him company."

She digs in. "It's different for women."

"Most everything is."

We're quiet for a moment.

"Why don't you get a dog?"

"I had a dog," I mumble.

She tilts her head to the side, curious. "There's a story there."

"There is." Talking about dead pets on a first date is right up there with mentioning exes or family drama. No way I'm going there.

"I'd like to hear it sometime," she says, sympathy in her eyes.

"Another time. Tonight I want to hear more about you." I sip my beer and wait for her to speak.

"Not much to tell," she finally says. "My life is exceptionally boring. I run a shop, I knit, I play trivia once a week."

"There's a lot more to June Moxee than those three things." Dipping my head, I grab her attention. "I really want to know you."

Her breath goes shallow. "You do? Why? I've been awful to you since we met."

The confession contains some truth. "Not always. You congratulated me the first time I beat you at trivia."

"Your team won," she corrects. "How many times? Two? Three?"

"So far," I add. I don't tell her my theory about Simon's crush stacking the questions in her favor, nor do I share that I've been researching crafts and crafting history at the library.

"That's all you have as evidence I haven't been a complete jerk to you?" Worry wrinkles her forehead.

"You let me give you a ride home," I offer.

"Okay, so I used you to avoid walking home in the rain and acted like a decent human by not being a sore loser." She cringes. "You must be a masochist to want to spend more time with me."

I laugh, not because she's right, but because she's revealed something about herself I don't think she intended: June defensively pushes people away before they can get close.

Takes one to know one. "Nah. I'm just stubborn enough to hang around until you like me."

"What if that never happens?"

I hold her gaze. "I think you already do, even if you don't want to admit it to yourself. What's not to like?"

June remains quiet for a moment—not long enough for the

silence to become awkward, though. "I didn't like you when we first met."

"I know." I tug on my bottom lip with my teeth to keep from grinning. "Also, notice you used past tense."

"Jury's still out." She lifts her eyebrows in challenge.

"If that's what you need to tell yourself, there's something else you should know about me."

"What?"

"Not only am I stubborn, I have the patience of a saint."

"St. Jonah?" she asks, amused.

"My namesake did spend three days and three nights inside a whale. If that's not an exercise in patience and faith, I don't know what is."

Her eyes narrow and her mouth curves into a closed smile.

"Weren't expecting Biblical references from a guy named Jonah?"

"Not at all."

"My grandmother on my mom's side was religious. Tried to scare us into going to church by sharing all the fire and brimstone Bible stories she knew, including Jonah running away from God, getting dumped off of a ship, and almost drowning before the whale showed up."

"Harsh," she says, horrified but amused. "Your grandmother was a stone-cold badass."

"Tell me about it. With the gray whale migration every year, she'd remind me not to ignore my calling *or else*."

"She sounds terrifying."

"She loved us and wanted the best for us, but showed it through criticism and judgment. My sister bore the worst of her disapproval." Ashley's story is hers to tell, so I move on before June can ask a follow-up question. "Are you close with your parents?"

The question is innocent, something typical you'd ask on a date, and yet it's a minefield for me. I hope she doesn't ask me the same.

"I guess, no more or less than the average family. Parents are divorced but get along pretty well. Dad is remarried and lives in Yakima. I have an older brother, but he's in California and we don't see him very often." She picks at her paper cocktail napkin. "What about you?"

"Now that my sister's living on the island again, we're close. We even run a business together. Our mom lives near Portland and visits more to see her granddaughter. Don't really have cousins we're close with and my grandparents are all dead. What about you?"

"You skipped your dad." Damn her and her attention to details. "Did he pass away, too?"

"I wish," I mutter under my breath. Louder, I say, "He moved to Mexico after my parents separated."

"A weekend in Mexico would be nice to break up all the rain and gray this time of year."

"I usually take the camper down there in the winter. There's a great area in northern Baja called Valle de Guadalupe that's like Napa, only more bohemian and chill. It's amazing."

"By yourself? Or do you visit your dad?"

I'm tempted to answer with *Hell no* but instead give a vague response about not going to the same area. The last thing I want to talk about is my shady father. I assume he scuttled back across the border to Mexico after randomly showing up two summers ago, but it's anyone's guess where he is these days. Ron's nothing but a human tornado who leaves a path of destruction in his wake.

"If you ever want to go to Mexico or Hawaii for sun and vitamin D, use Donna Kelso. She's the best on the island." I sound like an ad on the community channel.

"That would be amazing, but it's out of my realm of reality. The shop doesn't really turn a profit and the little money I make helping out at Diane's Pilates studio only helps cover living expenses. Someday, though. A girl can dream." Wistful, she rests her chin on her knuckles.

"I get it. Took me years before I made any money on the coffee hut or the roasting operation. The average is three to five years for a business to turn a profit and you've only owned the shop for a year. Give yourself time."

She nods.

Our waitress returns to take our order: salmon for June and halibut for me.

"Why did you move to Whidbey? You told me opening a store wasn't always your plan. Why come here?"

She pauses for a beat or two too long. "Timing, I guess. Seattle's crazy expensive, and I couldn't really afford to keep paying rent while selling scarves and shawls online. My bank balances were going down and my credit card debt was piling up. I was faced with the decision to go back to my old life in corporate America or move somewhere cheaper."

Surprised by this revelation, I try to imagine June working in a cubicle. "I can't picture you in an office job. What did you do?"

"Me neither." She sighs. "I was a project manager. Goes to show I shouldn't have been in charge of making a life plan at eighteen."

"What was the plan?"

"College, degree, first job on the ladder of the American Dream, followed by marriage, house, kids, and eventually retirement, all in that order."

"Not owning a yarn shop in a small town on an island. What happened?"

"How long do you have?" She laughs, ruefully. "Actually, it's a super short story. I woke up a few years ago and realized I hated my life of working long days in a soul-sucking job for people I didn't like at a company I didn't respect. I gave notice and walked away. Everyone thought I'd lost my mind, including my parents and most of my friends. I declared myself on sabbatical for six months and taught myself to knit."

"That's ..." I pause to find the right word.

"Insane?" she offers with a chuckle.

"Bold and brave came to mind first. When did all of this take place?"

Her forehead creases as she thinks. "Three years ago in May. A year before I moved here."

"Why Whidbey?"

"My grandfather died and left everything to me. He didn't have much and lived with my parents when I was little, so it was a complete surprise when we found out about the will and his life insurance policy. I knew I shouldn't waste his gift and decided to move to the island."

"Had you been here before?"

Focused on her silverware, she straightens her fork and then her knife on the table. "I'd visited a few summers as a kid. My grandfather loved it here."

I could picture June's mother as summer people, another reason she probably didn't like me. I didn't fit into her vision of what a resident of this quaint island should be.

"And then you found the Airstream? Lucky you."

"More like it found me. Living there isn't permanent. I'd love to build a little house in the woods someday. I don't need anything fancy, but it would be nice to have a bathtub and a full-size oven again." She peers at me through her glasses, a small curve to her lips. "Enough about me. Did you always want to run a coffee empire?"

Our food arrives. I tell her about business school and opening the Fellowship of the Bean. The fact that I have a marketing degree surprises her. We share stories about running small businesses on the island and the weirdest customer experiences we've had.

"I swear, the woman was completely naked, sitting in her car, waiting for her sugar-free caramel mocha." I cringe at the memory.

June's jaw hangs open. "Are you sure? Maybe she was just topless?"

I chuckle. "The service window is higher than car height. I had a direct view. Also, how would being *just topless* be better?"

She giggles. "Fair point. Did she say anything about why she wasn't wearing clothes?"

"Nope. Acted totally normal."

"When did this happen?" June fights back laughter.

"After the first Naked Whidbey calendar came out."

She nods, taking a bite of salmon. "That makes sense."

"How?"

"She must've thought you were a nudist. Like attracts like after all." She cocks her head at me, teasing.

I narrow my eyes at her. "You've seen that calendar?"

"Everyone around here has." She rolls her eyes.

"Did *you* own a copy?"

A beautiful blush spreads across her cheeks. "I don't know a woman on the island who doesn't. Some of them have their favorite months framed."

"Connie and Sally," I mumble.

She laughs. "How'd you know?"

"They were running a black-market operation selling non-authorized merchandise during the worst of Erik's infamy. The calendar was sort of their idea."

"At least this year you got to keep your pants on." She grins at me.

Staring at her mouth and thinking about kissing her, I brush my finger over my bottom lip.

"What? Do I have something on my face? Broccoli in my teeth?" June uses her napkin to dab at her mouth.

"You just confirmed you've seen my calendar picture." This could be another reason she's kept her distance. I'm guessing tattooed beefcake isn't June's type.

"I bought it to support the charities. That's my story and I'm sticking to it." She crosses her arms and lifts her chin.

"Very noble of you." I'm unable to fight the smile spreading across my face.

"It's a good cause. And, unlike Girl Scout cookies, calorie-free."

Enjoying her squirming too much, I don't say anything.

"In fact, I sell them in the shop, or did until they sold out. They were very popular with the knitting crowd this year."

"So it would seem." I rest my chin in my hand.

"Why are you smiling?"

"Just thinking about the fact that you've seen me naked."

The blush on her cheeks deepens. "Fine, yes. For what it's worth, I thought your picture was more artistic than the others. It was tasteful."

"Is that code for you couldn't see much?" My calendar photo is of me lying on my stomach on the bed in the camper, reading a book. Shot from the side, only the curve of my ass and my tattoos were visible.

"Cari did a great job. All the months are charming. Some are funny but not crass."

I nod. "Given it was full of naked man ass, that's high praise."

We finish our meals and I excuse myself. On my way back to the restrooms, I hand our waitress my credit card. There's no way I'm going to let June split the check. After hearing about her background, I don't plan to ever let her pay, not when I have more money in the bank than I need.

Back at the table, June protests when she finds out I already paid.

"You can buy me a coffee sometime," I offer.

"You own the coffee place," she protests as we put on our coats.

"That's right. How about you agree to go out with me again and we call it even?" I hold open the door for her as we exit the restaurant.

"And I'll pay next time," she insists when we get in the bus.

While I like that she said there will be a next time, I'm not quick to agree to her terms.

"Or you can give me cookies."

She pouts and crosses her arms. "A few baked goods don't equal the cost of dinner."

"You're hung up on this being an even-steven situation." I start the VW and let the engine idle. "Isn't my part of dating about taking you out and wooing you? How am I supposed to do that if I ask you for exact change on the dinner you ordered?"

"I don't want to be beholden to anyone or in someone's debt." Sighing, she meets my eyes. "It's a family trait. Moxees pay their way."

"Do you have that on a cross-stitch?"

"No, but I should make one for my mom. She'd love it."

We drive for a while in a comfortable silence as the head-lights illuminate the narrow road through the woods. The only sound is that of the engine sputtering along.

Finally, I break the stillness. "If it makes you more comfort-able, you can buy me lunch next week."

"Thank you," she replies softly, touching my hand on the steering wheel.

I open my mouth to ask if she wants to stop off somewhere for a drink but think better of it. It's too late for coffee, even for me, and a game of pool at the Dog House doesn't sound like something she'd be interested in either.

"Home?" I ask instead.

"Sure. I have an early morning tomorrow."

A vague sense of disappointment settles over me as I pull into her drive. I'm not ready for the evening to end.

I shift into neutral and take my foot off the brake, but don't kill the engine. "I had fun tonight."

"Me too," she whispers. "A really nice time."

June leans across the gap between the front seats and kisses me, brushing her lips against mine with the softest pressure.

Then she's gone.

SIXTEEN

If I'd had more warning, I would've prepared myself, and I
wouldn't be sitting here in the aftermath like a fish in a
bucket, mouth agape, trying to catch my breath and figure out
how I got here. A minute ago, I knew where I stood with June.

We weren't people who kissed each other goodbye on the
lips and then left without another word.

Light from inside the Airstream brightens the darkness
surrounding the camper.

June kissed me before I could kiss her. That wasn't in my
plan.

I'm out of the VW and striding across the mossy driveway.
What am I doing? I'm not impulsive and irrational. Normally, I
weigh multiple possibilities before acting. I'm a big fan of having
at least two options when making a decision.

All that is out the window now.

Crowding the top of the narrow metal steps, I rap my
knuckles on the siding. When she doesn't respond right away, I
swing the door open. June stands in the threshold, her hand
reaching for a handle that is now too far away to grasp.

"You kissed me," I tell her, in case she's forgotten in the
minute that's passed since she did so and ran.

For a beat or two, she says nothing. My rapid pulse and the sound of my heartbeat swooshing in my ears stretches and distorts time.

"Are you going to deny it? Pretend it didn't happen?" My tone is bewildered.

Her beautiful lips—the ones that briefly touched mine—part and she inhales sharply. "I'm sorry."

"Don't be sorry."

She frowns, her eyes wild and her cheeks flushed with shock, or maybe arousal. Maybe both. "I shouldn't have done that."

"What happened to the invisible line in the sand? The one you drew around yourself as protection?"

"From what?" She leans a hip against the cabinet next to the door.

"Me."

Her fingers twist in her sweater's cuffs. "Why would I need protecting from you?"

"I don't know. You'd have to tell me." I inhale the damp, night air.

"I shouldn't have kissed you because we're friends." Her teeth dig into her lip until the color drains away.

"Not sure that's true. I made it clear this was a date. Please don't make an argument about platonic friendship versus the infinite and often dangerous possibilities of ..." I stop myself from saying love. Why am I still talking? She kissed me and I was too shocked to reciprocate. That's not going to happen again. "June?"

My body is blocking the door from closing. She's inside, standing a step above me, putting her at almost my height. Our bodies are inches apart, so close I can feel the warmth of her breath on my face.

Her lashes flutter. "Yes?"

"I don't want to be friends with you." A dozen things I could say float away as soon as my mouth touches hers. I want to memorize the kiss in case she changes her mind about the potential of us.

I want to remember this lingering, perfect kiss.

My hand cups her cheek. I stroke the soft skin with my thumb as the feel of her soft lips against mine sears into my brain. I resist deepening the kiss. Not tonight. This is a proper good night at her door after a date. I'll only allow myself one more and then I'll go.

Yet my resolve weakens when her fingers grip my bicep, when she moans gently against my mouth. With a restraint I didn't know I possessed, I break contact, silently cursing myself for ending what was the best kiss I can remember.

"Good night, June." My voice is a low rasp as a war between good and evil rages in my head.

Her wide hazel eyes are dilated and her chest rapidly rises and falls with her quick breaths. "You could come in. I have cookies."

Closing my eyes, I tell myself to walk away. "Another time."

"Okay," she whispers and then worries her bottom lip with her teeth, drawing my attention back to her mouth and reminding how great the kiss was.

"I'm trying to be a gentleman." I step away from her and down the steps before I can change my mind.

"Still trying to impress me?" she asks, clearly amused by my self-torture.

I stop a few yards away from where she stands. "I am. How am I doing?"

"You're not at all what I expected," she replies, using the now familiar phrase.

"I'll take that as a good thing. Good night, June."

"Night, Jonah. Guess I'll see you around." Her full lips curve into a sly smile. With her rosy cheeks and mussed hair, she looks beyond sexy.

I point over my shoulder at the bus. "I'm going to go now."

Her delicious laughter follows me. I want nothing more than to kiss her again until she forgets what an idiot I am.

Instead, I dig my key into my palm, reminding myself to be good. No need to rush this and scare her off.

Driving down the road, it hits me again that June kissed me. I tap the horn and pump my fist. "Yes!"

Now to make her mine.

Tuesday morning I stalk the front windows of The Place, waiting to see June arrive for work. Most days she sets out a wooden sign with a pun or a snarky quote.

When it finally appears, I make a dirty chai and slip a ginger scone into a paper bag.

Layla and Amber are both working today. The two of them stop to watch me.

"Yes?" I lift an eyebrow.

"Nothing." Layla eyes the bag and paper cup. "Are we making deliveries now?"

"These are for … a friend." I quickly make my way to the door.

"That's … nice of you," Amber says.

"I'll be back this afternoon after some meetings. Think you can handle things on your own?" It's technically my day off.

"We'll be fine. Enjoy your day." Layla grins at me.

Amber waves. "Tell June we said hi."

Both women giggle before fake coughing to cover up laughing at their boss.

I pretend to glower at them. "Remember the new rule? My social life is off limits."

"I'll write that on the board," Layla offers. "Do you want it to say your name specifically or just the boss? Make it more generic?"

"Surprise me."

Outside, I cross the street and walk the short distance to In the Loop. Today's sign reads *Hookers welcome* above a drawing of a crochet hook.

June's in the front window, switching up the display. I knock on the glass and hold up the cup and bag.

"I brought you breakfast."

She mouths something, but I can't hear her. Pointing at the door, she pantomimes me walking.

Inside, loud music blasts from the speakers. No wonder she couldn't hear me.

"Let me turn down the volume," she shouts, jumping off the short ledge by the window and stumbling forward before catching her balance.

The moment reminds me of when we ended up on the floor of the closet. I wonder if she'd be open to the idea of making out in there.

"What are you listening to?" I try to place the song as the music softens.

"Some random girl power playlist on Spotify. I think this is Hailee Steinfeld's 'Most Girls'. The beat is good for motivating me to get my store chores done."

"Maybe these will help." I pass over my gifts.

Grinning, she inhales the steam from the cup. "Thank you."

"It's no big deal." I shrug, happy she's happy. "What are you working on?"

"I need to switch out the window decorations for next weekend's whale festival. There's a whole knitted diorama thing I made that I have to install."

"Can't wait to see it." I peep inside the large plastic tote near the window. A gray whale rests atop blue and green knitted blobs.

"No peeking. You need to see the whole vision when it's complete." She steps between me and the bag. "What are you doing for your windows?"

"Nothing?"

Lines form across her forehead. Based on her reaction, this is probably the wrong answer.

"Layla will create something later this week." Just as soon as I ask her to decorate our glass.

"Olaf usually refuses to participate, but Alexis and I are trying to convince him."

I chuckle. "He's probably not recovered from having to put up Christmas decorations for the annual sip n' stroll. Typically, he grumbles about that until at least June."

"Maybe Layla could add a couple of whales to the Dog House when she does yours?" Optimism shines in June's hazel eyes.

"If she doesn't get caught and banned, that could work. He'll be too lazy to wash the windows himself, at least for a few days."

"Does he really ban people? He seems too nice."

I about choke on my tongue. "Olaf? The guy with the white hair and matching beard? About this tall?" I hold my hand near my shoulder. "You might be confusing him with Santa after last year's Christmas miracle."

"He did fill out the suit really well." She snickers. "He's always been nice to me. I think he even flirted with my mom. Even stranger, she reciprocated."

"Olaf could be your stepfather."

We catch each other's eye and both crack up.

"If he made my mom happy, that wouldn't be terrible. There are worse men roaming around out there."

Olaf dating or being married is a strange thought. He's been a fixture behind the bar at the Dog House for as long as I can remember, yet I've never thought of him having a life outside of work. Not sure he actually does.

Shit. Maybe Ashley is right about me being a younger Olaf. Pretty sure he was younger than me when he had a wife and kids. This realization doesn't settle well in my stomach.

"Anyway, thanks for the treats. Are we still on for lunch this week?" She sips her drink.

"I'm looking forward to it." I attempt not to sound too eager.

"Are you going to let me pay?"

I exhale and stare at the ceiling. "If you insist."

"I do." She flashes a quick grin. "Are you doing trivia tonight?"

"Of course. You?"

"Wouldn't miss it. Want to give me a ride?" She picks up a ball of blue yarn and pokes at it.

First, she brings up lunch, and second, she suggests we go to China Ruby together? Men aren't supposed to get butterflies and swoon like women. I try not to let my happiness overcome me.

My eyebrows lift in surprise and a wicked smile tugs at my mouth. "Sworn enemies arriving together? Could create a scandal. Simon's head might explode. Let's do it."

"Why would his head explode?" She cocks her head. "Is there some sort of rule against fraternization between teams?"

"No. Also, how would they enforce that? I meant because of his crush on you. You haven't noticed?"

Her chin jerks back. "What are you talking about? He doesn't act any different toward me than the other women there. You're imagining things."

"Am I? Let's see what happens tonight."

"I think you're wrong."

"And I know I'm right. Should we bet on it?" I arch an eyebrow in challenge.

"What's the wager?" She crosses her arms and tilts her head up.

"You bring me cookies if I win."

"And what do I win?"

"What do you want? Name your prize."

Tapping her chin, she contemplates the possibilities before her full mouth spreads into a wicked smile. "Let me think about it. I'll let you know tonight when I win."

Please let her prize be something sexy, because I'm an idiot for saying cookies. "If—if you win. And it's a deal."

"We'll see."

"One more thing." I pull out my phone, unlock the screen, and hand it her.

She gives it a confused look, like she's never seen a phone before.

"I don't have your number. Might be helpful in making plans, like lunch." I lift my shoulder. "I won't be downtown most of the week. You might miss me."

She types in her number and sends a text. "Now I have yours, too."

"Feel free to use it. All I ask is one thing." I pick up a ball of yarn and toss it in the air before catching it again.

"What's that?"

"Please don't blow up my texts with sexy yarn puns." I tip my head toward the window. "Hookers? Really?"

She wrinkles her nose. "Too far?"

"Ask your knitting ladies."

"They're the ones who suggested it!" She rolls her eyes. "I'm more worried about the ice cream people. They're not above censoring freedom of speech while selling phallically shaped suckers to children."

Was not expecting her to say that. Good thing I'm not drinking anything or I would've done a spit take all over her locally sourced alpaca yarn.

"I'm not wrong." She takes the ball from my hands and replaces it in the pile.

Before I chicken out from nerves, I lean down and give her a quick peck. "You're perfect."

She beams up at me. "So are you."

Masculine moths flutter their wings in my chest at her compliment.

"Thank you," I whisper against her mouth, right before I kiss her again.

———

Simon's expression when he sees June enter the bar with me is priceless. The man has no game face, probably because he has zero game. In contrast to the red tint of his skin, his lips turn white from pressing them into a sharp line. For a moment, I think he might actually explode if he doesn't take a breath soon.

Simon practically runs over to greet June.

"Everything okay? Jonah's not trying to intimidate you or get into your head to throw you off your game, is he?" Simon fires a dirty look at me. "We take trivia seriously and don't tolerate sore winners or losers. Very unsportsmanlike."

Funny given this isn't even a sport.

"No one is playing dirty," June reassures him.

Placing my hand on the small of her back, I lean down to whisper in her ear. "Do you have any gingerbread left?"

Simon's eyes dart between my hand on June to her face and back to my hand. "Well, I have other teams to greet before we begin. May the best group win."

He storms off in the direction of the bathrooms.

Keeping my hand in place, I guide June through the tables to the booths near the windows.

"You didn't play fair," she whispers over her shoulder.

"Should I give you a list of my favorite cookies or do you want to surprise me?"

"I feel terrible. Poor Simon. He seemed upset." She glances over at where he disappeared to.

"You're not responsible for his feelings, or anyone else's." It bothers me that she cares how he feels when she didn't seem at all concerned about my crush. Then again, I hid my pining a lot better than poor Simon. "He'll be fine."

Cari, Erik, and Diane arrive and interrupt us. A few curious glances are exchanged when they see how close June and I stand, but no one comments. After greeting June with a warm hug, Diane takes a seat at the corner booth.

We split off to join our teams, but my eyes keep drifting over to June.

Pulling out my phone, I bring up her name to text her.

Hi

After hitting send, I wait for her to pick up her phone. A few seconds later, she reads the notification and lifts her gaze to meet mine. Instead of texting, she mouths "Hi" back to me.

With a shake of my head, I point at my phone. She purses her lips as she types a response.

You're going to get us disqualified.

No, I won't. We're not playing yet. Simon's still in the bathroom.

Someone should check on him.

Not it.

The man in question reappears, avoiding the row of booths as he walks straight to the bar. The bartender listens to his order and then pours a large shot.

My eyebrows head to my hairline while I catch June's attention. Her grimace says it all.

Trivia Thunderdome may have just taken a dark turn.

Simon downs his jumbo shot and stalks over to his microphone. "Everyone know the rules? Good. Let's get started."

"Someone's in a foul mood tonight," Erik mutters.

Cari laughs. "No kidding. Did someone steal his ugly tie collection?"

I was right about Simon's crush, but proving it might have been a bad decision.

The tension in the room is high as our host flips through his note cards, unceremoniously tossing several to the ground.

"Used in the title of a Shakespeare play, this word also refers to a rodent-like mammal."

"Oh, that's easy." Diane scribbles on her notepad.

June's eyes widen as she stares back at me. I dismiss her silent worry with a shake of my head.

The next question is about dangerous snakes. The one that follows asks for the name of a famous female spy from World War II. There's only a theme if you know to look for it.

Not a single question about crafts is asked.

I'm off my game, too busy searching out June's reactions and finding her worry increasing with each round.

With only the final two questions left, Simon tallies the ranking and then tears the paper in half before throwing the rest of his cards on the floor. "Yarned and Dangerous is tied with Ebey's Head. Because of course they are. Screw all of you. Trivia night is officially on hiatus."

With that, he stomps over to the bar, pours his own shot, and downs it.

No one says anything or moves. We're all too stunned to react.

Erik is the first to speak. "Who pissed off Simon?"

Cari's attention lands squarely on me, followed by Diane's.

"No comment."

My phone vibrates on the table with a text.

June's name in the notifications surprises me. I scramble to pick up my cell before everyone else sees it too.

What just happened?
I think I broke trivia night
Duh
What do we do?
Leave? Quickly?

A low hum of conversation replaces the stunned silence. Cassie speaks to Simon and then pats his shoulder.

Stepping up to the mic, she clears her throat before speaking. "We're going to declare this week a tie. Don't worry, though

—we'll be back next week." She glances over to the bar. "Or the week after. Check the website or call to confirm."

Whispering among themselves, a few people stare at our table—witnesses from the earlier encounter between June, Simon, and me, perhaps?

"Guess the evening's over." I pull out my wallet and drop a twenty on the table for my one beer. "No reason to stick around. I'm going to make sure they order a cab for Simon."

Diane slips out of the booth so I can exit. Her hand touches my wrist when I pass her. "Be good to her."

I nod. "Nothing but my best."

June's still seated, eyes wide as saucers while her team discusses Simon's freak-out.

"Mind if I steal her?" With my hand on her elbow, I coax June to stand.

Alexis focuses on the place where I touch June. "You should get out of here before someone asks you to step outside to brawl."

"She's kidding," I tell June. "No one is going to get into a fight."

A quick glance over my shoulder at the bar confirms Simon's still mad. He's shooting imaginary lasers out of his eyes and I'm the target.

"Ready?" I hold her jacket for her.

We escape into the parking lot and head to the far side where my VW is parked.

She darts between cars like we're truly on the run. "What just happened?!"

When we reach my rig, I rest my back against the side. "I think I ruined pub quiz forever. At the very least, I got myself blacklisted. Probably you, too." I laugh at the ridiculousness of my statements. "You okay?"

"I'm a bag of mixed emotions. On one hand, *what the hell?* On the other, I feel bad for Simon. On the other hand, this is the weirdest thing to ever happen to me."

"That's three hands," I point out.

She laughs. "You know what I mean. Do you think Alexis was right? Do you think he wanted to fight you? Over me? That's a first."

"I think you're enjoying this." Turning toward her, I brush her hair away from her face.

"I don't like him and I'd never lead a guy on. That's not something I do."

"I know. You make it clear when you're not interested in someone. Trust me."

She blinks up at me. "You think I didn't like you."

"Up until recently, I was right."

With a slight shake of her head, she disagrees. "Maybe I liked you but knew I shouldn't."

"Why?" I drop my hand from her cheek. "Because I'm not your type?"

Another shake of her head. Her teeth press into her lip.

"I'm confused."

"I didn't want to get hurt," she whispers.

June's confession lingers in the air between us.

"I promise I'd never hurt you on purpose." I take her hand in mine, sliding my fingers between hers.

"I don't have a lot of experience with guys, and the relationships I have had … well, they weren't great."

"This might surprise you, but I'm the same. I haven't had a ton of women in my life, short or long term."

Her brows draw together. "But look at you. You're hot and have the whole,"—she flicks her free hand in front of my body—"cool thing going on. I've seen the way women flirt with you."

She thinks I'm hot. Cue the moths in my stomach.

"Some women love the idea of a bad boy, which I'm not, remember? Potterhead, nerd. I get a lot of 'Thank you, next' after they get to know me."

"They're idiots."

"Says the woman who didn't like me because of my exterior

and the label she slapped on me based on my appearance." I squeeze her hand.

"Takes one to know one." She focuses on her feet.

"June?" I tip her chin up with my index finger. "You're not an idiot. You're beautiful, inside and out. Smart, funny, a little perverted. I like you—all of you."

Before she can argue, I kiss her, shifting our bodies so her back is pressed against the bus. Cupping her cheek, my fingers slide into her hair as she opens her mouth for my tongue.

She slips her hand from mine and wraps her arms around my waist, snuggling herself into the space of my open jacket. Her soft curves press against the front of my body, and it's heaven.

My paper-thin restraint shreds when her fingers brush the bare skin of my lower back. One hand tangles in her hair while I use the other to pull her even closer. She dips her head back and I taste my way down the soft skin of her neck. An unfamiliar fire burns through my body. I can't remember the last time I felt so consumed by desire like this. I'm not actually sure I've ever felt this way.

This is not how I imagined our train wreck of an evening ending, but I'm not complaining. However, making out in the parking lot at the scene of the crime isn't a good idea.

"We should go," I whisper against her mouth.

"I don't want to stop." She squeezes my waist.

"Never said we had to call it a night, but we can't stay here." I place another kiss on her swollen lips. "Come on, I can think of something better than making out in a parking lot."

Her energy shifts. "I'm not ready to go home with you."

"Who said anything about going home?" I give her a peck. "Trust me?"

She nods.

"Good."

I find parking on Anthes Street next to my building.

June takes in the neon sign of the Dog House. "You know bars aren't really my thing."

"I do. We're not going to the Dog tonight."

"Were you thinking dinner? Because I ate enough spring rolls to last me a week." She pats her stomach over her coat.

I motion to The Place. "How about a friendly game of pinball?"

"Is it open?" She peers through the window. "I thought you didn't have evening hours during the week."

I chuckle. "I know the owner. I hear he can be kind of intimidating, but he's actually a nice guy. Come on, I'll teach you the joys of pinball."

She doesn't release her seat belt. "What if I'm terrible at it?"

"Unless you turn out to be a pinball wizard, you're going to suck. No one is good when they first learn something. I imagine your first knitting attempts weren't perfect."

"Horrible." She still doesn't move.

"What do you have to lose? We don't make anyone use their own money on the games, and if pinball isn't your thing, we can play video games. You might like the virtual ass kickings of Mortal Kombat." I entwine our hands. "This will be fun."

"And what if I don't like any of them?"

"Then we'll have to think of some other way to spend our evening." I flash a wicked smirk.

"Honestly, I thought you were going to take me to some lookout point so we could continue kissing." Teasing, she quirks an eyebrow.

"On a school night? Scandalous." I close the gap between us and press my mouth to hers.

Soon her fingers are tugging on my hair and my hand is pulling her closer by the waist. Thoughts of the bed in the back of the van fuel the flames of lust I'm trying to control.

June pauses our kiss. "Windows are steamed up again."

"We've barely been talking at all," I tease. "What will people think?"

She giggles. "I can't believe I said that on the ferry."

"Were you *thinking* about kissing me? You barely tolerated me."

Briefly closing her eyes, she nods before peering at me over the rims of her glasses. "It crossed my mind. Fogged windows, enclosed space with a hot guy—who wouldn't go there?"

Her hair is mussed from my hands and her lips plumped from my mouth. The glasses and feminine dress are too much. She's incredibly sexy and irresistible.

"Pinball?" I hop out my side of the van before I lure her into the back and onto the bed, to break my three-year celibacy streak in a public parking spot on a Tuesday night.

"Right." Bemused, she runs her finger over her lips. "Lipstick okay?"

"Long gone, sorry, but you don't need it. If you put more on, I'll just end up kissing it off. If you're worried, though, we're not going to see anyone. This is a pinball party for two."

Inside the space, I only turn on my favorite, Medieval Madness, a game from the late '90s.

I sweep my arm in front of the machine as it comes to life. "Prepare to be amazed."

"What makes this one special?"

I pet the glass. "Well, there are castles, so already that makes it the best. You'll have to wait and experience the magic for yourself."

Giggling, she sets down her purse and removes her coat. "How about you go first and I can watch what you do?"

"You're still going to play." I drop my jacket on the back of a nearby chair. "Want anything to drink? Fancy seltzer? Green juice no one but Amber likes?"

"I'll take a seltzer." She follows me to the beverage cooler. "Even though you own the place, being in here after hours still feels like breaking and entering."

"Have you ever done anything you shouldn't, June?"

A worry crease appears between her eyebrows. "Nothing against the law, but there's a long list of stuff I did while drunk I wish I could take back."

"That's probably true for a lot of people." I crack open a seltzer for myself and toast. "To forgiving ourselves for the things we cannot do over."

She taps her can against mine. "Cheers."

I walk over to my favorite game and slip a quarter into the machine's coin slot. "Are you ready?"

"I am prepared for amazement." Her thumbs-up is cheesy but adorable.

"Keep your eye on the ball. The lights, sound effects, and super high-quality graphics are meant to distract you so you'll miss the ball and lose." I point out the buttons on the side and demonstrate their functions. "These are your controls."

"Got it. Seems straightforward." She positions herself to the side.

"Pull this to launch the ball, and that's it."

A deep voice welcomes us to the game. I keep the ball in play long enough for her to get a feel for the game before intentionally missing. I've probably clocked thousands of hours on Medieval Madness since discovering it in college and I had the high score on the machine in a dive bar close to campus for two years running.

"Your turn." I step aside.

June shoots me a worried look. "I'm not ready."

"Here." I take the seltzer from her hand. "Stand in front of me. I'll guide you through the movements."

Pinball pick-up 101—not that it always works. Back in college, I tried this move on Ceci before she told me she was gay. Luckily, she's almost let me live it down by now.

I place our drinks down on a nearby table. Then I motion for June to stand in front of me at the edge of the machine. "Give me your hands." Guiding our joined hands to the controls, I show her where to place her fingers. "Remember, pinball is a game of skill, not strength. You don't have to punch the buttons or shake the machine."

I lean closer until my chest brushes her back. Her breath hitches.

With my mouth near her ear, I whisper, "Ready when you are."

"I forgot what to do first." She turns her head slightly.

"Pull the plunger."

"Right."

I move our hands to the knob. "Here."

June tenses when the ball flies through the alley and bounces around the bumpers. "Now what?"

"We keep it in play as long as we can." I tap my fingers on the back of hers to remind her to use the controls.

A few minutes later, her tension gone, June's fully immersed in the game. "Ooh, there's a dragon and a damsel in distress!"

Lost in the excitement, she shifts forward and presses her full, round ass against my hips. There's a lot of wiggling involved in her pinball technique, along with delighted squeals and peals of laughter.

Which all becomes torture for me. Once I'm confident she has the hang of it, I remove my hands and step away.

"Where are you going?" She faces me and immediately stops tracking her ball, which slides past the flippers and out of play. Sad music bleats through the speakers. "Did I lose?"

"You have another chance."

"Why did you step away? I wasn't prepared."

"You were playing fine. Try it again on your own." Leaning against the other machine, I give myself some much-needed breathing room.

Her lips form a pout of concentration when she pulls the plunger and begins the next round.

Several games and many curses later, June wipes the sweat from her brow and glances around for me.

I've pulled over a chair and have my feet propped up on the table. "I think I've created a monster."

"This is really fun." She slaps her hands on the sides of her new favorite thing.

My grin says *Told you so* without speaking a word.

"You look smug."

"I might be." I stand and stalk over to her.

"Fine, yes, you were right. Pinball is fun with a capital F-U-N." Her happiness is infectious and makes her even more beautiful.

I snort. "So happy you added the N there at the end."

"Why? Do you have a swear jar like we do at our knitting circle?"

"F-U isn't a swear word."

"Tell that to Miss Cole."

I could ask who that is, but in this moment, the only woman I care about is June. Leaning forward, I cage her with my arms, palms resting on the machine. She arches up, her lips seeking mine as I slowly kiss her, sweeping my tongue into the heat of her mouth.

Deep inside me, a switch has been flipped. I never want to

stop kissing her. My rational brain knows we can't make out forever, but the body wants what the body wants.

Mine wants her.

"Mmm." She hums in pleasure, tugging me closer by my T-shirt.

Judging from the way she's softly moaning and grinding against me, the desire is mutual. We continue kissing and touching, exploring each other with our mouths and hands.

Voices from outside filter through the windows. June pauses and scans the sidewalk. "Why is there a crowd outside?"

I peer through the dim light at the clock on the wall in the kitchen. "Movie must've let out."

"Can they see in here?" She shuffles away, straightening her skirt and running her hand over the tangled mess of her hair.

"Probably." We never turned on the overhead lights, the glow from the glass-front beverage cooler and the game providing enough illumination for us to see each other. It's likely that anyone who bothered to peep through the glass would spot us.

"What if someone calls the police on us?"

"First, whoever responds to the call will know me and is likely someone I went to school with. Second, we're not doing anything wrong. Third, the incident will make a nice addition to the local police report log in the paper." I squeeze her hip to encourage her to return to me.

She moves farther away to collect her coat and purse. "We should probably go. It's late and I have a busy day tomorrow. I don't want to be the subject of a police log in the paper."

"In order to protect the guilty, they don't use names. More fun for people to guess who's behind the story." I pick up my own jacket and stride to the front door to make sure the lock's engaged. "We can leave through the back door if you're afraid to be seen with me."

"I didn't mean it that way," June mumbles.

"Are you sure? You seemed pretty concerned with the opinions of strangers a few seconds ago. Come on, I have to set the alarm and we only have ten seconds to exit." I lead her down the hall by the bathrooms to the door marked with a bright exit sign above it. After punching in the code on the keypad on the wall, I shove the backdoor open. Cool air greets us.

"I've never been back here." She examines the narrow alley that's more of a walkway, as it's too small for a vehicle.

"The movie theater and shops at this end of the block have access. Otherwise, there's no reason to come back here." I press my hand to her shoulder to spin her in the right direction. "Our ride is this way."

Once we're in the van, she announces, "Next week I should leave my car in Langley and you can bring me back here after trivia."

"Do you think they'll have it next week if Simon quits?" I lean over the steering wheel and watch for deer on the road.

"I completely forgot about him. Was that tonight? Seems like days ago." She hums to herself. "Thank you, by the way. I don't know if I said that already."

My eyes cut to her side of the van and I stare at her profile in the dim light. Her beauty still steals my breath. "For what?"

"For this evening," she says, voice soft.

"Anything in particular?" I anticipate her bringing up her new obsession with pinball, but I hope she'll address the change in our relationship over the last few hours.

"Everything. I had a really good time."

"So did I." I lower my voice. "And thank you."

"For?" she asks, turning to face to me.

"For taking a chance on something new."

And on me.

NINETEEN

I dropped June off with a quick kiss and a promise to let her know my schedule for lunch. We ended the night with text messages.

That was two days ago. It's Thursday and the week is almost over. I have a block of time free, so I text June about lunch. She doesn't respond right away. I assume she's busy with customers or knitting at the church. The weather is gorgeous today, so it's possible she went out on a hike, although she should know better than to go out in the woods without a phone. It's way too easy to trip on a root or rock and get hurt.

When I still haven't heard from her at three, I decide to visit her shop to make sure everything is okay.

"Hello?" I poke my head through the open doorway.

June's sitting in a chair by the window in the back, blowing her nose. Tears are spilling down her cheeks.

Lost in her grief, I don't think she heard me.

"June? Is everything okay?" My steps pound across the wooden floor, occasionally muffled by the small braided rugs scattered throughout.

Her needles lay ignored in her lap atop a partially finished pink blanket as she blinks away tears.

Gently touching her shoulder, I let her know I'm here. "Are you okay?"

Despite me alerting her to my arrival more than once, she still jumps with surprise.

Needles, yarn, and the blanket scatter to the floor as she presses her hands to her chest. "You scared me!"

"Sorry. Wasn't trying to sneak up on you. I said hello when I came in."

"I didn't hear you. Obviously." She laughs, but it comes out wobbly and sad.

"What happened?" I crouch in front of her. "Are you okay?"

I worry someone is dead or seriously ill due to the pile of tissues tucked next to her on the chair.

"Dash died." With a sigh, she uses one of them to dab under her eyes.

"I'm so sorry. Who's Dash?" I squeeze her other hand.

"Victoria's dog." Her voice trembles.

Quickly, I flip through familiar names in my head. "I don't think I know her. Is she a friend of yours?"

She tilts her head and gives me a funny look. "No, of course not. She's been dead for years."

With every answer, my confusion grows, but I plow ahead. "So her dog outlived her? Was another friend taking care of him?"

"He's been dead for a long time, even before she passed away." Her puzzled expression must mirror my own.

Now we're both confused. Classical music quietly plays in the shop, a soundtrack to our staring contest.

"Um, I'm a little lost here," I finally admit.

She points at the laptop perched on the small dresser in the corner. Tucked next to a basket of yarn balls, it's easy to miss. The end credits of a movie roll on the screen.

"This is about a dead fictional dog?"

"He wasn't fictional." She twists the tissue in her fingers. "Dash was Queen Victoria's beloved companion."

"Hold on—you're crying about a dog who's been dead over a hundred years?" Flabbergasted, I stand up before I tumble backward.

"I was watching *Victoria*. It's a series." She gestures at the laptop. "Victoria visited Lord Melbourne for the last time to say goodbye and had to pretend everything was perfectly fine even though they both knew he was dying." Her chin wobbles. "When she returned to the palace, she found Dash dead on the carpet."

"Do you need a hug?" I remember our conversation about the Langley bunnies and how she worried about them getting wet in the rain.

She hesitates then nods.

"Don't be embarrassed for feeling sad." I open my arms and wait.

"You don't think I'm a stupid, silly girl for crying over a long-ago-dead dog?"

"No. Well, not the stupid or silly part. I grew up with a little sister, so I've been exposed to the tears and tides of emotion that come with being a girl. Nothing you could do would shock me."

"Not even kissing you out of the blue." She smiles.

"That did surprise me. Shock? No. Ruined my plans to win you over with the most epic first kiss ever? Yes." Gesturing with my hands, I silently invite her to hug me.

"You'd thought about kissing me?" She stands but doesn't step into my arms.

"For a long time, longer than I want to admit right now." Closing the small gap between us, I wrap her in a hug. "Later. Right now, I'm consoling you over the loss of a Victorian dog."

She slowly relaxes into the embrace, hugging me back. Our height difference means I can rest my chin on top of her head, so I do, gazing out the window at the water.

"I'm better now." Her hold around my waist loosens. "You can let go."

"What if I don't want to let you go?" I murmur.

She gives me a squeeze. "Eventually, this hug will have to end. I have yarn to sell to the masses, and you have to return to whatever it is you do."

My head jerks back. "Excuse me?"

"That came out harsher than I meant. I just don't really know the details of your business. You seem to be around a lot."

"Plural." I step away, ending the embrace. "Businesses. I have several."

"See? That's what I mean." Walking over to the dresser, she closes the laptop.

"You want me to list my businesses?" I scratch my throat, mentally noting that I need to trim my beard. "Coffee, mostly. The roasting business with Erik and the chain of coffee huts with my sister. The Space." I pause before continuing, "And I have a minor stake in a green business with Falcon and several other partners."

Even though cannabis is legal in several states, including Washington, my experience is that it's best to avoid the topic because people are still uncomfortable with marijuana, and I never know on which side of the debate someone will fall.

June's eyes widen. "You sell pot?"

From her expression, it's clear she's imagining me as a drug dealer.

"Personally? No. I invested in a grow op. Completely hands off on the day-to-day operations, unless they need help at harvest time."

"So, you run a hangout spot for teens, but you also grow marijuana. You know it's considered a gateway drug." Her full lips draw together in judgment.

"Yes, so I've heard. Again, I don't personally grow or sell cannabis in any form. Think of it more like buying Amazon or Apple stock. Buy low, sell high." It's a cheesy joke, but it usually lands. Today, it crashes and burns. "Get it?"

She remains frozen, without even a twitch of her lips to show she's amused but resisting.

"Okay then." Stuffing my hands in the pockets of my jacket and rocking on my heels, I blow out a long exhale. We've gone from hugging to an uncomfortable standoff. Even the air in the room feels colder.

June still clutches the laptop to her chest while she worries her bottom lip with her teeth.

I dip my head to meet her eyes. "June?"

"I'm processing."

"Does this change your opinion of me?" I wasn't expecting her to have such a strong reaction to my revelation. "Because it shouldn't."

Ducking around me, she places her computer on the desk. "I'm having a hard time reconciling the guy who entertains sick children and opens a space for teens with this side of you."

"There's no other side, just me." I follow her to the counter. "Same Jonah. I'm multi-layered, like a cake, or a seven-layer dip."

Her shoulders loosen. "You're right. I'm judging you again without knowing all the facts."

My stomach growls. "Apparently, I'm also hungry."

Her frown fades a little. "Didn't you have lunch?"

"Nope, or breakfast, other than coffee. I texted you earlier about getting food, but you never responded." A thought occurs to me. "Want to grab something now?"

"Together?"

"That was kind of implied by the question. We can talk more about my investments and businesses if you'd like." Sounds boring as fuck to me, but I'll answer any questions she has.

"Another date? That's twice this week." She begins to thaw.

"I think Tuesday counts as a date, so technically, it's three. I'm not being subtle about it." Lifting my eyebrows, I shrug. My stomach growls again. "If you're busy, we can just go across the street for early happy hour at Salt and Water for food. They have half-price appetizers."

I wait as she mulls over the idea.

"I doubt anyone is going to need a last-minute yarn purchase at three-thirty on a sunny afternoon. Sales are better when it's cold and rainy. Let me grab my coat and we can go."

"Are you sure you want to close early?"

I watch as she goes through her closing routine, removing the cash drawer from the desk and placing it in the safe in the storage closet along with the laptop. Next, she turns off all the lights except the row above the front window display of an underwater scene for the whale festival. Green and blue scarves make up the kelp and water, and she's hung the gray whales from the ceiling with fishing wire. The entire diorama is as adorable as the woman who made it.

The closing process takes only a few minutes, but I spend the time browsing her non-yarn merchandise.

"Ball sack." Chuckling, I read the swirling text on a tote bag out loud. "You sell something that says *ball sack*?"

"Knitters have dirty minds and we love puns. We also need cute bags to carry our yarn and needles. That tote is a big seller."

"I never knew there was such a large crossover between people who knit and those who love a good pun."

"Huge. You should check out the card section."

"I'm afraid of offending my delicate sensibilities." I walk over to the standing rack anyway. "And I'm afraid I'll never be able to look at you the same way again, especially after your hooker sign."

"Perhaps that's a good thing." She pulls on her yellow rain jacket. I'm pleased to see it has a hood.

"I like big balls and I cannot lie. Knit me baby one more line. Knit fast, die warm." I keep reading as I spin the vertical rack. "All you knit is love. I'm sensing a musical theme."

"Song titles are easy to turn into knitting puns." She wraps a striped scarf around her neck and slings a green leather backpack over one shoulder.

Hanging on the wall next to the rack are several framed embroidery works. What first appear to be delicate florals with inspirational messages, instead contain more puns and snarky messages.

"I sell cross-stitch kits too. 'Knit happens' is our biggest seller, followed by that one." She points to a framed piece depicting two balls of pink yarn beneath the words *Knits out*.

"Perverts." I grin at her. "I feel personally deceived by all those sweet women at the farmers' market selling baby booties and scarves."

She giggles. "Better avoid the knitting circles, too. Things get pretty racy when you get a bunch of knitters together in a church rec room."

"I'm going to show up one of these days. You think I'm joking, but I'm completely serious."

A loud snort escapes. "That would be hysterical." She dangles her keys on the end of a finger. "I'm all set if you are."

Following her out of the shop, I wait for her to lock up. "Why would it be funny? Because guys aren't supposed to knit? Or is it the thought of me specifically being there?"

"The latter."

We only have to cross the street and walk up the block a few buildings to reach the restaurant, so I wait to clarify until we've hung up our coats on the rack near the door and we're seated in the corner of the bar, near the window. It's early and no one else is here. The nook feels cozy, and I'm happy it's just us. The difference between the inside and outside temperatures has fogged up the glass, making the rest of the world disappear, like we're the only two people left.

"Why shouldn't I join the knitting circle?" I ask.

"You could. You're not barred. Anyone can join." She unravels her long scarf and places it inside the sleeve of her jacket. "We've had other men attend. I was once in a co-ed knitting group in Seattle. Unfortunately, it was dissolved because of some misguided episodes of mansplaining and an extramarital affair."

"Maybe I should take up knitting."

"You want to learn to knit?" Her eyes widen like they did when I told her about my investments. I'm not sure which bit of news shocks her more.

"Everyone keeps telling me I need new hobbies. Can I come to the group sometime?"

"It doesn't seem like it would be your scene." She backpedals from her early statement about all being welcome.

"I have a scene?"

"I assume you do, sipping tea and eating cookies with a bunch of women who knit isn't it."

"We've already established that I like cookies. As for the tea, I can bring my own coffee."

She eyes me, doubtful.

"What if I told you it's because I want to spend time with you? Learn about the things you like, discover what your equivalent of Medieval Madness is?" I reach for her hand, lacing my fingers in hers.

"We have open groups during the week. I suppose you could come to one of those." Her offer lacks enthusiasm.

"I look forward to it." Leaning over the corner of the bar, I brush my lips against hers.

"Keep your expectations low, please." She casts me a wary look. "You're probably not going to find it interesting. Mostly, it's me and several senior ladies sitting around, Whidbey's own Golden Girls and me."

The more she tells me I won't like it, the more I want to go just to prove her wrong.

"Is it knitting only? What if someone wanted to crochet or cross-stitch?"

"I mean, if you show up with a craft project involving yarn, you won't be shunned. Embroidery is a whole different thing, though. Same with quilting. Most people love one or the other and stick with it."

"Like rival craft gangs?"

"Kind of?" She snickers. "I'm imagining a standoff on First Street between a group of women holding crochet hooks and another group armed with knitting needles."

"Doesn't sound like a fair fight."

"As my grandfather would say, nothing about life is fair."

"Sounds like a wise man."

"Wisdom comes from hard lessons." She twists a thin gold ring on her right hand. "He had a lot of those, too."

"I don't think anyone gets through life without a few painful experiences." I soften my voice. "I know I haven't. The thing is not to become bitter."

Her warm smile crinkles the corners of her eyes. "How did we go from dueling craft gangs to philosophical musings about life?"

"No idea." My expression matches hers. "Should we order food or explore the potential for bitterness further?"

"Food, please."

We order a seafood tower. Turns out June loves oysters as much as I do, which at first sounds like a good thing, but in reality means I have to share them with her.

Our conversation drifts from topic to topic as we eat and talk. Currently, we're discussing self-protection. Not sure how we ended up here. I didn't leave a trail of breadcrumbs.

June traces a swirl of blue ink on my forearm with the tip of her index finger. Her light touch sends a shiver through my body, raising goose bumps along my skin. "We all have our own version of armor. You wear yours on your skin."

"What about yours? Woven out of soft fibers?" I joke. She's a temptress in a hand-knit sweater.

She drops an empty oyster shell onto the crushed ice. "No, mine is tougher because you can't see it. Invisible barbs and thorns are more difficult to penetrate."

"What happened to you, June?" My tone is light, but the question is serious.

"Nothing." She focuses her attention on the discarded shells.

"Something happens to all of us. No one gets through childhood without a few scars, and I'm not talking about the ones we can see on our skin."

"Really, nothing remarkable happened. I mostly kept to myself. People have never been my thing. Introvert, in case that wasn't obvious. Over the years, I've made a handful of close friends. That's plenty. Not everyone needs to be prom queen."

"Did you go to your prom? I didn't go to mine," I admit.

Her eyes grow rounder. "You didn't? I thought everyone went but me."

"Eh. Wasn't my scene."

"Too cool for school dances?"

"Cool didn't have anything to do with it."

"I wasn't too cool. No one asked me," she confesses.

"Obviously, you went to school with idiots. Most seventeen- and eighteen year-old-guys are. Why didn't you go with friends?"

"They all had dates." A frown appears and quickly disappears on her face.

"I don't think we missed much."

"I've always wondered," she muses while stacking oyster shells into a little tower of their own.

"There's a weekly dance at Bayview in the summer. You can get your question answered there, discover if prom is your missing piece like the Shel Silverstein book."

She doesn't react right away, but then softly says, "I love that book."

"One of my favorites as a kid—another thing we have in

common." I pause. "We could go to the dance together, but we'd have to promise each other not to be wallflowers."

Her nose scrunches up, forcing her to use her index finger to push her glasses into place. "This is beginning to sound like one of those '80s teen movies. Nerdy girl gets a makeover, goes to the dance like a modern Cinderella, and meets her prince, who just so happens to be the guy who tortured her in math class. Everything is okay, though, because he's really a sweet guy with family issues that make him act like a jerk."

My eyebrows lift. "Not a fan?"

"Blech, no. Don't even get me started on the rapey overtones of some of the so-called classics. I don't care how good your swooped-back hair looks or how awesome your sideburns are or how well you rock a plaid shirt and drive a Porsche if you don't respect your girlfriend enough to make sure she gets home safely from a party at your house." Pink flushes her cheeks, not from embarrassment, but from anger. "Sorry. I get a little riled up."

As I process her rant, I smile. She's right about respect, but that's not what makes me smile. The hair and the plaid describe me perfectly. The Porsche, not so much. "You make excellent points. May I add that not all guys who fit that description are assholes?"

The color on her face spreads and deepens as her mouth forms an O. "I didn't mean you."

"I know. I don't own a Porsche. The only guy I know who owns one of those is Dan. I also didn't grow up rich and entitled either."

"That makes two of us. My family story is one of bad decisions and shrinking bank accounts."

For some reason, I decide to share about my dad, something I never do, because to speak his name is like conjuring Beetlejuice. "My father screwed us and a lot of other people over, emotionally and financially. There's probably not a person or business on the island who would be happy to see him."

"Must've made things difficult for you when you wanted to start a business here."

"He made life tough for both Ashley and me. That's why we changed our names after he left, switched to my mom's maiden name, not that the Kingstons were all that much better. They didn't steal and embezzle, but all their fire and brimstone did grate on our young souls. I'm not entirely convinced I won't burst into flames if I visit your church."

"Only one way to find out." She grins at me.

"Do you have a working fire extinguisher that's up to code?" I match her expression.

"We'll smother the flames of hell and damnation with the baby blankets." She pretends to pat out fires on my arms and shoulders. "You do all these selfless acts, but you don't let anyone see the real you."

Uncomfortable with the idea of being vulnerable, I give my standard reply. "I don't do what I do for attention to feed my ego or to brag to some stranger about all the ways I'm amazing."

"What sins are you atoning for?" She pins me with an intense look. "Your own? Or your father's? It almost seems like you're doing penance."

I've never thought about my actions as atonement for sins or guilt or a host of other emotions surrounding my childhood.

"Why does there have to be a hidden motivation behind doing good for others? Can't I just be a humble, nice guy?"

"Hmm. You are both of those things, but neither is what motivates you."

I haven't told her the details about my father or the tsunami of destruction he's left in the wake of his life. The shadow of Ron Curtis darkens my story and I'm not sure there's any way to escape it.

"We all have our reasons and patterns for doing what we do."

TWENTY

"Every spring the gray whales return to the waters off of Whidbey en route to their summer homes in Alaska. Often, they stop off for a shrimp buffet right here in Langley. Be sure to keep watch for their tails and fins making a splash," a woman dressed in a gray whale onesie tells a group of small children gathered around her near the dog and boy statue. The spot has the best view of the Saratoga Passage over to Camano Island, the perfect location for spotting whales.

I'm only half listening to her speech as I wait for Ashley and Rosie to arrive. Having grown up here, I've heard variations of the same talk for thirty-five years.

The annual whale festival is in full swing downtown today. Being on the migration highway is good for business whether or not a store puts out special merchandise.

Other than Layla's new designs on the windows, we're not doing anything else. Olaf noticed the "graffiti" on his windows yesterday afternoon. We could hear him cursing from across the street. Like many of his bouts of venting, this one didn't amount to anything other than a threat of banning the responsible party, or a Kelso brother, his typical scapegoat. I make a note to send one of the kids over on Monday to scrub the paint off the glass.

Sitting on one of the benches in the sun, I enjoy the warmth while I people watch. There are families with kids, couples, roaming groups of teenagers, seniors and a few loners milling around, all waiting for the parade to begin.

Langley is a small town and we find any excuse to have a celebration with a parade. Halloween? Parade. Christmas? Parade. If there's a semi-reasonable excuse to close First Street and have people walk down the middle of the road while wearing a costume, we're here for it. Bring us your vintage cars, your high school marching band, your scouts, and your dogs. I've marched or driven in plenty of these events, so it's nice to enjoy the festivities from the sidelines.

When I dropped off June's chai and scone this morning, I invited her to watch the parade with me. She's joining my sister, niece and me as soon as she closes up the shop. Given the route is a five-minute walk on a normal day, she better arrive soon or she'll miss the entire thing.

My sister's copper hair stands out in the crowd as she maneuvers Rosie's stroller around people. Whistling to catch her attention, I stand to greet them.

"You're looking happy," she tells me after we hug.

"I'm wearing all black and sunglasses. How can you tell?"

"For one thing, you trimmed your beard and appear more human, less Sasquatch. Also, you're smiling."

My brows pull together as I frown. "I smile all the time."

"Something's different about you."

Ducking her scrutiny, I focus on my niece, who is bundled up in a gray hat and a tiny sweater with a whale on the front.

"Someone's been buying hand-knit baby items," I accuse. "Maybe using her daughter as an excuse to spy and meddle in my life?"

"I can't help it that we live on an island with limited resources. Carter and I are trying to buy local." Avoiding my eyes, she tucks the soft pink blanket around Rosie's chubby body. "Oh, look, the source of your new grin and my favorite baby blankets is walking toward us," Ashley sing-songs, clapping her hands.

June approaches us, a happy bounce to her steps. She's dressed for the festival with a gray whale hat perched on her head and another whale tucked beneath her arm.

"Hey." I sling my arm over her shoulder as I kiss her cheek.

"Hi." She gives me a hug. "Wow, it's a madhouse out here. Who knew so many people love whales?" Spying my sister and the stroller, June releases her hold on me. "Hi, Ashley. So good to see you."

"Same." Ashley grins at me and then hugs June, surprising both of us. "Look, Rosie's wearing the outfit I bought."

The two women chat about the baby while I inwardly reassure myself this isn't a big deal. Small town means people make connections and get to know each other. Given they're both around the same age, becoming friends is natural. I'm sure they have a lot of things in common besides me. Still, this is the first time since college that I've introduced a woman I'm dating to family. Nothing to freak out about. Obviously, because they're already best friends.

June tucks her hand around my elbow and whispers close to my ear, "I like your sister."

"The feeling is mutual," Ashley says, not even pretending she wasn't eavesdropping. "All around, right, Jonah?"

I mutter something about meddling under my breath. Both women chuckle.

"Jonah doesn't like sharing," Ashley blabs to June. "It's probably better if I just invite you both over for dinner so he doesn't feel left out."

Smooth move, sis.

"I'd love to come to dinner. I can bring dessert." June squeezes my arm. "Doesn't that sound like fun?"

Ashley's right about me not wanting to share my time with June, but I agree to make a plan after we all check our calendars.

Another problem with small-town life: if June and I don't work out, I'll still have to see her around the island. I doubt I'll ever be able to go back to ignoring her.

———

On Monday, after a busy whale celebration weekend, I meet up with Dan at the Dog House to discuss business and catch up, mainly about The Place and his plans for the Dog.

I'm only partially listening to him, my attention focused out the front window.

June's walking down the street with a group of older women. Every one of them carries a bag of yarn and needles in each hand. There's a certain strut to their stride, like they're on a mission or marching in a protest. Yarned, dangerous, and ready to poke someone's eyes out … or knit them some mittens. Cute, but fierce. Like kittens.

The group turns the corner and heads up the street to the church. Given their serious expressions, I wonder if the knitting is a cover for more nefarious actions. Ever since I read *A Tale of Two Cities* in high school, I've been suspicious of women who knit.

"Jonah?" Dan asks, amused.

"Yeah?" I face him.

He glances between me and the window. "Didn't hear a single word I said, did you?"

I shake my head. "Nope."

"I'm also guessing you weren't distracted by a group of older church ladies. Going out on a limb here that they're not exactly your type."

We both know I'm busted. "Not that I have a type, but I draw the line at a ten-year age gap in either direction."

"Probably smart. I can't picture you as a boy toy." He chuckles.

"Well, there was this one woman in Seattle when I was in

college. She was nine years older, and that's all I'm saying about that."

His dark eyebrows lift before he shakes his head, a smile twisting his mouth. "Nothing you say should surprise me anymore, and yet … it does."

"Gotta keep people guessing." I rap my knuckles on the worn, wooden bar. "Want to fill me in on what you were saying when I zoned out?"

His eyes shift to the window again. "I was explaining that Olaf has decided to sell me the building."

"Wow. End of an era." I'm stunned even though this has been a long time coming.

He nods. "He wants to cash out while he can still enjoy life. I think the heart attack a couple of years ago shifted his priorities."

"Near-death experiences often do that to a person. Is he going to stop tending bar, too?"

"He's saying he'll cut back to one or two evenings a week, but I'll believe it when it happens. Remember how he was going to let us take over while he recovered from surgery?"

"Didn't happen." I shake my head. "We made all those plans for the space and he came back to work before we could implement any of them."

"Exactly. He's a stubborn old dog." Dan pauses. "Believe me, I've told him so to his face."

"You could always force him to retire. If anyone could, it would be you."

Dan frowns. "Not happening. He can stay on as long as he likes. After I sold my company, I swore I'd never turn around and do the same thing to another small business. Community is more important than profits."

"I agree, a hundred percent. Olaf's a fixture. Won't be the same around here without him threatening to ban the Kelso brothers or yelling about babies in bars."

We both chuckle.

Dan strokes his beard, near the corner of his jaw. "I benefit from not having grown up on the island. If Olaf had known teenage me, he'd have the same opinion. Luckily, my youthful indiscretions aren't common knowledge."

Tom Donnely walks through the main door and stops in the small corral formed by the old-timey, swinging saloon doors. He's wearing his welding coveralls folded down and wrapped around his waist. A rolled bandana keeps his blond hair off his face.

"Hey, you started the meeting without me?" He flicks his hand at our pints on the counter.

"We did," Dan admits. "Want to join us?"

"I'm not saying no." Tom slides onto a stool at the corner of the bar so he's able to face both of us. "I'm done for the day and headed home after this. I'll take a Mac & Jack." His eyes cut to me. "I heard you and the yarn woman were cozy at trivia night."

"You gossiping with Sally and Connie again?" I joke. "And her name is June Moxee."

"Speaking of lady business—"

I cut him off. "We weren't talking about anyone's lady business, and can we stop using that phrase?"

He eyes me, suspicious. "Okay, okay. I've been meaning to ask you something about last summer."

Shifting through my memories, I can't think of anything eventful that he'd need to bring up from almost a year ago. I shrug. "What's on your mind?"

"Why did you borrow Shaw for an afternoon under the guise of babysitting? You said it wasn't to pick up women, which I'm not against in theory, so I'm curious."

"Huh. I don't really remember." I attempt to dodge the question by sipping my beer.

"Hailey thought it might've had something to do with June." He studies me, both eyebrows lifted.

"Oh, that. I needed to figure out sizing for a baby gift. Shaw seemed like he was about the right age and size."

Both men eye me.

"That's it?" Dan asks, surprised.

"You could've asked us what size he wore. It's a pretty wide range when they're that small. It isn't like you needed a chest or inseam measurement for the tailor. Wait, you weren't ordering a custom suit for a baby, were you? Is that a hipster thing?" Tom's now laughing at his own joke.

"No suit," I mumble. "Quit calling me a hipster."

Dan places Tom's pint on the counter. "He does have a point though."

I throw him a dirty look.

"Whoa." He holds up his hands. "Not about the hipster part. I meant the baby stuff. They're all like baked potatoes with a floppy head and wiggly limbs at that point."

"Did you just—?" Tom cracks up.

Dan sips his pint. "Compare my daughter to a potato? Never."

"Moving on." I'm desperate to steer the conversation back to business. "You were saying about Olaf and the building …?"

"Let's wait for John. He just pulled up outside." Tom motions toward the giant Ford truck parked in the prime spot in front.

Dressed in a red and black flannel and jeans, John stomps his boots on the sidewalk before entering.

"I'm going to warn you, I probably have sap on my soles. Want me to take off my boots?" he announces as greeting.

"Nah." Dan waves him over to the bar. "These floors have seen worse."

Once all of us are seated around the corner of the bar, Dan lays out his vision for the future of the Dog House.

"She's going to need some major restoration and updates to her infrastructure, but because it's an historical building we're restricted on how we proceed. This process will take some time and we'll have to close down for a while."

"Close the Dog House?" John gapes at Dan.

"You're kidding, right?" Tom sounds shocked. "This place is an institution."

"If we want it to stick around for future generations, we need to intervene now before the whole building falls into the water." Dan's voice is more serious than I've ever heard him.

"How can we help?" I ask.

"I have the capital for the construction, but I wanted to propose a partnership between the four of us. Jonah and I have the business experience, and, pardon me if I'm wrong, but I believe John and Tom have strong emotional ties to this building."

Tom lovingly strokes the smooth edge. "A lot of good things happened here."

I snort. "Don't tell Olaf you had sex on his bar."

Tom flips me off.

Dan and I chuckle.

John clears his throat. "What are you suggesting?"

"Not to assume I know about everyone's financial situations, but I think we're all in positions to invest in shares and divide the ownership between us."

"Us? Own the Dog House?" Tom's mouth hangs open. "Is it my birthday?"

John sweeps a hand over his dark beard. "I'll need to discuss it with Diane. Are we talking about taking shifts and tending bar? Not sure she's going to be on board with that idea."

"No one has time to take on another job. We'd hire people to work here," Dan clarifies. "This is about having a stake in ownership."

"What about the Kelsos?" I ask.

Dan's mouth forms a hard line before he speaks. "Olaf's made a stipulation that forbids them from any ownership or role in running the business."

Tom bursts out laughing. "That's a ban if I've ever heard of one."

A snort escapes me. "Carter is going to be pissed."

Dan's shoulders shake from laughing. "Olaf specifically requested a clause about Erik's ass and public nudity be written into our contract."

"Who gets to be the one to tell him?" Tom asks. "Can it be me? I want that job."

Dan shakes his head. "I'll take care of it. So, we have a gentleman's agreement? My lawyers will draw up the paperwork and we can move forward from there."

We shake on it.

"Holy shit," Tom swears. "This is crazy, but I'm all in."

"It's only right we take over, given how many hours of our lives we've spent here." John turns and scans the room.

I glance at Dan and the other guys then back out the window.

"Have somewhere you need to be?" he asks, a knowing gleam in his eye.

"In fact, I do." I pull cash from my wallet. "I don't want to hear from Olaf about stealing beer. Make sure he knows this is from me."

Dan chuckles. "I'll be sure he knows you paid your tab."

After saying goodbye to the guys, I cross the street to The Place.

I pop my head through the door to tell Amber I'll be MIA for at least an hour. "I'm taking another hour for lunch. Got my phone if there's an emergency."

"Aye, aye, captain." She salutes me from behind the counter.

En route, it occurs to me that showing up empty handed to a knitting circle might be a little suspicious. It's too late to acquire the equipment now, though, so I forge ahead.

TWENTY-ONE

A painted rock decorated with the word *Faith* props open one of the side doors of the white clapboard building. If this were a quest, the door could be a secret passage or a trap. Either way, I open it and enter the long hallway on the church's lower level.

There's a scent that lingers in churches that reminds me of my grandmother: dusty carpet, smoke from extinguished candles, and perfume favored by older women. The combination equals judgment and disappointment in my mind.

Voices carry down the hall, and I follow the sound to one of the larger multi-use rooms. Well illuminated by overhead fluorescent lights, the space is mostly empty save for eight women on folding chairs, forming a circle. Laughter echoes off the linoleum, increasing the overall volume. Rather than shouting to be heard, I wait for a lull in the conversation to make myself known.

"Are you going to loiter in the doorway all afternoon, Jonah Kingston? Or are you here to join the fun?" Alexis asks without turning her head in my direction, her tone amused.

June tips her head back and peers at me through her green-

175

framed cat-eye glasses. She winks, knowing only I can see her face. "Can we help you?"

"I was curious about what goes on in these circles. Thought I'd stop by and check it out." Although I play along, I'm still uncomfortable being the focus of all their attention.

"Did you bring your needles and a project you're currently working on? Those are our two house rules," Alexis explains.

"I'm sorry. I didn't. I don't even know how to knit." I take a step backward. Softer, I say to myself, "This was a mistake."

"Don't be such a stickler." A woman I don't recognize pipes up. "If you'd like to learn, you can use my spare needles and yarn. We all have plenty of extra yarn."

Entertained by the ruse, June observes my exchange with the older women, her needles sliding and clicking against each other.

"Sit next to June. She can show you how to cast on. Best to begin with a garter stitch until you get the hang of it and can graduate to purling," another one of the women adds.

I catch June's attention before I commit to joining them. "Are you sure?" I mouth. She nods in response.

Picking up a chair from the stack against the wall, I circle the space until I reach June. She and the woman next to her slide their chairs away from each other, creating a narrow gap.

I could definitely use more elbow space. There's no way I can make use of the full range of my arms without jabbing someone in the arm or poking an eye out.

June scoots over a few more inches until I'm able to unfold the chair.

"Hi, I'm Jonah."

"Hi, Jonah," they echo back to me.

Alexis and June I already know. Miss Cole, Edna, Myrtle, Betty, Hilda, and Thea tell me their names. I know I won't remember all of them after this afternoon.

June sets aside her own project before handing me thicker needles and a ball of yarn she pulled out of her *Ball Sack* bag.

"What's with the act?" I whisper.

She ducks her head to whisper near my ear. "Don't want to be seen being biased because we're dating." She then taps the needles together like a drummer. "You think you're up for this?"

"Definitely," I reply firmly, and I'm not talking about knitting. "I'm all in."

The excitement of the meeting with Dan lingers. While I'm sad about Olaf's retirement, I know Dan will pay him more than a fair price for the building. With The Place and my other businesses running smoothly, I'm happy to have a new project in the works. There are so many ways we can make the old Dog House even better.

"Why are you grinning?" June whispers to me. "You seem way too happy about knitting."

"I'll explain everything later." I pick up my ball of yarn. "Show me how to turn this cat toy into a hat."

A few of the women titter.

Miss Cole levels me with her cataract-clouded eyes. "Hats are way above your non-existent skill level."

"We'll begin with a square and then you can move on to a scarf." June hands me the needles.

The majority of the women encourage me each time I mess up and have to begin again. I swear Miss Cole must be a retired teacher or librarian, or perhaps a former boot camp drill sergeant. She's tough and calls me out on every mistake. Given her thick glasses, I'm surprised she can even see me across the room.

Forty-five minutes of failed knitting passes quickly. As June promised, after everyone puts away their projects, the ladies descend on a tray of cookies and the carafe of hot water on a table near the back of the room.

June unravels the last bit of my "project" and winds it around the rest of the ball.

"I have nothing to show for my efforts now." Sullen, I bite into a cookie.

"No reason to save that mess. Keep practicing. You'll get better." She holds out the needles and blue yarn.

Confused, I accept them from her. "For me?"

"If you're serious about learning, you'll have to knit for more than an hour a week. Consider it your homework."

"I might need private lessons, lots of one-on-one tutoring." I smirk.

"What did you have in mind?"

"We can make an exchange: you teach me to knit and I give you after-hours access to Medieval Madness." I'm confident it's an offer she can't refuse.

"Tempting, but there's something else I want." She lowers her voice like we're co-conspirators.

"And that is? You're already getting free coffee and scones."

"True, and I'm very grateful for your daily deliveries, but this is something I can't buy on my own. You have one and I want it," she purrs, batting her lashes for good measure.

"You have my attention." I close the distance between us, momentarily not caring that we have an audience of senior ladies and we're in a church.

She lowers her voice to a faint whisper and cups a hand over her mouth. "Do you have a bathtub at your house?"

"There's an antique claw foot tub that is probably original. Why?"

Her eyelashes flutter and a soft moan of pleasure escapes her mouth.

"Are you okay?" I press the back of my hand to her forehead.

"Fine, fine. Do you have plans tonight?"

TWENTY-TWO

I've seduced women before using my tattoos and piercings as bad boy bait. Never before have I tempted a woman to come home with me by mentioning the claw foot tub in my bathroom.

June's excitement surpasses the responses to all my previous invitations to come to my house.

We've said goodbye to the knitting ladies and are walking back toward First Street.

"Can I bring a bath bomb? Is there a ledge for a candle? How good is your hot water heater? Are we talking a few inches of tepid water at the bottom of the tub or a deep, hot soak?" Her expression is pure innocence and joy.

"My hot water tank is more than adequate for the job." She may not be thinking about sex euphemisms, but I am.

"I'll run home and grab a few things. What time should we meet at your place?"

"Should we have dinner first? So I don't feel like you're just using me for my tub?" I rest my hands on her shoulders.

"I'd never do that. You should know this isn't something I do on a regular basis—or ever. I've never gone home with a man and taken a bath. You're special, Jonah Kingston." She almost makes it to the end without giggling. "You'll be my first."

179

"You are a terrible liar. I bet there's a long string of men wishing you'd come back and grace their tubs." I bend down and kiss her smiling mouth. "Pizza okay? I can pick something up at Sal's when I drop off Dan's coffee order."

"Mmmhmm. Yes, please. Nothing with garlic or onions, though."

"What are your thoughts about pineapple?"

"No fruit on pizza. I'm not a monster." Wrinkling her nose, she sticks her tongue out.

"Anything else?"

"No." She bites her lip and shakes her head. "I'm just … excited."

"I can tell." I squeeze her waist. "I'm excited you're excited."

Standing on her toes, she kisses me before grinning again.

We pause and simply stare into each other's eyes. This happy feeling reminds me of falling in love for the first time when I was nineteen. *Is that what this is? Love, or just a crush?*

"Six o'clock work for you?" I murmur, unable to break the spell.

"I'll be there," she whispers.

I'm in the warehouse at Whidbey Joe's when I get her text.

I don't know where you live.

Chuckling, I respond with my address and basic directions.

Can't wait!

Before Erik or someone else can comment on the stupid grin I'm sure is plastered on my face, I flatten my expression and rub my hand over the back of my head.

I remind myself that June is using me for my bathtub. She hasn't agreed to have sex with me. Just because she's going to be naked in my house doesn't mean I'll get to see her naked.

At that thought, my dick stirs to life.

I'm going to need a cold shower before she arrives.

———

At five o'clock, I take a non-cold shower in the freestanding shower next to the tub. Imagining June naked, covered in bubbles, her skin pink from the heat, brings my dick to life. Unwilling to spend the evening sporting a semi, I jerk off as hot water slides down my back, but coming barely takes the edge off of my arousal. After soaping and shampooing, I switch the water to cold and withstand the shock of the temperature change as I rinse off.

My hair is still damp when there's a knock at my front door.

June stands on the porch holding an overstuffed tote bag and a cookie tin.

"I'm a little early," she apologizes. "I brought cookies."

"What's in the bag?" I beckon her inside. "Is that a robe?"

"I …" She pauses. "I wasn't sure what the plan was and might have overpacked."

"Did you bring your toothbrush?" I ask.

"Was that presumptuous?" A blush warms her cheeks.

"Not at all. Better than borrowing mine and not telling me." The happy flutter is back in my chest at the idea that June plans to spend the night. I take the tin from her and place it on the table. "Pizza's hanging out in the oven. I wasn't sure what you wanted to do first, eat or bathe."

She nervously twists her fingers together as she softly states, "There's a third option."

My heart rate ticks up and my breath shallows at what she's suggesting. Closing the distance between us, I tease, "Knitting? I didn't know if you'd want to do that tonight. Wasn't going to presume."

"Jonah." The word comes out a plea.

My mouth crashes into hers, my hands cupping her face as I walk her backward until she's against the wall. Her bag tumbles to the floor, its weight settling against my leg.

She wraps her hands around my waist, slipping them beneath my flannel shirt. I jump at the coolness of her fingers against my skin.

One hand still tangled in her hair, I skim the other down her neck, over her collarbone, down to her breast. She arches into my touch, emboldening me.

Grinding my hips against hers, my dick hardens, reminding me that jerking off and a cold shower are pointless when June and her soft curves are right here.

Touches become desperate as we shift clothing out of the way. My shirt is the first to go, shoved up to my shoulders by June. I reach behind my head to pull it the rest of the way off.

Her greedy hands wander over my chest and arms, tracing the patterns of my ink.

"I've been dying to see this forever. You're a present I wanted to rip the paper off of, so I could see what's inside. This is better than I imagined." She presses her lips to a sacred heart done in grayscale above my real heart. Wrapped in thorns, it's one of the first tattoos I ever got.

Those moth flutters I felt back in her shop have turned into eagles, beating their wings in my chest. Her words, her mouth on my skin send a current of lust through my body. She has no idea the effect she has on me.

Her fingertips trace a small A as she reads a quote on my pec. "The best way out is always through."

"Robert Frost," I whisper.

"Who is A?" she asks, sweeping her mouth over the colorful ink on my shoulder.

"Ansel, my godson." My heart clenches with emotion for him. "He was the sick baby at Children's, the one who inspired me to volunteer there."

She pauses and peers up at me, a mix of emotions swirling over her face: lust, concern, worry, and something more. "Is he okay?"

I nod, overcome with the love in her eyes in this moment.

"I'm glad." She continues to gaze at me, her hands still exploring my skin. "I feel like there's a story for each and every one of these."

"There is." Her light touches are torturous.

"You've illustrated your life on your body. It's beautiful."

I'm not sure if she means the art or my life. Before I can ask for clarification, she presses her hot mouth against mine and palms me through my jeans. Like our first kiss, June surprises me.

Everything with her feels different, new. Her touch only increases my lust. I cover her hand with mine and then drag it over her head, pinning her to the wall. Lifting her leg, I wrap it around my hip.

We get lost in one another, grinding and begging for more contact, more skin, more of everything.

Trying to kiss her the entire time, I strip off her sweater, tossing it at the couch before lowering the zipper of her dress. Licking and nipping a path from one shoulder to the other, I glide the material down her arms until it pools at her waist and then drops to her feet.

Like she did with me, I take a moment to drink in the vision of her exposed flesh for the first time. Creamy, smooth skin, winding curves. The places where she's soft, supple. A simple white bra with a blue bow covers her full breasts. Blue under-wear matches the bow.

Gently, I move her hand from where it rests on her stomach. "Don't hide yourself from me. You're incredibly sexy."

"I'm squishy and wobbly."

"So? Those adjectives don't detract from your beauty." I squeeze her hips. "You're even more beautiful than I imagined."

She worries her bottom lip.

"Trust me. I've spent a lot of time thinking about you and this moment." I kiss my way down her chest, paying attention to the swells of her breasts as I unhook her bra. Once they're free, I cup and lavish her with more kisses, tonguing a pink nipple while squeezing the other with my hand.

Each of her moans and sighs encourages me. I drop to my knees in front of her, gazing up at this goddess standing in my living room in only her underwear and a pair of red shoes with tiny heels. She's a pinup girl come to life.

She tenses when I slide my fingers up her thighs, skimming the lace trim of the cotton covering her.

"Want me to stop?" I pause.

"No, no, please no. It's just …"

I wait for her to continue.

She exhales. "It's been a while."

TWENTY-THREE

"How long?" I ask.

"Two years," she whispers, tensing, her focus on the wall behind me.

"I have you beat by a year," I confess with a kiss to her hip.

Her wide eyes find mine. "What? You must've misunderstood. I haven't had sex in over two years. What did you mean?"

"Same thing." I kiss her other hip.

"That's impossible." She wriggles free from my hold. "Don't joke about this."

"Would you feel better if I told you it had been a week? Or a month?"

The familiar crease appears between her eyebrows right before she frowns. "No, that would be worse."

"Then you should believe me when I say I haven't slept with anyone in a really long time." The throb of my erection against the zipper of my jeans is a painful reminder of how long it's been.

"Why?" she asks, arm covering her breasts.

"Probably for the same reasons you haven't." I stand and lean against the wall, creating space between us.

"I doubt you had trouble getting dates."

"I didn't. I could've had sex with random people as often as I wanted." I cross my arms. "You could have too."

"No way."

"You didn't want to have meaningless sex with strangers."

"Sober sex with strangers was pretty much the worst." Her laugh is hollow.

And the pieces click into place.

"I came to the same decision. At some point, going home alone was better than the awkwardness of leaving after empty sex."

She blows out a long breath. "You're never what I expect."

I beam. "The good news is that I have three years of sex to make up for."

Her wide eyes drink me in as I cage her in with my hands on the wall.

"And so do you," I murmur.

Before she can answer, I scoop her up and flip her over my shoulder. Her red shoes drop to the floor on the way to my bedroom.

Gently tossing her onto my bed, I soak in the sight of her.

She takes off her glasses and sets them on the nightstand while I quickly undo my jeans and strip off my boxers. Climbing on the mattress, I remove the last scraps of fabric hiding her from me.

"Everything about you is perfect." I kiss her, pressing her into the mattress with my weight.

"Is it possible to combust from desire?" she asks, widening her legs to accommodate my hips.

I suck in a sharp breath as I glide against her heat. It's been forever, but I still need a condom.

First, I need to do something I've had actual dreams about. Shifting, I crawl down, trailing kisses over her chest and stomach until I reach her hips.

"Jonah." Her voice is a whispered prayer.

"Tell me what makes you feel good." I kiss below her navel before moving on to the spot no longer hidden by blue cotton.

Lapping and circling with my tongue, I slowly slide a finger inside her. The slick warmth clenches before opening for me. Her hands tug at my hair and her hips rise up to meet me. Lost in her, I want to be nowhere else. June's unfolding orgasm sweeps through her as she moans and writhes; I savor her breathless pants and whispers of "Please" and "Oh yes." I ride out the waves until she stills my mouth with a gentle press of her hand to my head.

"I think I left my body at some point," she murmurs as I kiss each hip and draw my chin across her stomach.

Her taste still floods my mouth as I kneel back. To give myself an ounce of relief, I stroke my cock. Small drops of pre-cum slide off the tip, June watching every movement with eyes filled with lust. "I need to be inside of you."

"Please." Her hand covers mine and squeezes. It's sweet torture and I have to move before I come from the world's quickest hand job.

Locating a box of condoms, I rip it open and pull one out.

"Fresh box?" she asks.

"Told you, it's been a long time." I cringe at the thought of how long. "This might be shorter than either of us wants. I promise to make up for it next time."

She laughs and pulls me down for a kiss. "I'm taking the box as a challenge."

My eyes bug out at the implication of her words. "Challenge accepted."

Slipping between her legs, I glide my tip through her wetness. I want to avoid causing her pain, so I push inside slowly, pausing when I feel the familiar tingling that warns I'm too close to the point of no return. She feels unbelievably amazing. Unable to resist the growing urge, I thrust and find my rhythm.

"You are incredible," I whisper to her. "I'm not going to be able to last."

Her nails dig into my ass as she encourages me. "Yes, please. Oh god, *yes*."

A blaze begins in the lowest point of my spine and flashes through my body as my orgasm hits. My thrusts become shallow as I come.

Once I recover enough to no longer feel like an exposed high-voltage wire, I kiss her and we're laughing and smiling against each other's mouths.

"Still want that bath?" I ask, standing to take care of the condom.

"Oh god, yes." Smiling, she stretches her arms over her head. The sight of her sprawled across my sheets tempts me to start round two, but I need a few minutes to recover before I'm ready to go again.

"Do you realize you said the same thing about your bath time—that you did during sex?"

"That's how much I love a hot bath. It's a bathgasm." She giggles and rolls to her side. "Want to join me?"

"I'm not sure we'll both fit."

Her face falls with disappointment.

I walk away, heading into the bathroom. After washing my hands, I turn the tap for the tub faucet.

June knocks at the door. "I heard running water."

I let her in and excuse myself to give her privacy.

A few minutes later, she calls me back. I find her in the tub, her hair in a bun to keep it out of the water, which is fizzy and pink.

"Come join me. You can totally fit." She points to the opposite end. "Smart to put the faucet in the middle so no one has to be jabbed in the back."

Water sloshes over the side when I do as she asks. Two people is a tight fit. I'm about to tell her she should enjoy her bath by herself when she leans forward, gliding her hands up my thighs until she finds me semi-hard under the water.

I love how she touches my body, like she can't get enough of me.

"Have you ever had sex in here?" She gives me a not so gentle squeeze.

I inhale sharply through my teeth as I harden in her grip.

"No, but I'm willing to try new things." I pull her forward and swallow her mouth in a kiss.

We start in the tub but finish in the shower after I make a wet dash to the bedroom for another condom.

Afterward, June wraps herself in her fluffy, rainbow polka dot robe and joins me on the couch with the pizza.

"That was the best bath I've ever had." Satiated happiness radiates off of her.

"Glad to hear it. For the record, that was some of the best sex I've ever had." Happy, drunk on lust and orgasms, I brush my lips over hers.

She giggles before sliding her tongue into my mouth, caressing mine in a deep kiss. "That too."

TWENTY-FOUR

My cell phone rings the next morning while I'm parked outside Whidbey Joe's.

June left early after admitting she brought her robe and toothbrush, but not a change of clothes, not wanting to be too presumptuous.

"Hi. Miss me?" Still riding a high, memories of last night and this morning on repeat in my mind, I'm pleased she's calling me so soon.

"Someone broke into the shop last night." June's voice shakes.

"Was anything stolen?" I switch to speakerphone and turn the key. "Did you call the sheriff?"

"I called you first."

"Did they break into the safe or steal merchandise?" The engine of the bus turns over and sputters to life. "Where are you now?"

"Standing inside the shop. How long until you get here?"

"Ten minutes. If you don't feel safe, wait for me outside."

The drive to downtown takes forever. Longest nine minutes of my life. Given the early hour, First Street is mostly empty, and I park right in front of In the Loop. I'm relieved the front picture window isn't broken and there isn't broken glass on the ground near the door either.

June paces on the sidewalk, waiting for me.

"Everything okay? Did they take money or break anything?"

"As far as I can tell, the safe hasn't been touched and there's no damage."

"Was the door locked when you got here?" I examine the doorjamb for forced entry.

"Yes."

Now I'm confused. "So the door was locked and nothing's been stolen? Why do you think someone broke in?"

"Come see."

I follow her into the shop, winding our way past the large tables filled with yarns and knitting pattern books. Nothing seems amiss.

"Look." She points at her favorite chair.

Next to the chair on the floor is a pile of blankets.

"What am I looking at?"

"The window is cracked open slightly. I know I didn't leave it open."

Curious, I step up closer and peer out. There's about a five-foot drop from the window to the embankment sloping down to the seawalk. Someone could make the jump without injury.

"Do you have an alarm?" I scan the room for a keypad, relieved when I spot one near the desk.

She twists her lips to the side and glances up at the ceiling. "I rarely bother engaging it. No one is going to steal yarn. They can't pawn it or trade it for drugs."

"June." Frustrated, I tug a hand through my hair.

"I know, I know. I should always set the alarm, and I would … if I still paid the premium." She grimaces. "Stop judging me. Cow's already out of the barn. No use beating a dead horse. Water under the bridge."

"You forgot the crying over spilled milk."

"That too." A small smile brightens her face.

"Okay, so we have an open window. Anything else?" Nothing seems out of place, but the shop is cluttered, making it hard to tell.

June points. "The pile of blankets. They weren't there when I stopped by yesterday before knitting group."

"Are you sure?" I eye the neatly folded stack.

"Definitely. I keep them in a couple different baskets around the shop, but never laying on the floor. Dusty, dirty blankets don't sell well."

"What do you think happened? Someone snuck in through the window and decided to take a nap like Goldilocks in the bears' house?"

"Exactly. Or someone wanted to have a sleepover."

"A sleepover on the floor of a yarn shop?" I cock my head to one side.

"It's possible." She picks up one of the blankets and holds it out to me using only two fingers. "Sniff this."

I jerk back. "No. Why would I smell that?"

"For drugs. Or sex."

Now I take a big step backward. "You think someone broke into the shop to have sex and do drugs on some hand-knitted blankets? Why?"

"I don't know." She studies the blanket before dropping it to the floor.

"Who would do that?"

She gives me a pointed look.

"Me?" I scrunch up my face. "The only person I've had sex with recently is you. At my house. Last night."

"No, not you, but maybe one of the kids who hang around The Place."

My jaw drops. "They're not delinquents running wild and committing crimes."

"Any of them talk about running away? Or having issues at home?" Her tone softens.

"What teenager doesn't think they have issues with their

parents at some point? Doesn't mean they're going to engage in breaking and entering. And why here? Why not sleep at one of the churches? Or at a friend's house?" *Like I did.*

"I think you should ask them," she suggests, digging in on the idea.

I balk at her suggestion. "Did you call the sheriff to file a report?"

"No. I told you nothing's stolen or damaged."

"So you called me down here instead? I'm not going to interrogate the kids."

"Okay, fine, but maybe pay attention and see if any of them are wearing the same clothes as yesterday or seem off."

I rub my eye and twist the loop in my brow. "That I can do. Can you do me a favor?"

"What?"

"Let me come over at the end of the day to make sure the window is secured? We can order a security camera, too."

"Deal."

———

I don't tell June this, but I'm more than a little worried about her break-in theory and how it relates to me.

My life has been going smoothly for the last couple of years. Business is good. Family is doing well. Dream project realized.

The entire time, I've been waiting for a giant shoe to drop out of the sky and crush me.

Because when I'm happy, that's when life goes to shit.

Two years ago, my dad decided to revisit his past on Whidbey. Ron Curtis slithered out from beneath his rock, tanned to the point of looking crispy and as soulless as always. Motivated by nostalgia or malice, he stalked Ashley until he showed up at her condo for a family reunion no one but he wanted.

We thought he was after our money, which was the logical explanation for any attention from Ron. After almost twenty years of avoiding her lawyers, he felt the need to show up in person and tell us he was in love and wanted to finalize the divorce with our mom.

Good riddance. Haven't heard from him since he returned to his life in Baja. He could be anywhere. He confessed to coming to the island and lurking around, checking things out, spying on us. Rationally, I know Ron breaking into June's shop makes no sense. He wouldn't bother folding the blankets and would probably steal stuff just to be petty.

Thinking about my dad reminds me of something Olaf once said about the man: just because you can't see the rats out in the open doesn't mean they're not hiding in the walls, lurking, waiting, biding their time until the moment is right to grab their prize.

June's probably right about the break-in being done by kids. Still, the unease I feel at the thought of my father showing up again and causing trouble for me and Ashley has me pulling out my phone to call my sister and make sure she hasn't heard from him.

She reassures me she hasn't had any contact or sightings.

"Does June know about dear old Dad?"

"Why would I tell her? I've finally convinced her I'm a great guy she should date. Why ruin that by spilling the family secret that our father is a grifter?"

"I think that's giving him too much credit. More like a sleazy, lying-ass, cheating con man."

Chuckling at her definition, I defend my label. "Grifter is quicker to say."

"True." She grumbles a few curses. "You should tell her so one of the island gossips doesn't spring it on her."

"Those women wield too much power around here."

"Preaching to the choir, dear brother. Explain the family history to June. You can have her call me if she has questions. I think she'll understand that his actions don't have any effect on your life."

———

After getting off the phone, I exit my office at the back of The Place and run into Lara and Theo in the dark hall near the bathrooms.

Actually, a better description is I slam into them while they're making out like the horny teenagers they are.

"*Ohmygod*," Lara squeals.

Stepping around their tangled bodies, I refuse to look at them. "New rule: no making out on the premises. That includes the hallway and bathrooms, and within a hundred feet of both entrances."

"That rule apply to you?" Theo snorts.

I pause in my step. Figuring if he's speaking, his tongue is no longer exploring Lara's esophagus, I face them. "Excuse me?"

"Nothing," Lara says, gripping Theo's arm.

"Saw some late-night action against the pinball machines last week after the movies."

June and I are totally busted.

He's only a few inches shorter than I am, but weighs at least fifty pounds less than I do—not that I'm thinking of taking him down. Theo's just a kid. He's a snarky kid who knows too much.

On a hunch, I turn the tables on him.

"Any chance you know of more private make out spots downtown? Maybe somewhere with a view of the water and lots of blankets?" I observe the color drain from Lara's face.

"Nope," Theo bluffs.

"Lara?" I focus on her.

Her gaze lowers to her feet.

"Lara," Theo warns. "They don't have any proof. Jonah's the guilty one for sneaking in here after hours and making out with June."

Closing my eyes, I take a breath and count to ten.

"You're so stupid, Theo! You just confessed." Lara groans. "Are you going to press charges?"

"No, June doesn't want to involve the sheriff. You both need to apologize to her and promise to never do anything like that again." I glower at Theo. "One of the good things about growing up in a small town is people know you and know your family so they'll be quicker to forgive idiocy. One of the bad things about living in a small town is everyone remembers all the stupid shit you did when you acted like an idiot."

"It won't happen again," he mumbles. "Can I say something in my defense?"

"This isn't a trial, but go ahead." I roll my hand to encourage him to speed this up.

"We were walking down on Seawall Park and noticed her window was open slightly. She should have an alarm on her store. Someone worse than us could take advantage." He finishes with a shrug.

"Point made." I hold out my hand. "Let's shake on the promise you won't turn into the island version of Bonnie and Clyde."

Both of them look at each other and then back at me. "Who?"

"Never mind. No more committing crime, got it? Or you'll be banned from here." Damn, I am turning into Olaf.

We all shake hands.

Feeling good about how I handled Theo and Lara, I decide to give the good news to June in person.

TWENTY-FIVE

There's a *Be Right Back* framed cross stitch sign on June's door.

I want to tell her about Theo and Lara in person, so I text her to say I'm looking for her and to let me know when she's back in the shop.

Not wanting to be around the law-breaking lovebirds right now, I stroll down to see if Olaf's at the Dog House.

"Guess you heard the news from Dan?" He doesn't bother with pleasantries like *Hello* or *How are you?* like most people.

"Nice day today. Good to have a break from the rain." I slide onto a stool. "How's your week going?"

"I'll take that as a yes. You want a beer?" His hand hovers near the pint glasses on the shelf behind the bar.

"Sure. I'm killing some time."

"Didn't ask what you're doing, asked what you want to drink." He pauses near the taps.

"Pick something you like. Doesn't matter to me." I study the grand old bar with its silver flecked mirror and carved supports. There's a lot of potential in this place.

He places my glass in front of me. "You seem like the kind of guy who likes a lot of hops in his ale."

I sip the crisp IPA. "Great choice."

"Don't see you in here much." He uses his white bar towel to wipe clean glasses before he puts them away. "How's business going across the street?"

"In general, good. However, I finally understand why you're always threatening to ban people."

"Teenagers are toddlers with hormones," he grouses. "You're insane to want to cater to that age."

I snort at his description. "You have no idea how true that statement is today. The whole point is to have a safe space for them to be able to hang out with their friends so they're not running amok and getting into trouble. Is it too much to ask that they not turn to crime the second I turn my back?"

"If anyone should've known better, it's you." He turns his attention to his knotty, wrinkled hands. "Can't blame it all on you, though. You had a shit role model for how to be a man. Amazing you didn't end up in jail."

I suck in a deep breath and then exhale. "I just look like a delinquent."

"It's your body. If you want to treat it like a coloring book, that's your choice." Olaf frowns and swallows like he's eaten something unpleasant. "Kind of ironic you ended up taking over that building."

My glass is midway to my mouth and I pause. "Why? 'Cause I hung around there in high school when it was Mike's Place? Life coming full circle and all that?"

"You know how Mike came to own that building?" Olaf drops his towel in the sink and rests both of his hands on the bar across from me.

"Bought it from the previous owner, I suppose. I don't remember when it was a gas station."

"Won it in a poker game. You're not going to like what I tell you about it." Olaf blows out a breath.

My stomach churns with foreboding. "Was my father involved? Fuck. I knew it. This has Ron written all over it."

"That's not the full story."

I grind the heels of my hands into my eye sockets and groan. "Tell me what you know."

"The poker game was a setup, not exactly high stakes, but a few hundred dollars passed hands on a typical night. Then Mr. Lloyd joined them. He owned the gas station and some undeveloped acreage in the woods. Mike and your dad saw a big fish on the line and got greedy. I don't like speaking ill of the dead, but Mike didn't believe in playing fair in cards, or in life. He and Ron made a fine pair."

"They deliberately cheated Mr. Lloyd out of the deed and the land? What was in it for my dad?"

"The only thing your father loves more than himself: money. Heard Mike took out a mortgage on the place to fix it up and gave your dad half, or Ron forged the papers. Either way, I heard your dad apparently walked away with a pile of cash."

"And the acreage?" My jaw ticks.

"As far as I know, Mike and Ron never got their hands on that. Mr. Lloyd left the island shortly after and no one heard from him again."

"Screwing over the Kelsos and cheating on my mom wasn't enough?" The muscles in my chest tighten from rage and adrenaline.

"There's more." He frowns, like he feels terrible for being the bearer of more bad news.

"I'm not sure I want to hear anything else about my father today."

He rests his hand on his whisker-covered chin. "It involves that pretty brunette I've seen you running around with lately."

"June? June Moxee? What does she have to do with Mike and my father?" Cold dread fills my veins at the thought of him telling me she's my half-sister from one of dad's many girlfriends. I both want to know and need to pour bleach on my brain so I never remember finding out. I feel lightheaded.

"Mr. Lloyd had a daughter. She never spent much time on

the island. Went off and got married young and had a couple of kids of her own. A son and daughter if I remember right."

"Okay." Relief flows through me as I try to follow this family history. I place both of my hands on the back of my head and exhale.

He continues to scratch his beard as he watches me. "The granddaughter's about your age, maybe a few years younger."

My brain is slow to process more information. "Hold on, are you talking about June?"

The nod he gives me is like the dropping of the blade of a guillotine.

"My father stole June's grandfather's building through a rigged poker game? What are the fucking odds of that?"

A soft female gasp fills the space. Glancing in the mirror, I spot June standing in the chute between the entrance and the swinging saloon doors. Our eyes meet for a second, shock, hurt, and confusion filling hers before she turns and leaves.

"Fuck." I glare at Olaf. "Did you know June was back there? How much did she hear?"

"She came in right at the end." He holds his hands up. "I didn't recognize her because she's not a regular. Don't think I've ever seen her come in here before."

Of course, he hasn't. "She doesn't drink."

My stool crashes to the floor as I bolt out the door to chase after her, not bothering to pay for my beer or say goodbye to Olaf.

"June! Wait." I yell at her back as she flees down the sidewalk. I stop a few paces away when she reaches her shop.

"Go away, Jonah." Her jaw is so tightly clenched she can barely spit out the words.

The pained expression on her face is a knife to my gut.

Panicked I won't be able to smooth this over, I babble, "I didn't know the connection. I swear. No one likes my dad or thinks he's a good person. The best compliment anyone ever paid me was to tell me I'm nothing like him."

She holds up her hands. "Don't. Just don't."

I take a step in her direction.

"Don't talk to me."

Plunging her hand into her oversized *Ball Sack* tote, she curses about not finding her keys. Frustrated, she dumps the entire contents onto the ground. A few painted rocks and an assortment of needles, balls of yarn, small hoops with thread hanging off them, lipstick, a wallet, a notebook, and a couple of pieces of chocolate spill out on the sidewalk. No keys. Patting the sides of her striped dress, she reaches into a pocket and extracts a set of keys. "Fucking pockets."

"Can I say something?"

"No."

"It might take your mind off of this revelation and make you feel better." I hold up my palms.

Her eyes are shooting daggers at me, but I keep talking.

"You don't have to worry about security and the break-in. Theo and Lara confessed to being the ones who snuck into the shop, to fool around."

As the words leave my mouth, I want to stuff them back down my throat, knowing I've made the situation worse.

June shoves her glasses into her hair and covers her face with both hands.

I assume she's about to start sobbing and I touch her shoulder. "Don't cry. Please."

She flinches away from my touch. Her features conveying pure anger.

"No one respects anyone else's property. Think they can just use what they want, take what they want and there won't be any consequences. Islanders are worse than Lenin with their attitude toward communal property. What's yours is mine and what's mine is mine."

I've never seen June mad before.

Annoyed, yes. Frustrated, yes. Purely angry? Not until this moment.

Only she would bring up Lenin at a moment like this.

"And you know what's the most rotten part about all of this is? I like you. I really like you."

"Why is that horrible?" My stupid face didn't get the memo about her being mad at me and spreads into a smile.

"You're worse than a regular bad boy. You're a bad boy with good guy intentions in a bad boy's body," she shouts. "I knew I was right to stay away from you even before I knew Ron Curtis was your father."

And then she slams the door in my face.

———

I decide to take a long walk to temper my emotions before my thoughts become actions or words that can't be erased. Unfortunately, Langley's a small town and I only have one block before I run out of downtown and either hit residential streets or the water. I opt for the water to avoid passing my building.

Or more correctly, her building.

On the slope down to the seawall, I kick a couple of rocks, cursing under my breath about too many men named Mike. Mike's Place. Mike's Gas Station.

People need to be more original when naming their children.

I slip my phone out of my pocket and call Dan.

"Hey, Jonah. How's it—"

I cut him off. "Did you do research on Mike's Place before you bought it?"

"You mean on the deed? I had my lawyers in Seattle go over everything two years ago. Didn't find any liens and there weren't any contingencies because the purchase was in cash. What are you worried about? I'm not planning to break your lease or hike up your rent."

"No." I blow out an exasperated breath. "I know you did

everything above board. I meant, how much do you know about the history of the previous owners?"

"Hold on." There's silence and then some muffled conversation. A minute later, Dan comes back on. "Sorry, I was in the kitchen. Too much chaos for conversation. Where were we?"

"History of Mike's. Did you know it was a gas station before?"

"Of course. Mike had to remove the tanks and pay for the clean-up before switching it over to a restaurant. Are you worried about toxins? Everything's been tested and cleared."

"And what about the guy who owned the gas station? What do you know about him?"

"Not much. That was over thirty years ago."

"What if I told you Mike didn't pay a fair price for the property?"

"I'd say it was none of my business as long as the deed transferred cleanly."

Not deterred by his indifference, I continue. "He won it in a card game. Any guesses as to who else was involved?"

"Your dad?" His voice is low. "Shit, I'm sorry. But, what idiot gambles using a building as collateral?"

"June's grandfather, apparently."

"June? Your June? I thought she was new to the island."

"She is, but her family isn't."

"How'd you find this out?" I can hear him typing on a keyboard.

"Olaf."

"Figures." More typing. "I don't see the name Moxee associated with anything on the island until June bought the yarn shop. Moxee's a name you don't forget."

"He wasn't a Moxee."

Dan's exhale is audible, and the pause that follows is long. "Is June trying to make a claim on the property? Why now?"

"She isn't." I shake my head even though he can't see me.

Another pause. "Then what's the issue?"

I growl with frustration. "It isn't right. On principle."

"Ah, I see. Principles are involved." Dan chuckles. "Are you sure hearts aren't the main issue?"

Ignoring him, I continue, "You know what I mean. We're profiting off of someone else's bad luck."

"That's one way of looking at it."

"Tell me another one," I mutter.

"Well, if a man is willing to bet his property deed, he's already made poor decisions that led up to that moment—bad financial choices. Betting the property means he was out of money or owed a chunk to a bookie. See the common thread here?"

"Point taken."

"What about the land she's living on now? Who owns that property?"

"I think she inherited it, not that there's much there. She's basically camping out there. No permanent structures, not even an outbuilding. She has water, electric and septic set up, but that's it."

"That's good. Someone was smart enough to keep it out of the gambler's hands. Not everything was lost."

"A couple of wooded acres aren't the same as a corner lot and a commercial building downtown. The difference is at least a couple of zeros."

"You of all people know we can't hold ourselves responsible for the sins of our father, nor is it our responsibility to right their wrongs." The line goes quiet for a moment.

"Can you call June and explain all of this to her?"

"I think that's going to be up to you." He softens his tone. "Guess she's not taking the news well?"

"I've never seen her angry before." The memory still stings like a paper cut. The fear of her not wanting to be with me is like salt on the wound.

"This fuck up isn't your doing. What happened between your dad and her grandfather is old news. We can't choose our blood family and we don't have to tie ourselves to their self-imposed doom."

My anger and fear dissipate. "When did you get so wise? What's your secret?"

"Age and learning from my failures. I've fucked up enough for a PhD in life lessons."

"If you don't fail, you're not trying hard enough." I echo one of the first pieces of advice Dan ever gave me.

"I stand by that on both professional and personal levels."

I get his not so subtle clue. "I shouldn't give up on June because she now thinks I'm a shady grifter like my dad?"

"You've shown her who you truly are. Let the dust settle from this revelation. Then remind her you're a good man."

"How do I do that?" I sigh, feeling hopeless.

"You'll figure it out." Loud yelling echoes in the background.

"I need to go. Jeff and Coop are acting like angry badgers today. Let me know if you need anything. My door's always open."

We hang up, and I tip my head back to glare at the blue sky.

The only thing to do is get out of town for a few days, sleep outside, and clear my head.

TWENTY-SIX

On my way out, I text Erik and let him know I'm disappearing for a few days. This isn't the first time I've left out of the blue. He responds with *Have fun*, so I know he'll take care of things. I follow up with another text to Amber and Layla, telling them to check in with Erik about schedules and staffing for the rest of the week. They've worked with me long enough to know what to expect.

I call Ashley, though. When it goes to voicemail, I leave a short message about the events of the day, ending with admitting she was right about controlling the story.

No plans or direction, I drive up the island and over to Fidalgo. I have camping gear in the van, but need to stop for groceries before settling in at my favorite campground near Rosario Beach. It's only an hour from home so I'm close in case there's an emergency, but far enough away so that I can think and regroup.

———

A few days alone clears my head enough to return. This is my pattern, which started in high school when I'd tell my parents I was staying at a friend's house and ask my friend to cover for me while I camped in the state park or slept on the beach. Then, in college, I'd say I was traveling during break, but instead stayed on campus while my roommates went home to visit their families. I've always found it easy to disappear.

On my way home on Friday afternoon, I swing by The Place to check on things. Given that it's the middle of the afternoon when I drive down First Street, I'm surprised I don't spot June's sign outside In the Loop. There are no lights on either.

I park the VW in a spot halfway between her shop and the Dog House and walk back to confirm what I already suspect. In the Loop is closed and there's a hand-written sign taped to the glass that says, *Gone Fishing*.

I doubt June actually fishes. Maybe she also requires time alone and it's another thing we have in common. This is of no comfort to me.

When I drop by work, Amber and Layla have more questions about June than answers. No one has heard from June since her big blow out on Tuesday afternoon, which apparently has gone viral through the gossip channels.

Wanting facts instead of rumor, I drive to the little Airstream in the woods. June's Prius isn't in its spot and the trailer is dark. I check my own house on the off chance she's left a note.

I'm sitting in the empty parking lot of the Saratoga Woods Trail when it finally occurs to me to text her. Then I quickly change my mind. I want to know she's okay, but I'm not sure if she's in a place to speak to me yet.

Instead, I head over to Ashley and Carter's house.

My sister greets me with Rosie on her hip. She wrinkles her nose. "You smell like a Sasquatch. Shower before we eat, please."

"Have you seen or heard from June?" I ask, ignoring her command as I follow her through the open floor plan of their single-story house.

"Bathe first and then we'll talk. The goats smell better than you do." She's wearing her mom face.

I give in, grab my pack from the camper, and then take a hot shower in their guest bath. It's the first one I've taken since the morning after June stayed over, and that time I wasn't alone. Frustrated, tired, and confused, I rest my forehead against the cool tiles and let the water pound against my back.

The only clean clothes I have left in my pack are a pair of boxers and a T-shirt, so I'm forced to wear the same jeans.

Ashley nods in approval when I enter the kitchen. "Much better."

Carter walks into the room carrying a baby goat in a pair of Spiderman pajamas. He hands it to me along with a bottle of milk. "Here. This one needs to be handfed."

And then he leaves.

So, I feed the baby goat while Ashley concurrently makes dinner and ignores me.

Carter returns right before we sit down at the dining table. This time, he brings Rosie, who is also wearing superhero jammies, albeit in the form of a Wonder Woman onesie. He places her in our sightline, in a baby chair in the living room where she can hang out while we eat.

This is a regular evening with these two. Only, I'm not feeling normal.

Midway through our meal of salmon and broccoli, I broach the subject of June again. After I fill both of them in on the details of my conversation with Olaf, I bring up what's been bothering me since I left the beach.

"You know, she lied to me too, by omission. The whole time she knew about the building. Never mentioned she owned the land where she's living. Forgot to point out that one of the only reasons she's on the island is because our dirt-bag dad conned her grandfather."

Carter swears under his breath. "How can one man be so toxic?"

"It's his super-villain power," I mutter.

"Are you done ranting?" Ashley stabs a stalk of broccoli. "You need to talk to June about all that. We can't give you answers."

"She's gone."

"Did you try her phone?" Carter asks.

"This conversation needs to take place in person, but I don't know where she is."

Ashley sets down her fork. "Diane called me when June left her a message about a family issue she needed to deal with out of town."

"Are her parents okay?" I can't help the concern I feel.

"Diane said June didn't give her any details but asked her not to tell you where she went." Ashley sips her wine. "Naturally, Diane called me to find out what happened between the two of you."

Carter chuckles. "You're becoming the next generation of gossips."

"Hush," Ashley scolds. "We're protecting our own, not spreading rumors."

"Are wingwomen a thing?" Carter asks me.

I shrug. "Apparently."

"Hashtag girl gang." Ashley snorts. "My point is: June left the island."

"Any idea when she'll return?"

"Diane said a week, so you have a few days to figure out what you're going to do." Ashley offers me a sympathetic smile.

"I'm not sure if I should fight for her or let her go."

Carter clears his throat. "Are you in love with her?"

I nod.

The truth hit me when I was alone this week, and now I'm scared I've lost her before we can begin.

"Then there's only one answer: don't give up." He slaps my shoulder. "Just don't wait ten years to make your move like I did."

Ashley agrees. "Timing is everything."

————

Knitting is harder than it looks. Each click-clack of the needles only serves to remind me how unskilled I am at this.

"You dropped a stitch," Miss Cole tells me from two seats over.

"How can you tell?" I lift my narrow rectangle. "Seems fine to me."

"I've been counting. You started with twenty and now you have nineteen in your row." Her look is both a challenge and a smug declaration of her rightness.

"Pretty sure I still have twenty." I count the loops on both of my oversized needles. "Nineteen. Damnit."

"Quarter in the swear jar, Jonah." Myrtle points to the jar they placed near my feet.

Reaching in my pocket, I pull out my wallet. "I'm putting in a five-dollar bill. Who carries quarters around these days?"

"Ha. You started out with twenty swear words and you're down to nineteen. Dropped a stitch and the d-bomb." Edna laughs.

If it would make any difference, I'd inform her d-bombs are really a thing. Damn is light swearing and d-bomb sounds like slang for an unsolicited dick pic. There's no way I'm going down that path with a group of Methodist senior ladies, though it's bad enough Betty and Thea recognized me from the Naked Whidbey calendar and requested my autograph.

I pull the loops off of my needle. "Should I start over?"

"No!" Betty shakes her head. "Well, now you do. Next time, we'll show you how to fix it before you frog the whole thing."

"Frog?" I ask, confused.

"What you just did—erase all of your hard work." Miss Cole tucks her chin and tsks.

"You are a tough group. Anyone ever tell you that?"

"We don't have time for bullshit." Thea clamps her hand over her mouth. "Damnit. I know, I know. Take mine out of Jonah's five."

"Hey now," I drawl.

"I'm on a fixed income." She bats her eyes at me. Stifling a laugh, I wink back. Out of all of the women in the knitting group, Thea's the biggest flirt. At the end of my first visit, she came right up to me with her walker and asked if I knew what a cougar was. I worried June was going to choke on her own tongue she was laughing so hard.

"Where's your girlfriend today?" Betty asks.

"I don't have a girlfriend," I reluctantly admit, avoiding looking in Thea's direction.

"What's wrong with June?" Myrtle interjects.

"Nothing."

Thea winks at me. "Then why haven't you tapped that?" It's possible she's trying to use lingo she overheard her grandkids using. Not likely, but possible.

"Can someone help me cast on again?" I hold up my needles and the mess of yarn.

Myrtle sets her own knitting in her lap. "Okay, but this is the last time."

"I don't think he's ready for knitting yet. Needs to practice the basics." Miss Cole clicks her tongue.

"Thanks for the vote of confidence, Miss Cole."

She glares at me through her reading glasses. "Back when I was your age, men didn't join women's groups. They spent their time at the Rod n' Gun or out fishing."

"Hush, you. If he wants to knit, let him. We're not the knitting police. Too many people trying to tell everyone else how to live their lives and who to love." Thea blows me a kiss. "One of my grandsons is gay and single."

"Oh, I'm not gay." Then I remember Erik's botched television interview where he somehow managed to out us as a couple.

"Then there's no reason you shouldn't be dating June." Betty's needles rapidly click together as she speaks. She doesn't even look at what her hands are doing. None of them do. Clearly, they're witches.

I hesitate before confessing, "Maybe June doesn't want to date me."

"Can't blame her."

"Edna! You're being rude. Put a quarter in the jar." Myrtle points at the floor.

"I will not. I didn't curse. I merely stated my opinion. He's probably single for a reason. Not sure he's good enough for our June."

Edna, keeping it real since 1942.

"Where is she today? She never misses our group. Is she sick?" Miss Cole shoots me an accusatory look.

"She's out of town for a few days," Alexis explains.

"Did you scare her away?" Edna glares at me.

"She overheard part of a story and I need to clarify some things," I confess.

"This about your father?" Alexis pauses in her knitting. "Connie was telling everyone at the bank about the poker game."

"Great. She gives new meaning to the word teller." At least I know the reason the story's spread like wildfire.

A brief squabble erupts, but their hands never even pause as they continue their work.

Myrtle gives me back my needles. "Ignore them. Try again."

I think she means knitting, but it's her soft smile of encouragement I accept.

The knitting circle lasts only an hour, but in that time I complete a few rows without dropping a stitch while the ladies make progress on their baby blankets. My yarn is about ten times thicker than what they use, but they manage to produce triple what I do.

"Will June be back next week?" Betty asks.

"I assume so," I answer, not knowing how much June told Alexis.

"You should call her and ask," Myrtle suggests.

"I don't want to bother her."

"You're really terrible at dating, aren't you?" Betty frowns at me. "How will you fix things with June if you won't call her? Send her a pigeon?"

"That's a good idea." I stroke my beard in contemplation. "I wonder where I can get a homing pigeon."

"Bah," Edna mumbles. "He's hopeless."

"Got any tips for me?" I ask the group, curious to hear their advice about relationships.

They give me a quick list of do's and don'ts:

*Flowers, but not red roses and especially not the ones that are sold at the gas station.

*Candy (preferably chocolate), but only if she's not on a diet (which is tricky because I should never ask if she's on one or comment about her weight).

*A poem, but not something I personally wrote unless I consider myself a proficient poet. I can make photocopies of the classics at the library for five cents a page. *If only I hadn't spent all my change on profanities.*

*A phone call to ask her out on a date, but only if I call a minimum of a week in advance and ask her availability. I should never assume she'll be free on a Saturday night. Oh, and if she tells me she has plans to wash her hair, I'm doomed.

Their advice is fascinating and complicated. Mostly, it serves as a reminder that courting a woman is a lost art these days.

"What are your feelings on cologne?" I ask.

This spurs a lively discussion.

"Don't overdo it."

"That Axe body spray period was hell for anyone with a nose."

"I still keep a bottle of Aqua Velva on the dresser to remind me of my husband. He's been dead five years now." Myrtle's eyes brim with tears.

"Avoid Old Spice, unless you want to smell like an old man." Miss Cole, a tiny woman with tight, lavender curls peers at me over her glasses. "Though that might be what you're going for with those suspenders. You know, they work better if they're over your shoulders instead of dangling down your legs."

Shade from an octogenarian is the darkest shade of all.

"It's a look. He's a hipster."

Gee, thanks for throwing me under the senior shuttle bus, Thea.

"Hamster?" Miss Cole asks.

"Hipster," Thea shouts before giving her the definition of the word, which apparently means I'm obsessed with old-timey ways and body alteration.

Come to think of it, she's not completely wrong.

"If you're trying to be old fashioned, cover up those tattoos and find yourself a good suit," Edna grumbles. "Unless you want her to think you're one of those traveling carney types, or a grifter."

The look she pierces me with is too serious for the joking, friendly banter of dating advice for the hopeless, her comment hits a bit too on the nose.

TWENTY-SEVEN

Ten days have passed since the fallout with June. I've decided to give her two weeks of space before I contact her. Once I stop stressing over events that occurred when I was five and that I had nothing to do with, anger replaces the guilt. *She* lied by omission. We could've avoided this pit of ugly emotions if she'd told me the truth about her family from the beginning, except she probably wouldn't have gone out with me at all if she'd known I was related to Ron. She never would have given me a chance.

I sulk and practice my knitting while resisting the urge to stab things with my needles.

The rocks start appearing on day eleven.

A small one with *Sorry* painted above a cactus shows up on the sill of one of the windows at The Place.

Another *sorry*, scrawled across a cloud filled sky, rests against the planter outside our front entrance.

Fangs and *I suck* in red paint decorate a flat rock propped on the front bumper of the VW when I leave work.

I ask everyone at The Place about the mysterious offerings.

"It's a thing. There's a Facebook page and everything," Lara explains.

"Who paints them?"

"Anyone who wants to can make one and then leave it for someone else to find, like a treasure hunt, but the prize is a rock." Dax pulls one such object from his backpack.

The surface has been transformed into the Milky Way on a star-filled background. The skill is more advanced than the ones I've found. "That's incredible."

"Yeah. I want to get a tattoo based on this painting. My parents are making me wait until I turn eighteen."

"Better hold on to that rock. Or, you know, snap a pic of it."

"Why are you asking about painted rocks?" Theo asks.

He and Lara still exchange heated looks but thankfully keep their hands and tongues to themselves.

"I've been finding them outside here and I was curious."

"Sounds like someone's sending you a secret message," Lara suggests. "That's romantic."

I pull the one with fangs from my pocket.

Dax snorts. "Or not."

"Are they telling you they suck or saying you suck because you now possess the rock?" Theo muses.

"I think it's an apology." Lara smiles.

The next day, a small, speckled egg rests on the railing of my front porch when I leave the house.

I recognize it immediately from the fairy house in the woods. Decorated to resemble a bird's egg, it must be another one of June's painted rocks.

Glancing up, I discover her Prius parked behind the VW. She steps out of the car, two paper cups balanced in her hands as she slowly walks toward the house. With her green coat and a darker green dress decorated with lighter green leaves, she's a beautiful wood nymph. My breath stalls in my throat and the weird, nervous fluttering returns to my chest.

"Hi." She stops a few feet from the base of the steps. "I brought coffee, hoping we could talk."

"Thank you. Did you at least buy it from one of my places?"

She climbs the stairs, extending the offering my way when she reaches the top. "I went to the Fellowship of the Bean and asked them to make your favorite."

Taking the cup, I gesture at the egg. "Are you the one who's been leaving me the rocks?"

"Guilty." She lifts both shoulders, looking sheepish.

"Why not text or call?"

"I acted like such a jerk last time we were together. Like a rabid cavewoman, I thought using rocks to communicate was more appropriate, and painting them felt like a way to show I'm willing to make an effort," she says, determined.

"Penance?" I ask, sipping my coffee.

"Exactly." Keeping her distance, she leans her hip against the banister.

"I particularly liked the vampire one," I declare. "Nice pun."

"That's my favorite, too." Her eyes brighten behind her pink frames.

I rest my back on the doorjamb. "How did we get here, June?"

"I'm not sure, but I think screaming about Lenin had something to do with it." She grimaces. "I can't believe I accused islanders of being communists."

"It would've been funny had you not said the rest." I dip my chin and gaze out at the woods.

"If I said I didn't mean it, could I take those words back?"

The catch in her voice draws my attention back to her. When I see the tears in her eyes, I cross my arms to keep myself from hugging her, my hurt still too fresh. "No take-backs."

"I'm a horrible person. I'm sorry." She swipes at her cheeks.

"I'll accept the apology, but I don't think you're a horrible person. We're human. We all have flaws."

"The list of mine is long. I'm sorry I wasn't honest about my grandfather. I was ashamed about his story, especially because you were doing amazing things with the building. I didn't want to put a damper on your excitement by telling you the sad tale of how he got swindled by some random con men."

"My father." I exhale. "Would you have given me a chance if you knew I was related to him? Be honest."

"No, but I lied when I said you weren't my type. Tattoos, leather, and piercings are my biggest weakness, especially back when I drank. Again and again, I'd fall for and try to tame a bad boy. It never ended well. That's why I avoided you, not because I thought I was better than you or you weren't good enough. I knew I'd fall for you if I let myself."

Our eyes lock and the love I feel for her tugs at my chest.

"Did you fall?" I ask quietly.

Holding my gaze, she explains, "I started to fall the day we found each other in the woods. You called me out for not liking you and I lied. After you left, I checked my fairy house and found the eggs had been disturbed. You were the first person to open the door, even though I placed it there months ago. I knew you were special."

"That was your work? Why?" I'm more than curious.

"When I was little, my grandfather told me bedtime stories about a place fairies would bring people to, an island full of magic where dreams could come true. He warned me that evil men also dwelled there and would try to trick me into giving away my heart and soul if I wasn't careful." Her lips curve upward. "He meant the boats, but when I was younger, I believed he meant the mischievous characters with wings."

"And so you built a fairy door in his honor?" I'm charmed by the whimsical way he told her the truth about what happened to him.

"I've hidden several around the island. You're the first to find one, at least as far as I know."

"I also spotted one in the stump beneath your mailbox." I straighten up. "Where are the others? Will you show me?"

She giggles. "Where's the fun in giving you a map leading right to them?"

My jaw drops open and I tease her. "I can't believe you won't tell me."

"I could give you a hint or two, but you have to find them on your own."

"Do you know how many trees there are on this island? The whole place is covered by woods. I'll need more than a single hint." My mind jumps to exploring the forests with her by my side and how much fun we'd have. I want her by my side on adventures.

"Not all of them are attached to trees."

She laughs when I grumble at her in frustration.

"You are a strange and wonderful woman, June Moxee."

"Do you forgive me?" She crosses the wide porch.

I meet her halfway. "I already said I did. Will you promise me something?"

With a nod, she agrees.

"If you ever doubt me, remember that I swore I will never deliberately hurt you. I may look like a bad boy on the outside, but I'm one of the good guys. Please don't forget that."

"I promise." She tilts her chin up, a silent invitation.

I soak in this moment, marveling at how different it feels from the first time we kissed. We stand here with open hearts and open minds, no longer acting from a place of fear or even reacting to perceived rejection. *This* is what falling in love feels like.

Gently, I slide my hand over her cheek, entwining my fingers in her hair. Inhaling, I breathe her in, savoring how her floral scent and warmth envelop me. Slowly, I sweep my lips over hers, barely making contact, teasing her mouth with mine. As her lips part, I increase the pressure slightly, still not giving in to the desire to capture and conquer her mouth, not until she's arching against me, her own hands pulling at my hair, attempting to guide my head down, closer to her waiting mouth.

Only then, when we're both desperate, do I fully kiss her, sliding my tongue between her lips and tangling it with hers. Moments later, breathless and panting, I whisper, "That's the kind of first kiss I wanted to give you."

The lenses of her glasses are fogged. Removing them, I reveal her beautiful hazel eyes. They're wide and dilated with lust.

Feeling the same wild desire, I ask, "Did you have plans for today? Other than randomly showing up at my house?"

"I have nothing going on." She tries to act nonchalant, but the rapid rise and fall of her chest says otherwise.

I drag my thumb over her full bottom lip. "You want to spend the day with me?"

In bed, I mentally add, but instead of telling her, I decide I'll show her.

Giggling, she allows me to drag her inside, past the living room and straight to my bedroom.

True to my silent vow, we spend the rest of the day making love. I'm not ready to say the words out loud, but my heart already belongs to her for as long as she wants, which I hope is forever.

TWENTY-EIGHT

Two months later

The weather's turned warm and sunny enough for us to keep the doors of the shop open. Late afternoon sunlight casts deep shadows around the tables and games.

"I'm heading over to Seattle tomorrow for my volunteer shift at the hospital. Want me to drop off blankets for you?" I ask June. She's stopped by for her afternoon game of pinball. Knowing she loves my favorite game pleases me more than it should.

"Can I come with you instead?" she asks.

Surprised, I blurt out, "But you don't like kids—especially sick ones! Last time you freaked out and you were only in the lobby. Probably not a good idea."

"I'm trying to be brave and do new things. Pinball was a huge success." She casts a loving glance at her favorite machine.

"You can't hog Medieval Madness all the time," I tease, stepping between her and it.

"I only play during my lunch hour. Most of the kids haven't even arrived by the time I leave." Going into defense mode, she assumes her Wonder Woman power pose.

I can't resist riling her up more. "You play so much, I should make you pay part of our electric bill."

"That doesn't seem fair." Her eyes widen. "Wait … are you jealous of the machine?

Chuckling, I pull her close. "You're hooked."

"I like the dragons and the part where the damsel with the valley girl accent gets rescued and it says"—she flashes air quotes—"Damsel Madness."

"I know. You quote it all the time." I place a quick kiss to her temple.

Her phone pings with a text. When she reads it, her face beams with excitement.

"I have some exciting news to share!" Before I can ask what it is, she bursts out with, "Carter and I are going into business together!"

"Is that wise?" I have no beef with either Kelso, and think they're both decent businessmen, but old habits die hard when it comes to treating them like my younger brothers.

She's bouncing on her toes. "He already has goats and knows how to raise them. What's a few more?"

"And Carter is open to this? He's pretty protective of his herd."

"He is. He wants to expand."

"Ah, you're getting in on the goatscaping." This makes more sense.

Goatscaping will always sound like a euphemism for manscaping to me, like Mr. Greatest of All Time tending to his body hair. Honestly, I prefer to avoid thinking about other men's grooming habits, thank you very much.

"More like the cashmere yarn business." She practically vibrates with glee. "I'll buy the goats and he'll raise them with the rest of the herd. They'll do the same work. Then in the spring, when they molt and it's time to shear them, I'll gather the fleece. Rinse and repeat. It's a win-win!"

"You? *You're* going to shear goats?"

Her hands return to her hips. "I could. I used to cut my dad's hair with clippers. Kind of the same thing."

"It isn't a matter of skill. You get teary every time you think of the Langley bunnies out in the rain."

"I'll make them sweaters as a thank-you gift."

She's so beyond cute in this moment, I'm tempted to bop her on her adorable little nose. "Let me get this straight: you're going to remove the natural fleece from a goat and replace it with a wool sweater. From a sheep."

"Or an alpaca."

"Aren't you robbing Peter to pay Paul?"

"Do you know the market price of cashmere?"

I shake my head.

"It's expensive, and each goat only produces an average of four ounces a year."

"How much is that in terms of sweaters?" I see the holes in this as a business idea already.

"Less than half a sweater." She frowns.

Doing a quick calculation of goats to ounces to sweaters in my head, I say, "That's a lot of goats."

"I know. We'll start with ten in the herd and see how they do. I already have local alpaca and wool sources. This is the missing piece. Even if we do blends with the cashmere to make it go farther, having locally sourced fibers is my dream." She's glowing with happiness.

Some people dream of seeing their name in movie credits or on a bestseller's list, maybe in Forbes magazine's roster of the richest people. June dreams of local fibers.

I'm in full support of her achieving her goals, whatever they may be as long as she's happy.

"I love you." I kiss her.

"I love you, too," she whispers against my mouth.

I envelop her in a hug. "Goats. Who knew?"

She squeezes me back. "Isn't it the best idea?"

"I think my brilliant plan might be a better idea."

Leaning away so she can see my face, she's suddenly serious. "What plan?"

"You'll see. You haven't made any plans for Saturday night, have you?" I tease.

She exhales, exasperated. "No. There are huge red Xs on all of my calendars and 'Busy with Jonah' scrawled in your handwriting on Saturday's square. Even my phone has the day blocked off with your name as an all-day event."

"Good."

"Still not telling me anything about it?"

"Nope." I give her a closed-mouth smile.

"What if I throw in a major clue about the fairy houses?"

"Tempting, but I've decided you're right—it's better to discover them all on my own."

"Can I at least know what to wear?" She pouts, adorably.

"Wear a pretty dress." I kiss her forehead. "I've got to go."

"That doesn't narrow it down."

"I know." I chuckle as I leave.

———

"We're really doing this?" I ask Ashley. I'm holding her ladder while she strings white lights over the beams of the community hall in Freeland.

"Throwing the best alternative prom that's ever existed? Hell yes." She pumps her arm in the air, causing the ladder to wobble.

I steady her. "This could be a disaster."

Grinning down from above, she corrects me. "Or the best night of your life so far."

I scowl back at her. "You think the bar is that low that a dance at the grange hall is going to shoot to the top of the list?"

I can think of multiple nights so far this year that will probably top this impending debacle, like …

When June kissed me.

When June came over for a bath.

The weekend after we reunited.

Tonight isn't even in the top five.

Ashely snickers. "Yes. I knew you in high school."

"Asshole," I mutter.

Cari joins us, a bag of yellow and black balloons in each hand. "I think you should do this every year as a great fundraiser for The Place."

"I'll keep that in mind if this doesn't backfire tonight."

"Can't be worse than the prom in *Carrie*." Erik exits the storage room, carrying another box of lights. "Or a dozen other prom nights in horror movies."

"Thanks for the trivia." Ashley rolls her eyes.

"Stop worrying, Jonah," Cari reassures me. "This is the perfect venue for you to win June over once and for all, forever and ever, till death do you part. This is your HFN and your HEA."

"My what and what?" I ask.

"Happy for now and happily ever after. Don't act like you don't know about fairy tale endings and fandom shipping lingo." Cari shakes her head as she wanders off.

"I'm not proposing tonight. June and I have only been together a couple of months."

"Stranger things have happened," Cari muses from across the open space.

"You better go home and change, brother o' mine." Ashely steps down from her high perch. "Make sure you don't smell like a Sasquatch."

The knitting ladies' cologne advice comes to mind, but I decide to forgo smelling like a man from the '80s or in his eighties.

"Are you sure you don't need me to stay?" I hesitate.

"Get out of here. We'll finish up and see you later tonight." Cari uses a bag of blue and bronze balloons to sweep me out of the hall.

———

"I feel overdressed." June smooths her hands over the layers of thin, pink fabric that make up her skirt, studying her dress in the full-length mirror on the back of my closet door. "You're not even wearing a suit and I'm tarted up like a … tart."

"This is formal wear for me." I point at my dark blue, collared shirt. "I'm not in a T-shirt or flannel."

"Still in your favorite black jeans, though." She catches my eye in the mirror. "Last chance to tell me where you're taking me."

"You'll find out soon enough."

"Are you going to blindfold me in the car?"

"Do you want to be blindfolded?"

"I might. We should try it sometime." She winks at me.

After a short drive to Freeland with June throwing out random possibilities along the way, I park her car in front of the building to avoid the crowded lot in the back.

She's wary when I come around to open her door. "This feels like a setup."

"Who said it wasn't?" I place a soft kiss on the corner of her mouth.

We enter the room and all of our friends yell, "Surprise!" and "Happy Birthday!"

June's eyes widen in genuine shock. "What is this?"

I'm delighted we successfully managed to keep this a secret. "It's your birthday party and prom all rolled up together."

Tears fill her eyes. "You're giving me a Harry Potter prom?"

Glancing around the room decorated in the Hogwarts house colors, I'm happy to see everyone agreed to wear the black Hogwarts robes I provided.

"I am." I lift her glasses and dab at the tears spilling down her cheeks. Soft enough so only she can hear, I whisper, "It's for both of us. I want you to have every happy thing."

"I have you." She wraps her arms around my neck and pulls me down for a kiss.

The crowd whoops and claps then Cari approaches us and places a tiara on June's head.

"This might be the best night of my life," she whispers between kisses.

"So far," I correct her. "This is only the beginning."

EPILOGUE

A year later

The sun is out and it's a fine day for the first farmers' market of the summer season.

Strolling past the vendors, I have a pep in my step on my way to June's green and white striped tent.

"I saw the new installation." I sneak behind her table where she's standing in the shade, out of the strong morning sun. Today's dress is a finer version of the tent's pattern.

She adjusts her glasses with the tip of her finger and straightens a few skeins of yarn in her display. "I have no idea what you're talking about."

Lowering my voice and keeping my tone serious, I whisper, "Then you should be worried that some other random knitting bandits are invading your territory. If there's going to be a knitting gang turf war, I need to be prepared. Gotta dust off my black belt from college." I'm teasing her, trying to draw out a laugh, because laughing June lights up my world.

"So dramatic. There's no turf war." She pushes on my shoulder, but her eyes hold amusement. "Don't you have a coffee truck to man instead of loitering around my booth and making accusations?"

"That's kind of a sexist term, you know. And, Layla is setting up today." I sneak a quick kiss. "Nothing I'd rather be doing than visiting my fiancée."

"Is that your new favorite f word?" she teases back. Her focus dips down to her left hand where the antique, pink sapphire ring sparkles on her finger.

Like I was going to buy her a boring, clear diamond? Pfft.

I proposed during our trip to Valle de Guadalupe in January, exactly one year later on the same date as when we tumbled ass over elbows together in her storage closet. At sunset in the middle of a vineyard, I got down on one knee and asked her to be mine forever.

Feeling sentimental over the memory of her saying yes and both of us crying among the grapevines, I wrap my arm around her waist and kiss the top of her head. Every time I think about the last year, my heart attempts to beat its way out of my chest with happiness.

"I really love the knitted squares in the old chainlink around the baseball field. Did you make it for the bunnies to have something nice to look at while they hang out?" I step away and pick up a skein of her new cashmere yarn, stroking the soft fiber between my fingers.

Pink colors her cheeks. "Not *for the bunnies*, but it's a nice bonus. The school district approved the project. No one wants to look at a boring fence all day."

"I love it, and you." That's not true. I like the knitted fence, but those feelings don't compare to my love for her. Nothing can.

"I love you right back. I'm not the only one with a soft spot for the Langley rabbits." She moves close and touches a spot on my left ribcage. "Mr. I Have a New Bunny Tattoo."

Busted. Her hand rests above the drawing of a small, brown

rabbit. "I got it in honor of you and to commemorate our beginning."

This time she kisses me. Well, she tries to but her happy giggle makes it impossible. Instead, we stare at each other for a moment, silly grins plastered on our faces. We are one of those nauseatingly in love couples that people love to complain about.

Breaking eye contact, I gesture at the three cashmere goats in their x-pen enclosure. "By the way, they look lovely in their sweaters."

"Aren't they adorable? I made the Weasley sweaters with a pattern for toddlers I found on Ravelry. Perfect fits."

"What are you going to use for the alpacas?" I dip my chin and lift my brows.

"Umm … why would you think I'm making sweaters for them?" she challenges with an arched eyebrow of her own.

I don't blink.

Glancing away, she admits, "Fine. Since they're all named after Hogwarts professors, I'm working on some black sweaters. Minerva's will be a cardigan. Of course."

"How could it be anything else?" I twist my lips to the side to keep from laughing at her reluctant confession. I'm head over heels for her, which she knows, but I try to contain my adoration in public.

She pouts. "You think I'm ridiculous."

"I'm trying to stop myself from telling you how adorable I think you are and then making out with you. Can you dial back the cuteness to like, say, a 9.5, so I can get through the farmers' market without ravishing you?"

She beams at me. "Not sure that's possible."

Releasing an exaggerated groan, I pull her into my side. "Please take pity on us regular folks trying to live our dull, boring lives."

"Can't stop, won't stop." She smirks and snuggles into me. "You should go before I maul you in front of everyone."

"No one is even paying attention to us." I scan the u-shaped formation of tables around the gravel parking area.

Sally happily waves at me from the CSA table where she's standing with both Connie and Sandy.

"We've been spotted by the gossip brigade." I spin June and myself so our backs are to the island's nosiest women. Can't a man kiss his love in public without an audience?

"Why are you hiding? They already know we're together. We live together." Her laughter shakes her shoulder against my chest.

"Did you tell them?" I mutter, sounding more annoyed than I feel because I would've happily hired a sky-writer to announce my love for June.

"You're hysterical." She ducks out of my grasp. "It's common knowledge I moved into your house."

I squint at the CSA tent and then down at June. "Because the post of our mailbox is covered with a yellow, black, blue and bronze hand-knit tube?"

With a shrug of her shoulders, she tilts her head to the side. "Might be their first clue."

"Speaking of crafting gone wild, when's the meeting at the property? I assume you want me there."

"Three o'clock. I'm so excited." She bounces on her toes.

"I'll meet you there. I need to swing by Whidbey Joe's to make sure Erik and Cari are making progress on the wedding plans."

"I can't believe they're getting married next weekend." Her sigh has a dreamy quality to it.

"Want to make it a double ceremony?" I wiggle my eyebrows.

"No, no way. I have a vision." She corrects herself. "We have a vision and we should stick with it. And we need to have the location finished before we can host a wedding there."

"Or we could elope like Carter and Ashley did. Be married

by Monday." I'm not a hundred percent serious, nor am I not somewhat serious.

———

Pulling to a stop on the drive of June's property, I spot a row of pickup trucks belonging to John, Tom, and Dan. June's Prius and Cari's car are parked near the Airstream she used to call home.

Everyone's standing around in a big clump in the meadow when I get out of the VW. Carter and Ashley pull up behind me.

"Great, everyone's here," June greets us as we join them.

Roslyn and Diane stand off to one side, observing Ione and Alene dancing around in the grass while Mac and Shaw try to eat dirt. Little Ellie Donnely studies everything her big brother does from her vantage point in her sling on Hailey's hip. My sister brings Rosie over to join them.

"Place looks amazing," Dan says approvingly.

"Thanks to all your hard work." June focuses on John. "Thank you for clearing out the woods so we have more useable land."

She continues around the circle. "Tom and Hailey, your work shed/studio space is incredible. I'm stunned. Truly. It's more than I ever imagined."

The barn-style structure sits across the meadow from June's original camper. With an open side for welding projects and studio space inside, Tom turned June's vision into a reality.

In the center of the meadow stands the heart of the camp. A simple, one-story, farmhouse building houses the kitchen, dining room, communal living room, and offices.

"To Dan for helping design the commercial kitchen, and Erik for promising all the coffee our crafters could ever want, thank you." June presses her hand over her heart. "Cari, I can't wait to see what you teach us in photography. You're so talented.

Thank you." She sweeps her arms wide and spins in a slow circle. "This is all because of you."

Surrounding these buildings is a circle of vintage campers, each decorated in bright colors picked out by June herself, for future crafters to stay in while they spend a weekend or week here. She also plans to host kid and teen programs here as well as at The Place. Turns out, teens and snarky cross-stitch are a perfect match.

"I could never have made Craft Whidbey a reality without all of you and your support." Finally, June focuses on me. "And to Jonah, my love, my life, for believing in my dream and helping to make it a reality, thank you, thank you, thank you. I love you."

She doesn't mention the part about me selling my shares in the green business to a Canadian investment group, which made all of this possible. We're keeping that part to ourselves and Dan, who advised me on the best way to manage a sudden windfall of money.

Before June finishes, I'm striding toward her. Enveloping her in a hug, I lift her off the ground and spin her around. "I love you."

A few people clap and there are a couple of feminine "Awwws" but I'm too busy kissing June to pay attention to anyone else.

Last summer, Trivia Thunderdome returned in a new venue: the Dog House. Without Simon Says, of course. Some evenings, I still miss his piano ties. Yes, the new name is all my doing, as is our new team. June joined Ebey's Head, and Yarned and Dangerous is now The Merry Hookers. Diane and Hailey formed a new group called the Wingwomen and invited Roslyn and Ashley to join. Amazing how a few years, marriages, and babies smoothed over the tension of old relationships and perceptions. Not saying Hailey and Ashley are ever going to be best friends, but it's nice to see them hanging out.

A couple of weeks after Erik and Cari's wedding, we gather together at the Dog House under the guise of a special Sunday afternoon of trivia, but we're really here for Olaf's official retirement party. He doesn't know it's a party for him. I can't wait to see his face, but I'm a little worried about his heart.

For the past year, he's been working one or two evenings a week when he's on Whidbey and not down in Arizona. Wanting to avoid the island's busy season, which is right around the corner, he's finally ready to hang up his bar towel. This summer will be the last one before we close down for repairs and restoration.

It's the end of an era.

We used June's mom as bait to keep Olaf away from downtown this afternoon. She volunteered eagerly, a little too happy to spend time with Olaf if you ask me.

The old Dog is packed with well-wishers and friends. Strange to be in a crowded room and recognize every single person here.

"Seems like June's mom has a crush on O." Tom leans against the bar next to me. "Who knew under all of his crankiness beat a real, human heart capable of emotions other than bitterness, anger, and disappointment?"

Standing with my elbows behind me on the bar, I nod. "June is happy about her mom and Olaf. If she's fine with it, I'm okay, too. Lisa told us she enjoys spending time with him, but isn't looking to get married again. Still weird to think he could be June's step-father."

"Even more bizarre, he'd be your father-in-law." Tom practically howls with laughter. "Wonder if he'd let you call him Dad."

The thought is funny, but part of me softens at the idea. Patting him on the shoulder, I admit, "Helluva lot better than my own father."

He flashes me a sheepish grin. "Shit, I always forget. Sorry. You and Ashley turned out okay, though—better than okay."

"Thanks for saying so, and I appreciate the apology. We've done all right for ourselves." I catch sight of her on the other side of the room, smiling and dancing with Rosie in her arms.

Tom lifts his pint and clinks the glass against mine. "You'll always have your island family. We may be dysfunctional and crazy, but we love hard and care for our own."

John strolls over to join us. "What are you two talking about that Tom thinks is so funny? He isn't reveling in the glory days of picking up women in this very spot with the geoduck line, is he?"

I snort. He knows his best friend well. "Not this time, but I swear ever since we started the partnership, he brings it up every time we're here."

Dan walks over to our little group. "Tom talking about phallic clams again? Remember when he suggested we change the bar's name to the Clam House?"

"It would be hysterical," Tom mumbles into his glass. "Geoducks are funny because they look like dicks. Come on, Jonah, back me up. You like a good pun more than anyone besides June."

"Can't help you out here." I chuckle.

From the other side of the pool table, Erik calls out, "Hey Tom, have you ever been geoduck hunting?"

Carter joins in the taunting. "Is that a geoduck in your pants or are you just happy to see me?"

Olaf stomps down the hall from the larger back dining room that overlooks the water. "When I owned this place, you'd all be banned for telling raunchy jokes in front of children and babies!"

"Where did you come from?" June asks from her lookout stool in the corner. "I've been waiting in this spot for half an hour and I know you didn't walk through the front door."

"Came through the side entrance. Driving down the street, I saw too many people coming here for a Sunday afternoon and knew something was up. To avoid any of you yahoos spotting me, I made a three-point turn and headed for home. Lisa convinced me to make an appearance. We struck a bargain that we'd take the stairs down to the seawall and cut around to avoid any of you screaming 'Surprise!' at me like you're trying to put me in an early grave. You assholes know I have heart troubles." Olaf finishes his tirade and is met with silence. "Well, if you're all just going to stand around gaping at me like salmon out of water, I can leave."

He makes a beeline for the front door before any of us can react.

Erik shouts, "Speech!" and begins a slow clap. A few seconds later, Carter joins in. Soon, everyone is matching the steady beat with their hands.

At the swinging doors, Olaf turns and pauses. The clapping ceases almost immediately.

He clears his throat and drags his nails through his beard. "Don't expect me to say how grateful I am to have had so many years standing behind the bar here, serving alcohol to a band of miscreants. I'm not going to tell sentimental stories about watching this group of idiots grow up into fine men who'd make anyone proud. I'm not going to say how much I appreciate people like Dan and his beautiful wife Roslyn helping to save this old building and the one across the street, and I'm sure as hell not going to take back all the lifetime bans I've issued on the Kelsos over the years. I tried to get those written into the sales agreement. Now, if someone would please get this old man a pint of IPA and a place to sit that won't get me battered in the head with a pool cue, I'll stay."

And with that, he stomps past the pool table, down the hall, and into the back room, leaving everyone hanging with their mouths open in stunned silence.

"Welp, that feels about perfect for Olaf's retirement party."

Chuckling, Tom lifts his glass. "To O, long may he suffer fools like us."

We all raise our drinks. "To Olaf."

"No toasts." His loud voice carries from down the hall. "Save it for when I'm dead."

The entire room dissolves into laughter.

Searching for June, I find her in the dining room, tucked into a booth by the windows.

"I love you," I declare, not caring who hears.

June's smile lights up her face. "I love you."

The room and everyone in it disappears as we gaze at each other.

"Thank you for loving me," I say softly.

For saving me from a life alone.

For becoming my family.

For letting me be the one who gets to love you every day.

I don't say the rest out loud, reserving those words for my wedding vows.

———

Thank you for reading *The Last Wingman*.
Make sure to subscribe to my mailing list!
You'll receive exclusive content, free stories, sales and new release alerts, as well as my monthly email with my favorite reads and current obsessions.

NOTE FROM DAISY

Thank you for reading *The Last Wingman*.

Please consider leave a review on your retailer of choice, Goodreads, and BookBub.

Jonah's book marks the end of an era. He and John first appeared in *Geoducks Are for Lovers*, my first novel. I've been writing my Whidbey books for over six years. It's bittersweet to end the series. I already miss these characters, who feel so real to me. All of the people who inhabit this fictional version of Whidbey will forever hold a special place in my heart.

Thank you for embracing these books and loving my Wingmen. If this is your first Wingmen book, keep reading for the first chapters of *Small Town Scandal* and *Ready to Fall*.

This isn't goodbye.

Be sure to subscribe to my email list to receive updates on my writing and new release alerts for my future books.

See you around,

Daisy

Chapter One

For the first time in my life, I'm cool.

Turns out goats are a hot trend, which makes me cool by connection.

If I'd known all it would take to be popular was a herd of goats, I would've joined 4-H in high school. Or Future Farmers of America.

Apparently, the ladies love the goats. At least in my case, they like the goat herder.

Yes, I'm the goat man of Whidbey.

People honk and wave when they spot my truck and goat trailer around the island. Small children practically lose their minds every time I show up with some goats.

Sometimes some jerk will yell "Goat Boy" at me. Like it's an insult.

Maybe it is.

I don't care.

No shame in being a goat boy. I could be a mythical creature. Half man, half goat. How cool would that be?

Although, I can do without the yodeling and the snark about

being a lonely goatherd from female friends, especially my brother's girlfriend and the wives of my friends.

Why does every woman seem to know the lyrics to the yodel song from *The Sound of Music*? Is this what girls do at slumber parties? Memorize movies? I thought they braided each other's hair and got in pillow fights. Or tried on each other's bras. Apparently, they all watch nuns fighting Nazis while singing songs about goats. Us guys watched scary movies and tried to out-gross each other doing disgusting shit, typically involving bodily functions.

Memories of teasing and torturing Ashley Kingston when we were kids skip through my mind.

Maybe if I wasn't such a guy, I mean if I wasn't dumb Carter Kelso and she wasn't so out of my league, she'd still be mine. Instead of becoming the island's own version of a jezebel, according to the woman herself.

For no reason other than thirst, I pull into The Fellowship of the Bean for an iced coffee.

The coffee hut being owned by Jonah, Ashley's older brother, is a coincidence of convenience to my current location.

I wait in line behind a black minivan, impatiently drumming my palms on the center of the steering wheel. A woman wearing a green and navy Mariners' cap leans out of the window of the hut to hand over a whipped cream topped beverage. I frown. I guess I secretly hoped Jonah would be working.

So I could catch up. About stuff.

Not ask about his sister.

I've been collecting the coffee grounds from Jonah and Ashley's coffee huts along with the ones from Erik's café. Packaged in large bags, we give them out for free to anyone who wants grounds for their compost or garden.

We're the Justice League of crunchy, earth loving hippies.

Without the patchouli and long hair. Or the mandolin music.

Or free love orgies.

In my rearview mirror, I spot a guy ride up behind me on a unicycle. He appears to be wearing a helmet shaped like a wolf's head, complete with a snout.

My frown deepens into a scowl.

Falcon.

He pedals past my truck, and cuts in front of me in line. As I glower at him, he stops by the hut's window, his bare feet working the pedals to keep his balance. Takes me a moment to notice he's wearing a skirt because I'm concentrating on imagining him face-planting off his clown bike. His rainbow dreads are wrapped up in a loose ponytail, which he tosses over his shoulder as he flirts with the barista.

Something she says must be hysterical because he leans his head back to roar with laughter.

Fall.

Fall.

Fall.

I chant in my head as he leans farther, precariously working the pedals to remain upright.

Then the moment happens.

He tips past the point of balance.

Fall.

I lean forward in delight.

His left leg kicks out to the side, and right before he goes ass over elbows, he catches himself. Hopping off the seat, he easily catches the unicycle in one hand. With a bow, he acts like he meant to do exactly that move.

Hippie asshole.

The barista leans through the window to hand him a plastic cup of pea green matcha. An auburn curl slips from under her cap.

My breath catches in my throat like I've swallowed wrong.

No wonder Falcon put on a show.

Ashley Kingston's laugh is worth making a fool of yourself.

I should know.

I've been doing it most of my life.

Annoyed and still thirsty, I tap my horn. Not like someone in Seattle cut me off, but harder than a friendly honk.

Ashley leans farther out the window and Falcon says something to her as he puts his cash in her hand. With a friendly wave, he hops on his wheel and pedals away.

I make sure he's gone before easing off the brake and pulling up to the window.

Resting my elbow on the door, I give her a friendly smile.

Not surprisingly, she frowns at me, her happiness fading. "Carter."

"Hi." Ignoring her frown, I wave.

"Was the honking necessary?" She doesn't ask what I want as she scoops ice into a large cup.

I stare at her profile while she works. A universe of freckles dot her high cheekbones and nose, which has a slight swoop at the end. Pink colors her cheeks and I'm not sure if it's makeup or too much sun. Long, dark lashes frame her ever-changing hazel eyes. Even in the baseball cap, her fiery hair hidden, she's beautiful.

"Falcon looked like he was going to perch on your counter for the day. Didn't want him to scare off honest customers."

She pours black coffee into the cup of ice, leaving about two inches at the top for milk. "Ha ha."

Her laugh lacks any warmth and the fake sound bruises my ego.

"Where's Jonah?" I ignore the way my palms get clammy with rejection.

"He's working with Erik, roasting a new blend." Again, without asking, she adds cream to my coffee and then presses on a lid.

I should probably know this, but I'm not my younger brother's keeper. Not since he moved out to live with his girlfriend, Cari, who's way too cool for him.

Ashley hands me the cup and I pull out cash to give her.

With a flick of her hand, she tells me, "Falcon bought your drink."

"What if I don't want him to buy my coffee?"

"Why wouldn't you want a free coffee?"

"I don't want to be indebted to a guy who can't afford a bicycle with two wheels."

Her frown deepens. "What do you have against him? He's legitimately the kindest guy on this island. Did you know he's on his way to give a free show at the senior center? He creates balloon animals and does magic tricks."

"He's a one man sunshine brigade," I mumble as I take my coffee from the counter and leave the ten-dollar bill. "Pay that forward to the next customer."

Fucking Falcon. He probably lives in a tiny cabin in the woods without running water and bathes in a spring fed creek, drying off with moss before namastaying his naked salutation to the sun. She can't be sleeping with a wood sprite with the same name as our high school mascot.

Can she?

"Anything else I can get you?" Impatience flattens her voice.

"Any coffee grounds to pick up?" Despite this being one of our worst conversations among many awkward ones, I don't want to drive away.

"Oh, right. Let me grab the bag." She steps away.

A few moments later, she walks around the corner of the cedar-shingled hut, holding a large garbage bag against her chest. I open the truck's door to help her, but she shakes her head and mutters, "I've got it."

Ignoring her, I step out of the truck and jog around the front in time to push the bottom of the bag over the side into the truck bed.

"I told you I had it," she says, drily.

"You're welcome."

"I'm not saying thank you. I didn't need, or want your help." To emphasize her words, she crosses her arms and widens her feet. She's either bracing for a fight or trying to appear bigger in the presence of a threat.

A small snort escapes my mouth at the thought of her going up against a grizzly.

Poor beast wouldn't stand a chance.

In her apron, she looks like a beautiful, fierce, but pantsless warrior.

Note I left off the princess part.

Don't call Ashley Kingston a princess.

She will kick your ass like an adorable raccoon who happens to have rabies.

I speak from experience on that one.

Summer after fifth grade.

I have a scar on my elbow from where I fell onto the gravel after she pushed me for asking if she had a soul. In a flower print dress her mother probably picked out, she managed to be fierce. More Princess Leia than damsel in distress.

"You're welcome." She brushes her hands on her green apron. "Tell Jonah he needs to be back here before closing. I have to catch the five-thirty boat."

"Hot date tonight?" I shouldn't ask. I don't want to know.

"Hopefully." Her smile shows all her teeth but it doesn't warm her eyes.

"Well, good luck with that." I flick the brim of her hat.

We stand facing each other for a few awkward beats before a car pulls up behind my trailer.

She walks ahead of me to the side door and I stare at her ass covered in a pair of faded jean shorts.

Watching her walk away from me is the story of my life.

At least it's a nice view.

———

After dropping off the ten goats at their new job site, I find Jonah and Erik in the warehouse of Whidbey Joe's, their coffee roasting business. The two of them are bent over a roaster, examining a scoop of beans. Some days I envy their working bromance.

My coworkers have horns and horizontal pupils.

At least they don't take long smoke breaks or spend their paychecks on beer.

Unlike my business partner.

I could never work with my brother. Up until last year, we lived together. That was enough. But I'd take him over working with our dad most days.

If I had the chance, I'd do things differently.

I used most of my savings to buy the goats. Tom Donnely helped me build their custom trailer. Those were the major business investments. Pretty straightforward, unlike the dynamics of the Kelsos.

Family is a bramble of blackberry bushes. A tangled mess, with a nearly impenetrable bond. Sweet, but can easily cut you deeply. I've learned how to protect myself over the years.

When Mom or Erik ask how things are going, I lie.

Both to cover for Dad and save them from worrying.

Saving face is something ingrained in the Kelsos.

Pretend everything is okay and maybe it will be. Fake it until you make it. Or can't anymore. Or it all goes to hell in a spectacular, public way.

No one knows what goes on behind closed doors.

The perfect Sunday churchgoing family hides a history of conditional love and dirty secrets.

A married father of two boys and the nicest wife turns out to be a serial cheater.

The owner of the tavern and the crankiest SOB on the island, who might as well be a troll under the bridge, writes a huge check to the local domestic and sexual violence support group.

The island slut who—

"You going to stand there staring all day?" Jonah interrupts my thoughts by bumping my shoulder, shaking me out of my list as if he knows I'm thinking about his sister.

As far as I know, the only person who knows anything about my opinion of Ashley is Dan, friend and owner of Sal's Pizza. A few months ago I was doing work on his property, helping him build a fire pit and patio for his girlfriend for Valentine's Day. Because she wanted cozy fires outside and that's the kind of guy he is. He'd do anything for her. I must've felt inspired to spill about Ashley.

Or I'm terrible at hiding the truth behind a closed door.

"I brought the grounds from the Bean." I shove my hands in the pockets of my hoodie. "Where do you want them?"

Erik points at the long steel table in the center of the room away from the roasters and storage containers. "I'll have the crew handle them tomorrow."

People say Erik and I could be twins. We have the same dark blond hair and lanky builds, but his eyes are brown. I'm the only one in our family to get blue eyes. The same people who joke we could be twins also like to tease my mom about the milk man. Make up your minds, folks. Opinions, everyone has more than their share.

Where Erik and I have light hair, tall and lean builds, Jonah's all darkness. Dark hair, dark eyes, and enough black in his wardrobe to clothe a goth club. I lost track of the number of tattoos he's gotten over the years. Jonah has at least five piercings you can see when he's fully clothed.

If people compare Erik and I to golden retrievers, then Jonah would be a bat. Broad shoulders, tattoos, gauges in his stretched lobes, a pierced eyebrow and who knows what else, he's the dark to our light. We look like the all-American guys in a Tommy Hilfiger ad. Jonah's the bastard child of a hipster and a pirate.

I laugh at how far from the truth of his parentage those two things are.

He and Ashley couldn't be more different. If anyone around

has a secret baby daddy, it's probably their mom. I snort at the idea of super uptight, judgmental, and conservative Karen fooling around on her husband. Icicles in hell would be more likely.

If you only met them now, you'd never guess he and Ashley grew up in an ultra-conservative family. Then again maybe it's obvious. They're each rebels in their own way.

We all are.

By the time I return with the bag of coffee grounds, Jonah and Erik are done with their roast. I sit on a pallet of burlap sacks of raw beans. The scent of coffee makes me think of Ashley. Lately, it seems like everything does.

Coffee.

The color red.

A combination of orange and sweet flowers that reminds me of her shampoo.

Morning wood.

The general loneliness I feel hanging around my brother and his girlfriend or our married friends. Couplehood spread through my wingmen like a hardy flu strain. So far Jonah and I are the only two left standing.

"Hey, Jonah."

He looks up from where he's wheeling a garbage can of beans toward the wall.

"Want to go over to town tonight and blow off the stink?"

"What about me?" Erik sounds like the little brother being left out. Which he is. "Cari and I like to go to town."

I ignore the opportunity for a sex euphemism, but Jonah jumps in with, "Especially downtown."

Then laughs at his own joke.

Erik's grin is smug and unapologetic.

"I was thinking of a guys' night. Maybe go to Pioneer Square and hear some live music."

"Pick up women? Is that why you don't want me to go?" Erik whines. "I can be your wingman. The honey for the bees."

"You mean pollen. Bees are attracted to pollen. They make honey." I correct him. I can't help it. Once a little brother, always a little brother.

"Fine, whatever," Erik huffs.

Jonah observes us before speaking, "Sure. There's a punk country band I like who have a gig tonight. Probably not your scene, but the music's excellent."

"Will there be women there?" I ask.

Jonah lifts his eyebrows in confusion. "There usually are."

"Then it's my scene." I nod to emphasize my point.

Chuckling, Jonah brushes a hand over his beard. "Suit yourself. Should make for an interesting night."

READY TO FALL

Chapter One

A high pitched wailing entered my dream. Slowly, I shook off the warm breeze and sunshine from the catamaran and opened my eyes to my bedroom. It took a minute or two for me to determine the sound wasn't from my dream, but coming from next door. From Maggie's house. Her smoke detector was going off.

From where he stood on the comforter facing the window overlooking the beach, Babe's barks drowned out the noise. Tossing the comforter and blankets off of me, I leapt from the bed, followed by Babe, and headed downstairs. Kelly rolled over and put the pillow over her head, grumbling about it still being dark out and what the hell was wrong with me for waking her up. Ignoring her, I grabbed my jeans and thermal from the floor, and raced from the room, not bothering to zip my jeans.

I reached the door to the deck where Babe pawed to get outside. The second I opened the door, he bounded out and barked at Maggie's cabin.

I peered through the pre-dawn gloom, but couldn't see any flames or smoke. As far as I knew, Maggie was in Portland with whatshisface. There shouldn't be any reason for her smoke detector to be going off. The battery could be dying, and if that was the cause for the ruckus, I'd give her an earful about changing her batteries with the time change next time I saw her.

The breeze shifted and I could smell the distinct scent of smoke coming from her cabin. Where there was smoke, there was fire.

I ran across the narrow yard separating our properties. Luckily, I knew she hid a key under a frog at the foot of her steps. Searching for the damn frog, I bent over, peering into the dark when the door to the deck flew open and slammed into the wall.

What the hell?

A petite brunette I'd never laid eyes on swung a throw blanket over her head while she attempted to chase the smoke pouring from the door.

Who the fuck is that? I stared at her. Now she ran around the living room, opening windows as the smoke detector continued to squawk its annoying beeping into the sleepy morning.

The smoke appeared to be coming from the wood stove. Miss Blanket Waver probably hadn't opened the flue. She must not be from around here.

Walking through the open door, I coughed and waved the smoke away from my face as I headed toward the stove.

Without introducing myself, I said, "You forgot to open the flue."

The woman stood at the kitchen sink, trying to open the window, and jumped at the sound of my voice.

"Cheesy Rice and Joseph!" she shouted and turned to face me, clutching her hand to her chest. "Who the fuck are you?"

Leaning over, I swung the lever to open the flue on the chimney stack. "I'm the neighbor. Who the fuck are you? Cause I know this isn't your house."

With the doors and windows open the room began to clear of smoke, but the smoke alarm continued its piercing cadence.

Where the hell was the damn thing? I stared at the ceiling and followed the beeping until I spied the red-lighted beast in the hallway. I reached up and knocked it from its perch, removed the batteries, and set it on the kitchen counter.

"Ah, silence," I said. Observing the woman, I noticed she had wrapped her blanket weapon around her shoulders. Sticking out below the blanket I could see a pair of flannel pajama bottoms and mismatched socks. "You going to tell me who you are and what you are doing in my friend's house? Or am I going to call the sheriff?"

She tightened the throw around her shoulders and glared at me, but not before I noticed her eyes linger at my waist and my jeans hanging off my hips.

I smiled at her to let her know I'd caught her staring before closing my jeans.

She didn't blush or glance away, but continued to glare at me. "Do you always barge into people's homes at the crack of dawn?"

"I do when the alarm wakes me up and smoke fills the air." I crossed my arms and waited.

"I'm renting the place for a few months. Arrived on the ferry last night."

She didn't tell me her name. Nope, definitely not from around here.

"Well, that explains what you are doing here, but not who you are. I'll go first. I'm John Day. I live next door. The yellow lab out on the deck is Babe. Your turn."

"Diane. Diane Watson. Well, Woodley, but Watson soon."

"Nice to meet you, Diane Woodley-but-Watson-soon. Is that hyphenated?" I stuck out my hand to shake hers, figuring it was the polite thing to do.

She laughed, but it sounded hollow, not a real laugh. Somehow the smile didn't reach her brown eyes. She shook my hand and said, "Just Woodley. Watson is my maiden name. I'm thinking of changing it back."

"No more Mr. Woodley?" I asked.

She scowled. "No more Mr. Woodley. Or there won't be soon enough."

"If you are planning on murdering your husband, don't tell me. I don't want to be an accessory. I'm here to open the flue and prevent you from burning down my friend's house." I smiled at her. "Plus, it's way too early to hear all the gory details of your personal life."

She laughed this time and it was real. "No, no murder. Not that it hasn't crossed my mind. Sorry about the smoke detector. I thought I knew how to build a fire. The fire part I figured out, but not the flue. Obviously."

"Obviously."

"Thanks for coming over and saving the day."

"No problem. I keep an eye on the house for Maggie, it's what neighbors do around here." I surveyed the quiet beach. "In January, not many of us live down here on the beach, we have to band together."

"I appreciate it. I'd hate to have the fire department show up on my first morning here. Sorry to wake you so early. I guess I'm still on east coast time."

"Honestly, no problem. Nice to meet you," I said, backing toward the door. "Well, I'll leave you to it. You probably want to change out the batteries on all the detectors. Who knows the last time Maggie changed them."

She looked forlorn standing alone in the living room with the blanket falling off her shoulders. The Soon-to-be-not-Woodley blinked at me before remembering her manners.

"It was nice to meet you. I don't know anyone on the island, so it's nice to meet my neighbor. I hope to see you around again."

"You probably will. Island's a small place, and the beach especially. Give a holler if you need anything." I turned when I opened the door. "And don't forget to open the flue when you start a fire."

She seemed embarrassed, but smiled. "Thanks, John."

I gave her a wave and headed back over to the house with Babe on my heels. It was weird to have someone besides Maggie living in the cabin. Diane appeared nice enough, but she was no fiery redhead like Maggie.

I crawled back into bed after shedding my jeans. Kelly rolled over and curled into my side, mumbling about barking dogs and smoke. I stayed awake for a while, thinking about the woman next door and the expression on her face as if she didn't have a friend in the world. I'd have to text Maggie later to let her know about the wood stove. And find out more about her new tenant with the sad eyes.

ACKNOWLEDGMENTS

To Whidbey and the real life residents who inspired this fiction-alized world, thank you for embracing me as one of your own. Someday I'll call the island home again. Until then, send me all the Happy Hippie!

To the readers who have been here from *Ready to Fall*, thank you for sticking with me through the long wait between books. Thank you for loving this series.

Thank you to Julianne Burke for another gorgeous Wingmen cover. I am in love with the new branding.

Thank you to Heather Lyons for volunteering your time to beta read the early version of this book—it is infinitely better with your input. To my editor, Caitlin, I owe you a saison and some oysters. To Janice, thank you for proofing this book. Any remaining errors are entirely my fault.

All of my love to my husband, whose steadfast support of me and my writing keeps me going even on the hardest days. Thank you for giving your perspective and insight to make these fictional men the best they can be. Each of the Wingmen contain elements of you and they're better for it. For my family, who encourages me to follow my dreams, thank you for nurturing my roots with your love.

To the Indie book community, thank you for continuing to be a place of support and fellowship. To the BSGs, you are amazing. Special thanks to Tina Gephart, Julia Kent, Helena Hunting, Heather Lyons, Katana Collins, Penny Reid, EL James, Autumn Davis, Becca Mysoor, Katherine Stevens, April White, Elizabeth Hunter, Hilaria Alexander, Benita Botello, Tina Lynne, Fiona Fischer, the Modern Inklings, the Nerdy Little Book Herd authors, and so many others who offer a word of support, a laugh, or a kind gesture. Your friendship and encouragement have kept me afloat during a tough season.

Thank you to Jennifer Beach for being my incredible PA. I'm lucky to have you on my team. All the love for Christina Santos and Sarah Piechuta. Thank you for your friendship and keeping me sane. To KP and Emilie at Inkslinger, thank you for helping me navigate the ever-changing waters of Indie publishing and marketing. To Meire Dias at Bookcase Literary Agency, thank you for your unwavering faith in my writing.

To everyone in my Facebook reader group, Daisyland, thank you for hanging out with me and chatting about sloths, books, and life.

To all amazing the book bloggers and bookstagrammers, thank you for sharing your passion for reading. I am forever in awe over the time, energy and creativity you put into your reviews, blogs, and pictures. Thank you for your continued support for me and my books.

Finally, if you are reading this, thank you. There are millions of books in the world. Thank you for spending your time and money on mine. I'm blessed to be able to write and publish books as my career. I couldn't continue to do what I love without you, and I'm forever grateful.

I love hearing from readers. Come find me on social media and say hi, or email me at daisyauthor@gmail.com.

OTHER BOOKS BY DAISY

Wingmen
Ready to Fall
Confessions of a Reformed Tom Cat
Anything but Love
Better Love
Small Town Scandal
Wingmen Babypalooza
The Last Wingman

———

Love with Altitude
Next to You
Crazy Over you
Wild for You
Up to You

———

Modern Love Stories
We Were Here (prequel to Geoducks)
Geoducks Are for Lovers
Wanderlust

———

Tinfoil Heart

Bewitched Series

Bewitched

Spellbound

Enchanted

Charmed

———

Wicked Society

Get Witch Quick

Someday my Witch Will Come

Four Witches and a Funeral

———

Want a reading list?

www.daisyprescott.com/books/

To keep up with my latest news and upcoming releases, sign up for my mailing list.

www.daisyprescott.com/mailing-list/

ABOUT DAISY

Daisy Prescott is a USA Today bestselling author of small town romantic comedies. Series include Modern Love Stories, Wing-men, Love with Altitude, as well as the Bewitched and Wicked Society series of magical novellas. Tinfoil Heart is a romantic comedy standalone set in Roswell, New Mexico.

Daisy currently lives in a real life Stars Hollow in the Boston suburbs with her husband, their rescue dog Mulder, and an indeterminate number of imaginary house goats. When not writing, she can be found in the garden, traveling to satiate her wanderlust, lost in a good book, or on social media, usually talking about books, bearded men, and sloths.

Mailing list
www.daisyprescott.com

facebook.com/daisyprescottauthorpage

twitter.com/Daisy_Prescott

instagram.com/daisyprescott

bookbub.com/authors/daisy-prescott

www.ingramcontent.com/pod-product-compliance
Lightning Source LLC
Chambersburg PA
CBHW031957050726
47590CB00006B/1936